The Keepers of the Key

The Keepers of the Key

(Book 2 of the Gate of Fire Series)

B. J. Vanderhoof

Also by B. J. Vanderhoof
The Gate of Fire Series
The Prophecy of the Gate
The Keepers of the Key

Other Stories
Tales from the Kingdom of Tyndall: A Short Story Collection

The Keepers of the Key
(Book 2 of the Gate of Fire Series)

The Kingdom of Calridian
Malick *(Elf)* - King of Calridian
Esmeralda *(Dragon)* - King's Advisor
Vurth *(Dwarf)* - Captain of the Guard
Jyres *(Human)* - Keeper of the Key
Lalatco *(Elf)* - Keeper of the Key
Percy *(Gargoyle)* - One of the King's envoys
Mit Merrituk *(Human)* - Ambassador

Tomackus
Lord Kapel *(Delga)* - Leader of Castle Mystic
Demorous the Fierce *(Delga)* - Former Knight of Enchantment at
Castle Mystic
Felix, Sigmon, Digmon *(Delga)* - Former Knights of
Enchantment at Castle Mystic
Tagro *(Dwarf)* - Dwarven leader and Vurth's son
Shepherd Rowland *(Human)* - Warden of Skystair

Alhazar
Crimson *(Dragon)* - One of two dragons still in existence
Simamar *(Elf)* - Elven leader and nephew of the King of Calridian
Ogla *(Orc)* - Self-appointed leader of the orcs and goblins
Elonda *(Elf)* - Skilled warrior
Leah *(Human)* - Hunter from the Old World

The Stone Way
Gargan *(Gargoyle)* - Clan leader
Bram *(Gargoyle)* - Clan leader
Hawkins *(Gargoyle)* - Member of Gargan's clan

Secord
Zar *(Delga)* - Wizard
Lumpkin *(Dwarf)* - Dwarven alchemist
Flick *(Unknown)* - Friend of Zar

Heritage
Constance Octavia *(Human)* - Empress of Heritage

Other Characters
Cyna *(Human)* - Young girl in care of the elves
Rajeem *(Elf)* - Watches over Cyna
The Silver Shadow *(Delga)* - Former Knight of Enchantment
Bartholomew the Bold *(Delga)* - Former Knight of Enchantment
Brigand *(Delga)* - Former Knight of Enchantment
Karth *(Delga)* - Former Knight of Enchantment
Rutu (Yixl) - Kin of the yixl leader
The Horde - The reason for the Gate of Fire

*Interested to hear how the author pronounces all the characters
and places in the Keepers of the Key? Just scan the qr code.
(You are also free to pronounce them anyway you like)*

THE KINGDOM
Small River Town
Gargan's Clan
SECORD
THE STONE WAY
Bram's Clan
The Gate
Stone Heights
HERITAGE

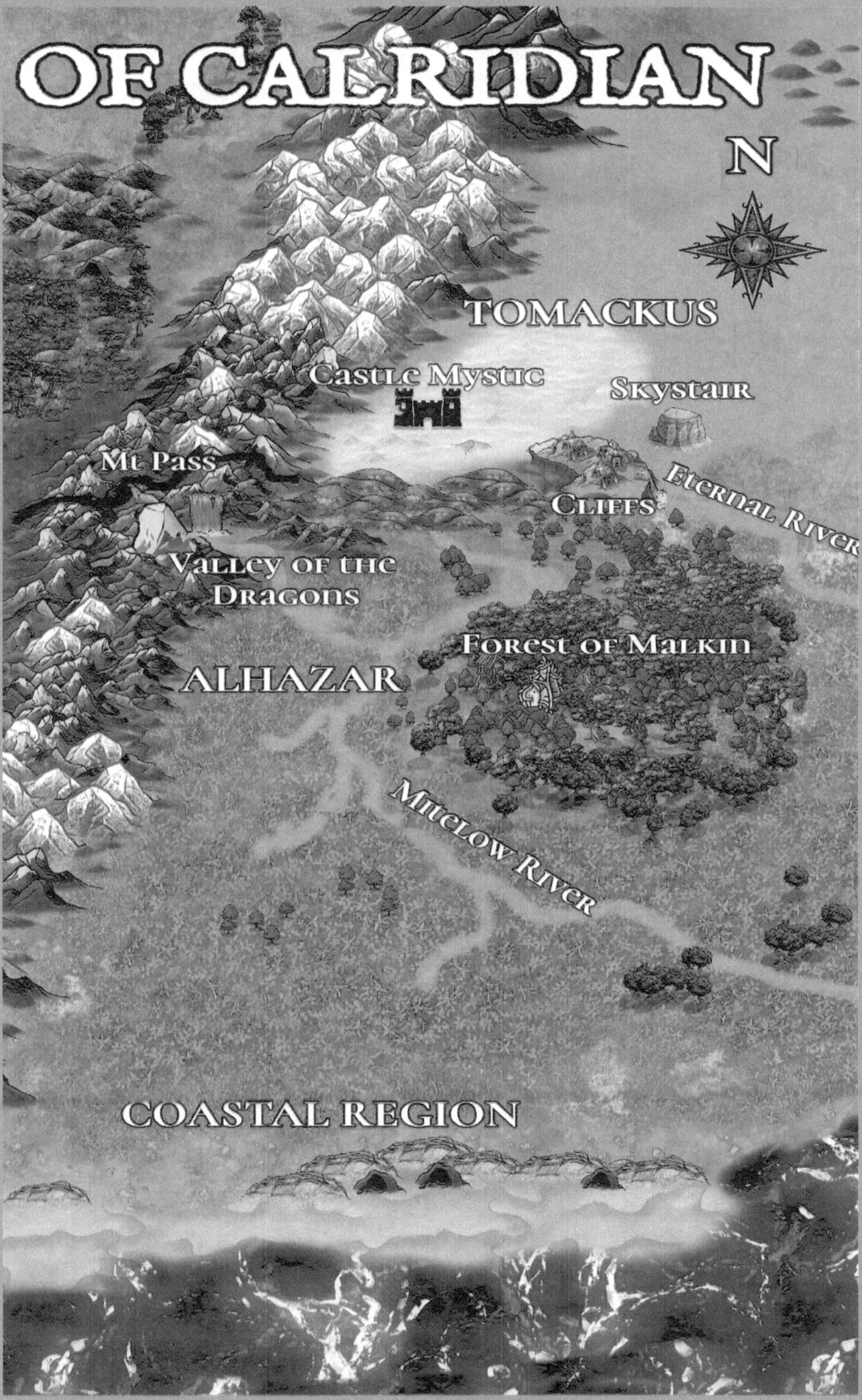

OF CALRIDIAN
N
TOMACKUS
Castle Mystic
Skystair
Mt Pass
Cliffs
Eternal River
Valley of the Dragons
Forest of Malkin
ALHAZAR
Mitelow River
COASTAL REGION

Table of Contents

Prologue 1

1 Jyres and the Key...3

2 Elonda's Wild Spirit 10

3 The King's Work..15

4 A Keeper's Work 22

5 Chase The Horizon 29

6 Trust Must be Earned...36

7 Merrituk 41

8 Lumpkin 46

9 Another Day..52

10 The Shepherds of the Isles 58

11 Stovea..65

12 Cyna 72

13 Lalatco Delayed 81

14 A Dragon Pericarp and a Reunion 87

15 Departures 95

16 Heritage 101

17 No More Waiting for Lumpkin or the Silver Shadow......... 109

18 Armant 114

19 Hide And Seek 121

20 Hero?.. 127

21 Discoveries 137

22 Alive? 143

23 Sands 150

24 Preparations.. 158

25 The Day of Two Moons 164

26 The Black Donosin 173

27 A Sound in the Night.. 181

28 Fights and Flights... 190

29 Recovery... 200

30 Tracks And Dragons... 207

31 The Two Lost Sands.. 218

Epilogue 224

Acknowledgments.. 230

About the Author 232

PROLOGUE

Centuries before, there was the horde. They were an ancient and evil plague upon the world. Whether there was one of them or many, they were simply called the horde. No individuals, no names, no personalities. A leaderless race, a race that followed the desire of their masses. That desire, to cause chaos. Going from town, to city, to village, to farm. Where they left death and ruin in their wake. The horde were chaos uncontrolled, they were relentless.

But the races of the world united against them. The strongest and wisest among them put their combined talents together and developed a spell of such power and complexity that it had never been outdone. With it they created the Gate of Fire and its protective ring of fire.

The horde, driven by their common goal of destruction, were fooled. They were drawn toward the gathering of their enemy, who were waiting for them and well prepared. Soon the horde was trapped forever in another dimension, in a place held at bay by a mighty magical gate. A gate of fire. A gate of power. That Gate of Fire and its ring of fire had stood untouched for years upon years. It was a gate created to grant relief and safety from the chaos known as the horde.

For years the horde waited, waited with nothing to do. Unable to go anywhere. Forever trapped by the gate in a magical domain not of this world. The horde lived a miserable existence, an existence worse than death. But now, one of their own had escaped. After all these years closed off from their old world, a chance was born. For so long one word had haunted their existence, despair. Now a new word had taken the place of despair. Patience. They wait patiently, their desire united in their quest for release and their thirst for revenge.

1

JYRES AND THE KEY

The horse was breathing hard as it trotted up the winding path. Horse and rider had ridden hard during this last leg of the journey. Jyres had wanted to reach the small outpost before nightfall and to do that required a lot of effort from the horse. Jyres could see the outpost just ahead and off of the path. It was not much more than a small, two-room hut. Quickly dismounting, he led his horse to a small stream just behind the structure. The horse, who Jyres had named Gerti, seemed to relax as she drank from the stream.

After a little while, both man and beast headed for the small hut. Jyres gave her an encouraging pat on the neck as he tied Gerti's reins to a small post. Then he took a deep breath. He savored the night air and the slight chill it carried. A long ride on a nice day had the tendency to work up a lather for both horse and rider, and this ride had certainly done that.

Another moment or two, and Jyres retreated inside. Both habit and sound thinking won out over the need to rest and Jyres quickly investigated the outpost's two rooms making sure there were no unwanted visitors, be it someone or something. Deeming it safe, Jyres opened the secret compartment in the wooden floor of the entry room and pulled out two boxes.

Each box was supposed to contain some essentials and in this case Jyres was happy to find what he was looking for. Wrapped up in cloth were two small loaves of bread and a few bright orange carrots. Looking them over quickly, and seeing they had not spoiled he removed them from the boxes before returning the boxes to their hiding place.

The food and the cot called to Jyres, but he knew he was not done yet. He retrieved the pail in the corner and taking two carrots with him he stepped back outside. Gerti's head popped up at the sound of his approach and he held out the carrots for her. She hurriedly snatched them from his hand, chomping on them greedily. Jyres filled up the pail in the stream and left that by Gerti before finally collapsing on the cot inside the hut.

This was just one of many small outposts aiding those in the service of the king. King Malick, the elven patriarch, had ordered them built and they were one of his earliest projects to be completed. Members of Vurth's army had used these at times, but Jyres and Lalatco, who are the Keepers of Key, had used them the most. They had come in very handy and Jyres silently thanked Malick for his wisdom on every occasion he put one to use. King Malick had also had the foresight to assign the task of keeping them stocked to a small group of individuals referred to as the King's Envoys. Although Jyres was not aware of the group's other tasks, restocking these outposts was just one of the group's assignments.

Jyres, realizing he still had more to do as part of the usual routine, was finding it hard to get up off the cot. Finally, he sat up and undid his sword belt from his hip. He placed it directly under the cot. It was not the same sword Malick had given him for his first journey, which now seemed long ago, but it was a quality sword. Upon returning the elven sword to Malick, Malick had given him another sword for him to keep. No fancy inscription this time.

Jyres then removed the knife from his boot and placed that under the straw pillow. Finally, he stood up and pushed the cot over a little ways revealing another small trap door in the floor. He removed the key from his inner shirt pocket and placed it in the small hole under the trap door. He returned the cot to its rightful position and, after kicking off his traveling boots, he laid back down on the cot.

The key. The small shield-shaped piece of metal. It was gray in color and raised silver dots were placed in even intervals around the outside edge. Then, on the inside of the dots, a raised orange metallic trim bordered the interior of the key. Emblazened in the middle of the key was a depiction of flames, which glowed so fiercely they appeared almost red. This was the key that really had been at the center of his journey. The reason for his Keeper of the Key title. It had been three years now since he embarked on that incredible journey. A journey that had been full of danger, prophecies and death. The dangers that seemed so real and so insurmountable at the time. But somehow he and his friends prevailed. The prophecies proclaiming doom and destruction and claiming a hero would arise. The prophecies seemed to have been proven true.

Meslar, the delga wizard, on a quest for more power, had sought to open the Gate of Fire. This ancient gate held back a power of unspeakable evil from being released on the world. This power turned out to be some form of creature. These creatures had been locked away by some unknown power of old. It was as if the gate led to another place, a place not of this realm. Meslar had achieved his goal just long enough for one of these creatures to escape that place before Meslar had died.

Jyres had killed him. Flashes of that moment were ingrained in Jyres' memory. His sword, his movement, Meslar's death. The immediate lunge against the fiery gate and the vivid recollection of jarring the key loose as the creature escaped. Everyone said he had fulfilled the prophecy of the hero. He had stopped the opening of the gate. What they chose not to see was what Jyres saw, what he saw almost nightly. He saw the prophecy was only 99 percent right.

Something had escaped. This thought was with him again tonight as he drifted off to a restless sleep.

Jyres woke earlier than he hoped and did not feel entirely rested, but he started his day anyway. Jyres ran his hand through his dark hair and rubbed his eyes. His stomach growled, reminding him he didn't eat anything last night. He tore off a chunk of one of the loaves of bread and bit into it eagerly. The bread tasted fresh and his belly asked for more. After finishing another piece of bread, he checked on Gerti.

Gerti was happy to see him and pulled on her reins, anxious to be free. Jyres obliged her, untying her from the post and giving her freedom to graze. As she did so, Jyres patted her side and walked along with her. Gerti had been his horse for about two years now. He had found her, a horse free in the wild. So untrained and leery of people it had taken them a while to see eye to eye.

Although other horses could have been provided for him, the opportunity to help train his own horse had factored into his decision to go through the extra work. He had a lot of learning to do himself as a rider and Jyres thought it best if horse and rider learned together. And the work had paid off. Gerti responded to him in ways an already trained horse would not have been able to do.

Gerti and Jyres had seen some interesting times together over the last couple of years and Jyres was happy to have the horse. He had found Gerti to the east of the Eternal River. A few herds were known to frequent the area. Jyres thought she was a beautiful horse, a nice light-colored brown with a dark brown mane and tail. As of late, Gerti was the only one around, or so it seemed. All of his friends each had different missions or roles, just like Jyres did. Everyone seemed to be always going in different directions.

A lot had changed over the course of time following the death of Meslar. King Malick had immediately begun the process of expanding and protecting the kingdom. He declared that inviting others to be in fellowship with, or part of, their kingdom would be the best way to preserve the peace they had fought so hard for. With that as his goal, work on many projects commenced.

Each race in the kingdom was asked to serve. The dwarves not serving in the army put their skills of craftsmanship to work. Commonly traveled paths were enhanced to make traveling easier and some paths were even laid out with gravel or stone. Outposts, like the one Jyres stood by, were built along these roads to help offer protection by allowing members of the army to guard the paths and move from outpost to outpost. The biggest task that was given to the dwarves, however, was the construction of Serenity Castle. The construction of the castle at the end of the Valley of the Dragons was almost complete.

Jyres could picture Vurth, the Captain of the Guard, standing in the new castle, barking out orders and earning the respect of those he commanded. Even though the castle had not yet been completed, the Valley of the Dragons had been the home for Vurth and the elven king. Tents had been set up in the valley and had served as the shelter for those in service to the kingdom. With that being the case, Jyres had not seen Vurth since the wedding. The valley was too obvious a place for the key to be located, so it often prevented Jyres from seeing his dwarven friend.

As Jyres belted on his sword and retrieved his knife, his mind wandered back to the wedding. Lalatco and Leah had wed just five months ago. It was a beautiful fall day in the forest of Malkin. Leah had looked so lovely, and Lalatco so happy. Jyres had never seen a more poetic sight. The magnificent elven forest was the backdrop for the marriage of two of his great friends, both who were radiant. The party that followed would not be easily forgotten, nor the majestic singing by the elves.

Although Jyres could not be happier for his two friends, the wedding had changed Lalatco. Over the past three years Jyres and

Lalatco, the two Keepers of the Key, had developed a complex schedule of hidden locations for the key. Only the two of them ever knew where the key was. Sometimes it was on one of them, sometimes it was hidden near, and sometimes far. Lalatco had stressed the importance of the key not always being carried by one of them. He thought if that would have been the case, that would make it too easy for those who sought it.

It seemed to Jyres, however, that Lalatco had started to forget that. Since his wedding, Lalatco's willingness to travel had decreased, as had his need for extra precaution as it pertains to the key. Jyres found himself trying to stick to the same complex schedule and locations, but was now having to do more of the work. He had understood, and actually expected it for a little while, but he had hoped that enough time would have passed now for the newlyweds and Lalatco would return to his normal workload.

Jyres again saddled his horse and they searched the area close by, as had become their practice when they were in the same location for a few days at a time. They looked for threats often. This outpost was located in the forest of Malkin, but to the north and east of the elven home and location of that wedding not long ago. The outpost was not far from the village, which was now called Skystair, a place Jyres knew well and which had prospered since the humans made the plateau their home. Jyres would be stopping there for a visit.

Jyres and Gerti traversed through the forest both to the north and south before finding the nearby dirt path and traveling on it from the west and heading east back toward the outpost. Although they did not see any other travelers, Jyres' trained eye could pick out recent boot marks heading to the west. Jyres pulled on the reins and brought Gerti to a halt as they stood for a moment, quietly listening for anything out of the ordinary. Gerti gave no indication of such, nor did Jyres sense any threat. In fact, no threats have been occurring anywhere. The mysterious creature that had escaped from the gate had not been seen for almost two years. This peace had settled into the kingdom.

Jyres was glad for this peace, but he would not let down his guard. Zar had warned him of the danger the creature could represent, and he dare not let this peace be interrupted. But it was getting harder and harder to stay vigilant. So few people even gave the key, the creature, or the gate a passing thought. So quickly are things forgotten. And now, Lalatco, was he growing too comfortable? Was he letting his guard down?

It did not surprise Jyres at all that his three-day stay at the outpost went by relatively uneventfully. He had talked briefly with two travelers on the road on the second day, but nothing noteworthy was told to him. As he prepared for departure, he retrieved the key from its hiding place and returned it to the inner pocket of his shirt and pulled his brown leather vest over the top of his tan long sleeve shirt. He whistled for Gerti, who responded quickly, trotting up to his master. "That's a good girl," said Jyres, as he mounted the horse. "Another day for just Jyres and Gerti, and another day of travel."

2
ELONDA'S WILD SPIRIT

Elonda and four other elves rode their horses at a comfortable trot. They were traveling south and had just entered lands that had not yet been explored. The king and former elven leader, Malick, had given the elves an assignment following the events of three years past. That assignment was to explore the world on this side of the mountains as had never been done before. And that is what the elves had been doing, nearly nonstop for three years.

When Malick had been named King, a new elf had to be given the role as elven leader to replace the seat Malcik had held for many years. Malick's family, known as the Malkin, were by far the biggest family group amongst the elves. They were the group that originally traveled across the mountains and the forest they live in was now known as the Forest of Malkin. Since then other family groups had developed, but none compared to the size of that of the Malkins. With that being the case, it was natural for the next elven leader to be selected from the Malkins. Many elves were considered, both male and female, and in the end the honor fell to a blood relative of the king, Simamar.

Simamar, a nephew of King Malick, had taken the task of exploring the world to heart. Eager to impress his uncle and King, he continued to send recon missions. This particular mission had them far to the south. They had already traveled for multiple days. At first, these missions had excited Elonda. It was well suited for both her skill set and her need to take action. However, the task had become mundane. Rarely had their explorations turned up much that had been useful. This fact only fueled the desire of their young leader to discover something of significance to impress the king. He sent more and more of his people out to explore and sent his best on very long expeditions.

Each expedition often contained members from different elven family groups and in this particular group both Elonda and one other elf represented the family of Malkin. Elonda was a Malkin by birth, but only distantly related to King Malick. The other three elves along were from the smaller family groups.

Each expedition team was tasked with mapping out the world. A capable artist was sent with each group and once they entered territory that had yet to be mapped the real work began. Although an important task, this also took time, which made long trips even longer. Groups could be gone for weeks or even months at a time, a hard thing for those who had families or easily missed home. Even Elonda, no stranger to the long road, had trouble stomaching this particular trip. A trip that took her a long way from home and far from Jyres.

The five elves made camp and talked about the coming days and how they would begin to map the new area. Elonda fell silent, letting the others take the lead. All four of them had been on multiple trips and all of them were capable of the task ahead. They were prepared and well suited for the task, but Elonda struggled to find the adventure and thrills she so desperately sought. Not since she led Jyres to the Gate of Fire itself had she felt content. She was an untamed soul, as was her horse, appropriately named Wild Spirit.

In the morning the work began as one of the elves got out ink and parchment to begin mapping their immediate area to use as a starting spot. It was a beautiful morning, just a slight breeze keeping the summer day from being overly hot. They were settled in a small copse of trees and out in front of them lay what seemed like never ending and unhindered grassland. The grass had a multitude of different colors of green and brown, and the long grass waved in the breeze.

Elonda unconsciously looked down at her clothing. She was wearing her customary dark blue shirt and pants with black stitching, but left her gray cloak packed, as it was not needed on this warm day. The elves around her blended in nicely to their surroundings with their different shades of green clothing. Elonda had always chosen to stand out and her clothing was an expression of that choice. Some of the other elves had made comments to her over the years about the colors of her clothing, but they had little effect on her.

Elonda continued to stare out over the land, the unending sea calling to her. She looked over at Wild Spirit, the horse as black as night, its muscles tense, power waiting to be released. She looked back to the sea of green again, and unconsciously took a step towards her horse. Did she perceive a slight nod from the stallion, or had that only been in her head?

She took two quick steps before leaping onto a rock and launching herself from the rock and into the horse's saddle. The horse responded immediately, thundering out from under the trees as surprised shouts from the other elves rose up behind them. Wild Spirit plunged into the grasses, not slowing a bit, the grass reaching as high as his rider's knees in spots. Elonda let out an excited cry as they sped through the grassland.

No one had been able to tame this horse. No one could match its fierce need to run and play. Not until Elonda had met him just a couple of months ago. He had been found with an injured calf muscle. The elves nursed it back to health, but he would not allow anyone to ride him. So many of the young male elves so wanted to, the horse's obvious power and speed calling to them. But it was Elonda with whom it connected, Elonda in whom it saw that same fire behind the eyes. This connection was much to the dismay of the other elves, who grew envious. It hadn't even been that hard, in Elonda's estimation. Yes, the horse had tossed her once, but after that, they connected. They had been inseparable ever since.

Elonda let him go, and he flew, going at full speed. The wind and grass whipped at Elonda, her black hair flying out behind her. So long had she been waiting for a moment like this, something spectacular. Both Elonda and Wild Spirit felt a happiness they had not felt in ages! She yelled with excitement once again as they continued their wild ride. She extended her arms out wide, trusting her horse and her experience to stay saddled while at full speed. The wind was cool on her cheeks, and the sun was warm on her body. She took a deep breath and closed her eyes, trying to soak up every moment, every sensation.

Then the terrain started to change, the grass becoming shorter and thinner, and Elonda realized, perhaps too late, they were starting to go uphill. She grasped the reins again and tried desperately to rein Wild Spirit in, to slow his charge.

Finally, he responded, slowing his gate. Elonda pulled back again as she saw the approaching cliff, Wild Spirit saw it too, and tried to slow down. The cliff was coming, coming too fast. Elonda closed her eyes and leaned down grabbing her horse around the neck. Then the sudden skidding stop came and the horse's hooves were desperately trying to stop their momentum. Wild Spirit stopped drastically close to the edge, but the momentum was too much and Elonda went flying out of the saddle, up and over Wild Spirit's head.

She held on as hard as she could, her arms still locked around the horse's thick neck. Her whole body went over the side of the cliff, her weight and force all pulling on the horse. But the horse refused to be pulled from its spot. Every muscle taut, Wild Spirit, stood firm. Elonda dangled over the cliff. She looked down and saw nothing but rocks and grass far beneath her. A fall from this height would be life ending, but no fear had come to her. The thrill of the ride still burned hot and she only felt exhilaration and contentment.

A huge smile was on her face as the horse backed up and pulled Elonda back to safety. Elonda fell to the ground, breathing hard. Then she jumped up and screamed, full of joy. She wrapped her arms around the horse, resting her head against it. The horse neighed in response, and she chuckled.

She patted the horse gently. "Well, that was fun." She stayed in the position a moment longer, feeling the rise and fall of the stallion's chest.

Then, as she focused on her surroundings, she saw something that seemed odd to her. Out past the cliff, there in the distance, it looked like two different color blues were combining and went flat. And that was for as far as the eye could see. She had never seen anything like it. She mounted her horse again and continued to stare. Then a hint of recognition came to her. Was that water? A lake meeting the sky? It was too big for a lake. What could it be?

Questions continued to occupy her mind and she wondered how far away it was. It couldn't be that far. Would they journey that far on their current trip? They must! Finally, after all their exploration, perhaps they had found something that could be of interest to the king.

Something stirred in her again. After the ride and exhilaration it appeared that the excitement might continue. She had found it. Her next adventure. And she and Wild Spirit had found it together.

3
THE KING'S WORK

King Malick sat on his wooden throne at one end of the very large tent. When he had become king he replaced his dark green cloak for a bright blue one trimmed with white. The cloak was long and while sitting on the throne the bottom of it rested on the floor. His fair long hair was pulled back and a silver crown lay on the floor next to him. It was made for him soon after he was named king, but he seldom wore it, reserving it for special occasions.

Where he sat was the temporary seat of the Kingdom of Calridian. The new kingdom was created in the wake of the events of a few years past. The name "Calridian" was an elvish word that stood for alliance or treaty. The name had been suggested by the dragon Esmeralda and Malick had taken a liking to it. It was a great word for what he hoped this kingdom would become. A group of united races from both the new and old worlds.

A small twelve-year-old girl had just walked away, having just completed her conversation with the king. Only a handful of people knew about the girl's existence and Malick hoped to keep it that way. An elven female waited for the girl and escorted her out. The elf, Rajeem, who was from the Malkin family, was the girl's protector and even she did not know the girl's ancestry. As the king considered the girl, a messenger entered into his presence.

"Sire," the young dwarf said, "we have received news from Ambassador Merrituk. He has reached the human city of Heritage. The gargoyle Percy brought us the news."

"Excellent," said Malick. "You are dismissed."

The City of Heritage was the last remaining fortified city the humans had held after the Battle of Ages. It contained a vast population of humans and the king had hoped to welcome them into the new kingdom. His efforts, however, had failed thus far. For three years they had resisted. This time, the king decided to send another human, Merrituk. Malick understood the city's reluctance to join them.

The city had basically been on its own for over a hundred years and survived, even thrived. But Malick believed they could benefit so much more by being part of the Kingdom of Calridian. Things like trade and travel would now be open to them.

Each city, race, stronghold, or region that was part of the kingdom also received a seat on what was being called The Council of Peace. The Council of Peace was derived from the Week of Peace that had been in existence until a few years ago. The idea behind the creation of the Council was a way to unite the lands together and give everyone a voice in the overall rule of the land.

Merrituk had just recently drawn attention from the king. He was a young human male, who had shown promise by organizing the trade for the city of Skystair. One of their main exports was a healing salve that the people of Skystair had been making long before they had founded the city. Merrituk was able to help the city make it with more regularity and then use it to trade and bring in food and needed supplies for the city.

Malick had decided to bring him on as an ambassador after his accomplishments with Skystair. His first assignment had been to go to Castle Mystic to maintain good standing with Lord Kapel, who now led the castle, and to also, in a subtle manner, keep tabs on the knights. Merrituk had performed admirably and found out that two knights had died, supposedly of natural causes, and others had decided to move on from the castle. Although Malick understood what had happened to the knights in the past, he made it a point to know about the delga and keep watch on them.

Merrituk had found out that Oliver and Oscar had died in the past year. Lemont the Lost had died at the battle by the gate three years before, leaving nine knights to account for. The castle was still a home for the knights, but it had also brought in those who had nowhere else to go and Lord Kapel saw to taking care of the castle and all its occupants. Merrituk had reported that Demorous, Felix, Sigmon and Digmon were also still at the castle. This left Brigand, Karth, the Silver Shadow, and Bartholomew the Bold. Karth and Brigand had supposedly left together, headed south, but the Silver Shadow and Bartholomew had basically disappeared.

If Malick was honest with himself, this was a concern of his. Not knowing where a few of the former knights were was like a bell that rang in this distance. It was always there at the back of his mind, but never close or loud enough to really grab his attention. But he was glad for the information. Merrituk had done well.

Malick knew this latest task he had given Merrituk would most likely be much harder than the trip to Castle Mystic. The city of Heritage was really the last holdout in joining the kingdom. The other small towns that were also on the other side of the Alhazar mountains, as Heritage was, had agreed quickly to follow the king. There was, of course, Bram, his castle and his clan of gargoyles that also remained on the outside of the Kingdom of Calridlan. Bram would not even entertain the idea, though Gargan assured Malick that it was probably for the best.

Malick sighed, and was about to retire for the evening when the dwarven messenger returned.

"Sire, sorry to disturb you again so soon, but your Captain of the Guard has requested an audience."

"Very well," a tired Malick replied. A king's work is never done.

*****

Ambassador Mit Merrituk was about to enter the palace of the city of Heritage. The end-of-the-summer sun was beating down on the thin, light-skinned man who was sweating from both the heat and his nerves. His blond hair was combed neatly to one side and he wore a thin long sleeve shirt with an angled stitching pattern at the neck and end of the sleeves. He took a deep breath and stepped through the open doors, two guards closing the door behind him.

Mit looked around the palace quietly as he followed a third guard through the clay brick building. Openings in the walls let in the sunlight and created light and shadow in the rather large hall. A few tapestries were hung as well, though Mit could not guess what the symbols meant on most of them. They turned down a hallway, which had less windows, making it a darkened walk. The guard continued to lead him through the palace and into the main audience chamber.

The chamber itself was rather humble, not overly large or heavily decorated. Simple is the word that came to Mit's mind. Mit made a note to remember that. He approached the wooden dais and gave a courteous bow. He then straightened and glanced at the woman who was referred to as their empress. Mit had to force himself to not show his surprise. The woman before him was not who he had expected. He was told the empress was an aging woman well past her prime. That is not who stared down on him from her raised seat.

He quickly remembered his role and began his introduction. "I am Ambassador Merrituk from the Kingdom of Calridian. I come in peace and friendship. Well met, Empress." After finishing, he gave another bow.

"I am Empress Constance Octavia. I welcome you to our city." She spoke in a quick and concise manner. "I assume you were expecting someone else. I am sad to report that the empress who your people last communicated with has left us. The city mourned her passing just forty days before."

Mit observed the new empress as she spoke. She was dressed in all black, a stark contrast to her very light skin. The garment she wore was simple, except for the rope belt around her middle with a flower pinned to it. Her blonde hair was pulled tight above her ears and then loose behind her head, a small and dainty crown holding back the hair. Never did a smile grace her face, her face set and matter of fact.

Mit was unsure if his normal tactics would work. His charm and humor were his normal approach. *Well,* he thought, *let's test the waters.* "I am sure you didn't expect such a young and handsome man either," he said with one eyebrow raised.

No reaction. She simply ignored the comment.

This was going to be a challenge, he thought, and he looked forward to it.

The rest of the conversation went as expected. She offered Mit a room in the palace to stay during his time in the city. He graciously accepted. The empress then left him with instructions to talk with the Palace Official who would coordinate their next meeting. After being shown to his room, Mit left his few belongings in the room and returned to the palace entrance where he received permission to leave and return as he wished.

Once out in the city proper, Mit began to observe the city with a curious eye. The city itself seemed more colorful than the palace had. This gave more evidence to his belief that the former empress was more outlandish than the women currently seated on the throne. Many of the wooden huts were painted different colors, and the clay buildings had rugs of different colored threads at their front doors.

Mit turned down another gravel road and he came upon the main trading hub of the city. Many different merchants were lining the street, some he guessed were traveling merchants while others were residents. He graciously turned down a seller who called out to him to buy clay pots and then another selling tomatoes. He was stopped a few moments later by a female merchant claiming to be selling items of the former empress. As he surveyed the items he saw two men with a rough appearance approaching him from the opposite side of the street.

"Greetings," he said to them, ignoring the small fear growing in the back of his mind. They nodded their heads in his direction, but said nothing right away. Mit started to wonder if he was in trouble when one of them spoke.

"Is it true? Have you traveled here from the other side of the mountains?"

Thankful that the man's tone was neutral, Mit replied, "Why, yes, I have come with orders from the king himself."

"The king?" One man laughed. "Who does he think he is, that he can call himself king over us?"

"Take it easy, Joff," said the other. "Tell us, have you met the one called Jyres?"

Mit smiled easily and said, "Yes, of course, I have had the pleasure of making his acquaintance. He is a fine fellow, a hero, if I do say so myself."

The rest of the day, Mit ran into more conversations with much the same theme. The citizens of Heritage wanted only to be left alone and wanted nothing to do with King Malick. But, many were also very curious about Jyres. This assignment the king had given him would be no easy task. The populus seemed to be against a union with the Kingdom of Calridian and the empress would not be swayed by his smooth talk. The silver lining was their interest in

Jyres. Jyres, a fellow human, had been the talk of the kingdom and, apparently, of Heritage as well. Now, Mit would just need to use that to his advantage.

After eating supper at the palace, Mit ventured out into the city again, this time looking for someone, as opposed to information. It didn't take long to find Gargan and his companion, the gargoyles who had escorted Mit to the city. Gargan, large and green, stood out in a crowd, as did the other gargoyle with him, who was almost as large.

"There you are Gargan, I was searching for you." Mit had had enough interactions with Gargan now to be comfortable talking with him. But he understood why others could be intimidated when talking to the large muscular gargoyle. Gargan also had massive wings that made him look even larger when they were spread wide.

"We are here, not much has changed since I was last at Heritage."

"Perhaps that is the case in the city, but I think the palace has," replied Mit, remembering his observations he had made earlier.

"I have never been inside the palace," replied Gargan.

"Well, they have a new empress for one thing." Mit paused for a while before speaking again. "I wanted to let you know that I do not think this will be a quick process. It may be a while before I am ready to leave."

"We understand, we will stay here unless other matters force our departure."

"Very well, would you like to stay in the palace? I am sure I could secure you a room?"

"That is not needed. We are known here and will stay in the city."

Mit nodded his head in the gargoyle's direction, and smiled at the gargoyle who was as matter of fact as ever. "You know, your friend Jyres seems to be a household name around here."

"As he should be," responded the gargoyle. But this time with a little more joy in his voice.

4
A Keeper's Work

Jyres let a smile come across his lips as Skystair came into view. The plateau it sat on had been the home of humans for just three years. Jyres had led the people out of their previous village as it burned and he and Gargan had led the people here. Since then the village had made a lot of progress, including the adoption of a name. Skystair. Skystair was fitting, since as you walked up the stairs that had been cut into the side of the plateau it appeared as though you were walking up to the sky.

Along with the improvement of the steps, the shelters had been improved upon and more had been built. The original structures, while well built, had been built in a hurry. Jyres was proud of the city; not for himself, but for the people who have been there and done the work to bring it to where it is now. Although Jyres was fond of the place, it was not his home. Right now, his home was wherever he laid his head. But deep down he knew his true home was where his friends were. Right now it just seemed a rare day when he saw them.

Jyres arrived at the base of the plateau and was greeted fondly by a few humans who recognized him. There was a small stable there and Gerti was led that way. Jyres waved his hellos as he started to climb the stairs. Although it was an easier way to arrive at the city than it used to be, it was still a long climb. As Jyres continued the climb, he remembered not so fondly the crude ladder that was used when they originally had settled here.

He stepped up over the final stair and was immediately greeted by those nearby. After exchanging greetings and pleasantries he was shown to a small hut where he could spend the night or stay for as long as he wanted. Jyres took a look around the city, nodding to himself as he viewed the strong wooden structures and picking out the ones that were the original buildings. It wasn't long before the Warden of Skystair, Shepherd Rowland, walked up to him.

"Jyres, good to see you again. What brings you back to Skystair?"

"Just needed a place to sleep, I am thankful for your hospitality again," said Jyres, shaking the older man's hand.

"Of course, please join me and my family for dinner tonight."

After dinner Jyres, returned to his hut. There he waited a long while, until he was confident the city would be asleep. Then he left his hut and entered the dark of night. Very carefully he snuck away from the huts and made his way to the far side of the plateau. Ensuring that no one was watching him, he swung his legs over the edge, his arms propping him up. His feet quickly found the ledge he was searching for and he let his weight fall back on his feet.

He found himself thinking of Lalatco, the nimble elf would make this look easy. Very carefully, he bent down, his feet solid on the small ledge. He reached into his pocket with his right hand removing the key, and then, brushing aside a few hanging vines, he revealed a small natural cut out in the rock face. Jyres placed the key carefully in the hiding spot and then let the vines fall back over the opening.

Jyres let out a breath he didn't know he was holding and reached up and grabbed the ledge above him and pulled himself back up to more solid ground. Quickly looking around for any unwanted eyes and seeing none, he made his careful way back to his borrowed hut.

As usual, it seemed to take him too long to fall asleep. The unknown whereabouts of the creature always haunted him. It always gnawed at his mind. He was out there somewhere. For some reason the creature remained hidden. But why? What was it doing all alone?

Like most people, Jyres assumed it would come after the key, but that hadn't happened. Two years ago the creature had been spotted by Jyres' good friend Gargan, the gargoyle. Gargan had seen the creature in the jungles of the old world, but nothing came of it. And the creature had not been seen since.

Jyres spent the better part of three days at the city of Skystair, one more day than planned. But this was the part that Jyres always hated. According to the schedule, the key was to be left in its hiding place here in the city until Lalatco retrieved it seven days later. Every fiber of his being wanted to go and get the key and bring it with him, a pull that he had to resist every time he left it somewhere. Just leaving it there unprotected was foolish in a way. But at the same time, who would ever look for it there? Finally, Jyres said his goodbyes and descended down the stairs.

Jyres saddled Gerti, offered thanks to those working the stables and urged Gerti into a trot. *Now what?* he thought. The key had been hidden, relatively on schedule and Jyres had a little free time until he would be needed again. Most travelers would probably take the opportunity to spend time at home.

Home, he thought again. *Friends.* He went through his list in his head.

Elonda, no longer a friend, but a girlfriend. Just the thought of her brought joy to his heart, but it was quickly followed by a longing to see her again. But he knew she was off on another long exploration journey, and would not return for some time. He let out a sigh and continued the horse's trot in no particular direction.

Lalatco was next to spring to his mind. The two had been through a lot together, and he considered him to be his closest friend. He was also the first real true friend that Jyres had made. Unfortunately, he felt like an uninvited guest as of late when around Lalatco and Leah. It was nothing intentional on their part, it was just the way of things. Three is an odd number, after all.

His friends Gargan and Zar were both currently on the other side of the mountains and Jyres would not be able to travel that far and return in time for his duties.

Well, Jyres, thought. *Let's see what is happening in the valley.* He had not seen Vurth for a long while, and now seemed to be as good as time as any for a visit. Jyres turned Gerti to the southwest and toward the Valley of the Dragons and his friend Vurth.

Vurth, the Captain of the Guard, was seated at his desk at one end of the tent, the temporary home of the King of Calridian. He was pouring over lists of tasks, supplies, soldiers and the like. Being Captain of the Guard had sounded so grand three years ago. Leading soldiers was something that came easy to Vurth and it was something he enjoyed. But mostly his tasks of late had been sending supplies here and building this there.

Vurth didn't mind the work; it was just not what he had signed up for. He sometimes longed for the days where he was leading his dwarves. Or sometimes, despite the harsh circumstances, he even looked with fondness on the events of three years ago, when he had battled alongside dragons to save the world and preserve the future for his kin.

He leaned back in his chair and stroked his very long orange beard, which was finally starting to show hints of gray as if it was trying to catch up the gray on the top of his head. He leaned back a little more and put his feet on his desk and relaxed for a moment.

The moment didn't last too long, for someone yelled, "Surprise!" as they stuck their head around a temporary canvas wall. Vurth jumped a little in his chair and started to lose his balance, and before long his chair fell backward. The dwarf yelled in surprise as he fell to the floor with some of his papers falling around him. The dwarf looked up and was about to let out a fierce retort, but then he saw who had caused him such hardship.

There stood Jyres, his cheeks a little red in embarrassment. The dwarf let out a hoot, and started laughing hysterically as he tried to get up from the floor. Jyres, also laughing, came over and offered a hand down to the dwarf, who readily accepted it and Jyres pulled him to his feet.

"Jyres, you young devil, you sure made me look foolish."

"It is so good to see you again Vurth," replied Jyres, still chuckling.

"You, as well. Tell me, what brings you to the valley?" asked Vurth, who grabbed Jyres hand again and gave it a firm shake.

"Just to see my friend."

A big smile came to the dwarf's face and he reached up and slapped Jyres hard on his shoulder. "Well, that calls for a drink. Come." Vurth led Jyres through the maze of tents and to another corner of the camp where three dwarves were sitting around some wooden barrels, each with a mug in their hand. "Friends," cried Vurth, "we be needing a couple of our own."

Jyres and the four dwarves talked long into the night, laughing plenty, and drinking more. Although at times the dwarves started talking about things going on here in the valley in which Jyres was not involved and could not contribute to the conversation, Jyres still enjoyed the banter. Finally, it was just Jyres and Vurth left sitting around the barrels.

"So, Vurth, tell me, how is it being a captain?"

"I am not going to lie to you lad, it's more work than when I was leading my clan. Constantly, telling men what to do, where to take things, what to build. I think Malick thinks everything has to happen all at once. Who decided to put him in charge?" The dwarf finished his mug of beer and chuckled. "I am kidding, of course, the king is doing a fine job. What about your task?"

Jyres, knowing he was asking about the key, simply nodded and said, "It is safe."

After a pause in the conversation, Jyres said, "Hey, how about you and I go hunting tomorrow. Just the two of us, find a nice stag to catch."

Vurth sighed. "I wish I could. But you messed up all my papers, it will take me half the day to get it all straight again." The dwarf laughed. "But it was mighty fine to see you again. It has been too long."

"It *has* been too long! Sorry about the papers."

The dwarf laughed again. "Don't think about it for another moment. It was well worth it."

The next morning Jyres decided he should pay a visit to the king, since he was here in the valley. He informed the dwarf at the entrance to the king's temporary throne room that he wished to pay homage to King Malick. As Jyres waited to be ushered in, a girl who couldn't be much older than 13, left the throne room in an exasperated fashion. She had a scowl on her face and was stomping in frustration. A few moments later the dwarf let him in to see the king.

Jyres gave a slight bow and said, "Good to see you, Your Majesty."

"Jyres," said Malick, "to what do I owe this honor?" If possible, Malick's tone was as worldly as ever.

"I was just in the area and it seemed only right to greet you."

"Well, of course, it is good to see you. Tell me, all is well?" To the king's credit, he seemed engaged in the conversation, despite not knowing that Jyres would be coming.

"Yes, sire, all is well, and I thank you again for the outposts, they have come to be most helpful."

"No need to thank me. The kingdom is in your debt."

"I do have one question, if I may," said Jyres. It was the same question that he was always thinking about.

"Of course," replied the king who gestured with his outstretched hand as a sign for Jyres to proceed.

"Has there been any word of the mysterious creature?"

Malick smiled and shook his head. "No, not at all, I dare say we can put that prophecy behind us."

The short conversation was at an end as the dwarf who had let Jyres in to see the king returned to inform him of other business. Jyres left to find Vurth and say goodbye, and that put an end to his short stop at the Valley of the Dragons. As Jyres mounted Gerti later that day, one thing stuck in his mind. King Malick had seemingly written the creature off as meaningless.

5
CHASE THE HORIZON

Elonda and her fellow elves continued their work and today they happened to be on the very cliff that Elonda had almost fallen off of just a few days before. Elonda, astride Wild Spirit, her sword strapped to her back, informed the others she would search for a way down the cliff as they mapped out the area from this great view. The drop from the cliff was almost straight down from where they were, and directly before them was more land, which appeared to be much the same as the land they had just traveled.

Elonda led the horse to the side and slowly found a way for horse and rider to descend. Once at the bottom Elonda searched the area for any unwanted creatures. Satisfied with the result, she looked again to the horizon. Ever since her eyes laid upon it, it called to her. She almost kicked Wild Spirit's flanks, letting him loose, when an elf called from above.

"Elonda, find a suitable place to camp, we will stay here for tonight."

Elonda reached down and whispered in the horse's ear, "Not yet, not quite yet."

That night the group agreed to continue on until they had reached the point about which they all had grown so curious. The coming together of the water and the sky. Even though it would create a much longer journey, they all thought it was well worth it.

As the days went on, Elonda's desire to chase the horizon grew. They continued in that direction, but the going was slow. The map making and scouting was too slow for Elonda. It had already been 38 days since she had seen Jyres. At this pace, it would be at least another 38 before she saw him again.

That night, as she was tending to Wild Spirit, she made up her mind. Quickly and quietly she mounted her horse. With her sword on her back, and a few supplies hanging from the saddle, she slapped the reins and kicked the horse.

It shot out from camp like lighting. The elves gave shouts for her, asking where she was going. But she was gone. With each hoofbeat on the ground, she was growing closer to her adventure. The night was dark, and the wind whipped against her as Wild Spirit thundered on. They rode long into the night.

Two nights later Elonda had arrived at her destination. Saddled on Wild Spirit, they stood on a small natural overlook. Elonda stared out over the water. The water went on and on. And the night moon, bright in the sky, sent moonbeams off of the water. The effect showed the water in a magnificent color blue, one that reminded her of Jyres' eyes. She couldn't believe her eyes. The land had ended, and water began.

As she sat, captivated, she had no idea of what was happening around her. She closed her eyes and took a deep breath as the wind came from behind her and blew her gray cloak about her. While her eyes were closed, Wild Spirit suddenly flinched and started to turn its head. Elonda's state of calm vanished as something plowed into her, knocking her from the saddle. She landed hard and before she could do anything creatures were all around her. She tried to fight them off, but before she had any chance of it, her arms were pulled out in front of her and forced still by many hands. Her arms were quickly bound and then she was blindfolded. Her sword was yanked out of its sheath on her back and she heard Wild Spirits' neighs, but he too was being corralled.

She was led away by someone or something pushing her from behind and someone or something else pulling her with the rope that was binding her hands together. Without her sense of sight, she tried to hone in on the sounds around her. She heard many voices. The noises made by those voices were of a click-clack nature. She had no idea what they were saying as her captors talked with one another.

Suddenly, her feet were traveling across what felt like ground that was not all that different from the desert sands of the Desert of Despair. She struggled to keep her footing as her captors continued to drag her along. Finally, they stopped and she fell to the ground, her knees hitting the sand, or what she assumed was sand. She stayed there, catching her breath as the click-clack voices talked amongst each other.

Her thoughts drifted to her fellow elves. What would they do? Would they continue on their path and maintain their slow pace of mapping the area? Or would they rush to catch up with her? No, they would continue their mission. She had left them to follow her own path, her own desire and she was paying the consequences. She could not expect immediate help from them.

She was jarred back to the present, as rough, almost scaly hands grabbed each of her arms and hoisted her up. She was dimly aware of the surroundings changing as she was pushed along again. The ground she walked on was now cool and rough and the air felt closer and cooler than a moment before.

She was pushed down again, this time the ground was not as forgiving as the sand was to her knees. Then the blindfold was pulled off and she blinked a time or two, her eyes adjusting to the dim light. As she looked around, she first tried to establish where she was. She was in a dimly lit cave, torches attached to the walls fighting off the dark. In front of her and a little above on a natural rocky platform stood two creatures she had never seen before. She cast her gaze to the side, and on each side of her stood one of the creatures as well.

The creatures were smaller than her, and had an almost animal look to them. They did not stand straight up; there was a bend to their posture. Their skin looked rough and scaly and their heads reminded her of the lizards often seen near the Desert of Despair. They also had small horns or spikes that protruded from their skin in places. Their large dark eyes were set in on their face, which had little more than slits as nostrils and a wide mouth.

The creatures in front of her started talking in their language and they were looking at her as they said it. Unsure of what to do, Elonda said back to them, "I don't understand." First in elvish, and a second time in the common tongue.

The two in front of her talked to each other and then one walked away, leaving her field of vision. Then, for a long time, nothing happened. Everyone just stayed where they were.

Eventually, new voices could be heard behind her, from the direction she had entered the cave. She could hear one that sounded much different than the creatures around her, but it still spoke in their language. She heard footsteps coming behind her and to her surprise she saw two humans follow one of the creatures to the rocky platform above her.

"Well, this is not what I suspected, that is for sure," said one of the humans. She recognized that voice, but couldn't place it and she did not recognize the face, either. Then the other human spoke.

"The elven warrior, Elonda, has somehow made it to the coast."

That voice she did recognize. But no, how could that be, that didn't make sense. Elonda couldn't keep a look of confusion off her face, and shook her head in disbelief. She could have sworn that the former Knight of Enchantment, Karth, was standing before her.

"Karth, is that you?"

"Why, yes, it is. I know, we are not wearing the armor you became accustomed to all those years. This is Brigand, I am sure you remember him as well," said Karth, gesturing to the other human as he did so.

They were certainly not wearing the armor of the knights, but were clad in all black, each with a sword sheathed at their side. Elonda smiled, suddenly realizing she may not be in as much trouble as she feared.

"Wait, so you know these creatures, you can get me out of this mess!"

"Perhaps," said Karth. "But first you will tell me what you are doing here, as your presence has distressed our—" Karth paused as if searching for the right word. "Clients," he finally finished.

"Clients?" Elonda repeated.

"Yes, the yixl hired us to help them with a particular problem, and we have stayed here ever since. Now why have you come?"

Elonda sighed and responded, "We are on a mission to explore the world and as I was watching the water they kidnapped me. I mean them no harm."

Karth turned to the creature next to him and talked to it in its own language. After a moment or two he turned back to her. "What assurance can you give them that you do not mean them any harm?"

"You can talk to them," Elonda said, surprise clearly evident in her voice.

Karth and Brigand both looked at each other with smiles on their faces and Brigand shrugged. Karth looked at Elonda and said, "Each of the Knights are a delga and had their own inherited power, but somehow Meslar had suppressed it and some of us even forget what our power was. I am able to speak in any language it seems. I can't explain it, my mind just comprehends it and spits back out what is needed. Brigand here has the ability to heal injuries and wounds, which brought us here in the first place."

"Amazing," Elonda said quietly, and then in a louder voice, "Tell them I have no reason to harm them, and will prove it in any way they see fit."

Karth translated the message, and satisfied, the leader of the yixl ordered her to be untied. Karth did so.

"You are allowed to move about, but you must stay within sight of the entrance of the cave. Brigand will show you where you will sleep." After saying that, Karth nodded to Brigand and exited the cave.

Elonda followed Brigand through the cave and through another side passage made in the rock into a much smaller cave. Brigand offered Elonda her sword and she silently replaced it in its sheath on her back.

"Where did they take my horse?" Elonda said, agitation in her voice.

"Just leave the cave and turn left, you will see."

After thanking the former knight she left the caves and went back into the night. She found the horse as Brigand had said she would. Wild Spirit was still showing signs of unease. The horse was tied to two stakes that were driven into the rock and it was not happy at all. Three of the yixl creatures stood around it, not daring to get any closer.

Elonda walked right up to her horse, and with a soothing voice and gentle strokes she calmed Wild Spirit. She stayed with him a few more moments before giving the horse a final pat and climbing on top of the rocks nearby. The yixl stared at her as she did so, whether that was because they were instructed to watch her or she was just odd to them, she could not guess.

Standing on top of the rocks, she looked around her. The area in front of her was full of sand, which led down to the water that lapped upon the shore. She glanced to the left and right and she saw the same thing as far as she could see. Her heart thumped in her chest. The thought of technically still being a prisoner of these creatures was far away from her as she took in her surroundings. What an amazing sight! She only wished Jyres was standing next to her, for she doubted she could do this sight justice by merely speaking of it.

The rocks she stood on were adjacent to others. Many different rock formations dotted the coastline, and many appeared to have caves either naturally made or somehow created by the yixl. As she looked out over the water she thought she could make out something in the distance, but with the darkness she could not be sure what it was. Satisfied for now, she jumped back down to the sand and, startling the creatures near her, she ran straight towards the water.

Some of the yixl ran after her, not sure of her intentions. But she slowed down as she neared the water. Taking off her traveling boots, she stuck her toes in the water. The water was cold, but she kept her feet there anyway. She stood there a long while, enjoying this new experience. Finally, she picked up her boots and started walking back to the cave, the sand sticking to her feet as she did so.

6
TRUST MUST BE EARNED

The next day Elonda was presented with the challenge by which she would need to prove herself trustworthy to the yixl. Further down the coast from the caves in which the yixl resided, birds had made the rocky slopes near the beach their home. The birds were called isle crows by the yixl and they had nests. In these nests were eggs highly prized by the yixl. Her task was to retrieve one, a task that Karth claimed was not easy.

Elonda stood at the bottom of the cliffs and watched as the birds came and went from their nests. The first step was to get to one of the nests. As she gazed at the rocky terrain, she tried to spot some sort of course that she could take to reach the nests, which were located high and built into crevasses in the rock. As she stared up, she heard a chuckle behind her. Karth, Brigand, and two yixl had come to observe her as she attempted to complete the challenge. Elonda whipped around and directed a warning glare toward the group.

Karth threw his hands up. "Sorry, we will be quiet."

Giving him a weak smile in return, Elonda undid the straps holding her sword to her back and handed it to Karth. One of the yixl handed her a small pouch which she tied around her waist.

Elonda did not see an easy way to reach one of the nests, but she knew that she had to be successful. Elonda proceeded to the rocky face, and finding a hand hold for each hand, she began the climb. As she climbed, getting higher with each reach and step, she looked back down toward the ground. A brief second of fear from the sight of the distance to the ground took hold of her, but then her adrenaline kicked in. A smile came to her face and she continued the climb. A few moments later, her foot slipped and she was momentarily only hanging on by her hands. Her fingers, already blistering from the climb, hung on tight. Her feet soon found a delicate hold on the rock face and she continued the climb. After climbing a little further, she found a path that would take her close to a nest.

She was now within an arm's reach of the nest, but one of the birds sat in it protecting two large eggs. The birds were big black birds, with long beaks and sharp talons. The bird in the nest eyed Elonda with malice as Elonda drew close. She tried to wave off the bird with exaggerated movements, but the bird stayed put. Then she tried yelling at it, and it responded by snapping its beak at her. She pulled back quickly to avoid being pecked at more than was necessary.

Elonda let her weight on her legs, giving her hands a break and shaking them to restore normal feeling. She stayed in the position a moment longer, trying to come up with something to try next. Looking below her and to her left she saw a small ledge and it gave her an idea. She turned her body so she was sideways with the rock face and no longer flat.

She shifted her focus towards the nest to find the next hand hold she would need and then without hesitation she jumped. Elonda grabbed the hand hold and used it to continue the momentum towards the nest. Elonda was then in midair, no longer anything keeping her safe from falling. As she came at the bird, with elven quickness she put her left arm up in defense while her right arm came up and grabbed an egg.

The bird pecked at her mercilessly, her left arm taking the blows. She cried out in pain as she began to fall, the egg safely in her right hand. She looked down, quickly spotting the ledge she was counting on. Like only a trained agile elven warrior could manage, she bent her legs and landed on the ledge. The ledge was barely wider than her feet, yet she had landed, avoiding what surely would have been a fall to her death.

Blood trickled down her arm in multiple places from where the bird had pecked her. The isle crow was making an incredible amount of noise, and nearby birds were joining the agitated bird. Not wanting to wait around to find out what would happen next, Elonda tucked the egg away in the pouch the yixl had given her and quickly started to descend.

More and more birds started to take up the annoying bird call and fly in her general direction. She continued her descent, reaching the halfway point, and now multiple birds began flying directly towards her.

Throwing caution to the wind, she jumped, and with her dark hair flowing behind her she landed on a small ledge much like she had done before. She moved quickly this way, leaving the birds behind her. She completed a couple more jumps before landing safely on the sand.

"Now that was something," said Karth as Elonda approached them. "Impressive."

Elonda shrugged it away and handed the pouch with the egg to one of the yixl. "Do they trust me now?"

Once back at the main cave, Elonda was asked to wait while they discussed matters. After spreading some salve on her arm, Elonda wrapped her arm with a bandage. Elonda always kept some of the healing salve that Skystair produced with her. It had proved useful on more than one occasion. Elonda chose to spend her time waiting by standing in the sand looking out over the water.

Now, with the light of day, she could see what she could not make out the night before. There were small land formations out on the water, and she even saw one tall building in one of these areas. This intrigued her greatly. How would one even get to the building? As she thought this over in her mind, Karth approached her.

"Well, they finally have decided you are not currently an enemy. This is the first time they have ever seen an elf, you know."

"I assumed so, as I have never seen them before. Well, I am glad that is out of the way. So I am free to do as I please?" Elonda's statement was more asking for confirmation than it was a real question.

"I don't know if I would go so far as to say that. They are a race that scares easily, and they have lived in their little part of the world for a long time with very little interaction with anyone else. They have few threats, save the natural elements."

"I don't understand," replied Elonda.

"They are afraid more of your people will come. The two who watched you steal that egg were quite impressed with you and they told their leader as much." Karth had emphasized the words "quite impressed."

"I did what they asked," expressed Elonda.

Karth sighed. "I know. But you did it well, how an elf would do it, with such skill and movements they have never seen before. I mean, you even impressed me, and I have seen plenty of elves! The way you were able to do it so gracefully has worried them as they, as I said, scare easily."

"Well, I will not lie to you Karth." Elonda paused and looked Karth in the eyes. "More elves will come. Either searching for me, or to expand the Kingdom of Calridian. But no harm will come to them, we wish only to help them and expand our knowledge."

"I believe you. Your race and the king helped us knights when we didn't even know we needed it. You have given us a second chance, a chance to redeem ourselves." Karth broke eye contact before adding, "You are just talking about things they don't understand."

"How do I make them understand?" pleaded Elonda. "How have you and Brigand fit in so well?"

"Brigand and I had decided a while ago to take our leave of Castle Mystic and set out on our own. We traveled far and wide and eventually we came upon this vast bit of land touched by water. As it so happened, I had taken a tumble down the rocky landscape and scraped up my face. Brigand, as I told you, had already learned that his power to heal had returned. He pressed his hands to my face and took away the pain and the cuts. Unknown to us, we were being watched by the yixl who saw what Brigand had done." Karth paused as if remembering, and then continued.

"The leader's young child had been badly injured by a blade. After they saw what Brigand did, they approached us for help. To my astonishment, I could understand what they were saying. Brigand saw to the healing, and we have been with them ever since."

"Injured by a blade?" asked Elonda, wondering who could possibly have found the yixl in the first place.

"Yes, they have but one known enemy, a race not unlike humans, or perhaps they are humans. They live out on those isles that you see. They call themselves the Shepherds of the Isles."

"I was wondering about those buildings on the isles." Elonda paused as she stared out at the water and the isles. "So, somehow I need to be accepted, as you have," Elonda thought out loud. "Dealing with those shepherds may be the way to do just that."

7
MERRITUK

Mit Merrituk awoke a frustrated yet determined man. He had yet to make any progress with the empress and the City of Heritage. But he had been tasked with bringing the human city under the kingdom's banner and he was not one to give up easily. Past experiences had taught him to be persistent. This was not the first challenge he had faced in his young life. In the years that followed the humans throwing off Meslar's oppression, many things had to be done for their village to survive.

Jyres had started them off on the right path, and was seen as a hero. And he was; Mit would agree with that statement. But Jyres was not around for the hard work that had taken place over the last three years to bring Skystair to where it was today. And now, at only 19 years of age, Mit had positioned himself as one of the King's Ambassadors.

He had started by simply helping his village get things they needed to survive. Food, water, clothing and the like. He quickly became the one everyone looked to for supplies. People wanted more than what he could provide, which became his first challenge. So he had to acquire more supplies, and at the young age of just 16 he left the village on three consecutive trips to visit the elves, dwarves, and Castle Mystic in order to open up communication for possible trading relationships. By age 17 he was actively trading for the human village, the healing salve that the humans had long been making being the most traded good. The salve was made from a mixture of sand, water, and the root of a cactus that grew in the desert which had healing properties.

The next challenge he undertook was to establish himself and the village as a person and place of substance. He knew the people needed to take pride in what they had created in this new settlement, so he pushed for the people to establish a name for the village. At first, the village leaders were not open to the idea. It had required Mit to be persistent. But after numerous conversations, the village leaders started to come around on the idea and thus finally the city of Skystair was born. The name soon brought both pride and recognition to the city.

Historically the village had struggled to maintain a stable population, as the people tended to die young. But since the village's rebirth, and the founding of Skystair, the population had slowly begun to grow. With this growth, lineage and family became more important. The humans of Skystair had moved on from just trying to survive to trying to live. The people took pride in their city and wanted to leave something to their children. Thus, family names were born. Almost all of the humans in Skystair took on family names, something that had never been done before in the history of the human village.

Mit, with no living relatives, chose his family name of Merrituk all on his own. He had no particular reason for the chosen name, other than to stand out from the other names. This seemed to work well for Mit, as he started to make a name for himself with the other races and which had led him here, on a mission from the king himself. If he could make this work, he would be as close as anyone to King Malick, something others his age could only dream of. With that in mind he set off to meet again with the empress and her Palace Official.

The empress was dressed simply as always, her hair he noticed, was not as neat as it usually was. Thinking nothing of it, Mit bowed before he took his seat at the table. The usual small talk ensued as they ate a light lunch. The food was excellent. After lunch, servants came and cleaned up the table and took away any evidence they had eaten.

The empress was the one to start the more serious conversation this time. "Mr. Merrituk—"

But Mit interrupted her. "Empress, please. How many times must I ask? Mit is fine, you honor me far too much with your formality."

Pretty much ignoring him, the empress continued, "Mr. Merrituk, you have been with us now for multiple days and we still have not come to any sort of agreement. Although we have enjoyed our discussions, I think it is safe to say that the City of Heritage will remain as is, self-reliant."

"I understand why you would say that," responded Mit in a conversational tone. "But there is still one thing that I have not discussed with you, and that may yet change the minds of you and your citizens." Mit was going to have to play his final card.

The Palace Official responded in a dismissive tone, "We appreciate your boldness, however, I don't see what could possibly change the city's or the empress' mind."

"Perhaps you could humor me, your highness?" The empress nodded in return. "Very good. Now the city of Heritage is a proud city. A city of honor, a city of independence, and of history. There are few things it holds to be worth more than honor. Would you agree?"

The Palace Official responded again, "Yes, we have discussed this in the past; this is not a new direction for this conversation."

The empress, however, quickly chided him. "We will hear him out. Please continue."

Mit smiled a sly smile and bowed low. "Thank you. Now where was I? Oh, yes, honor. Many things can bring honor to a city. For this great city, much of your honor comes from your past. Your long years of prosperity, and your ability to still be here despite the War of Ages. The city of Heritage still stands. Another thing that can bring honor is your people. Your people make up the largest population on this side of the mountains. Your city was the last city of the human race, and it is full of humans. But what human has brought more honor to your race than Jyres?" Mit paused. The rest of this conversation would be the thing that sealed his seat by the king...or relegated him to some minor role.

"Jyres, although human, has no connection to Heritage," replied the young empress in a calm manner.

"Doesn't he, though? How much do you or others in your city know about the humans of the new world?"

"We will admit, our knowledge is limited," replied the official, his tone of voice showing his renewed interest in the direction of the conversation.

"Well, did you know they have no records, and only recently even bothered with family names? Take me for example, I am the only Merrituk living."

"I don't see how that applies to our current situation, other than the fact there is no proof of where any of their families have come from."

"Official, you have just said it, don't you see? Is there really no proof? Perhaps the empress does see?" Mit turned towards her, sitting calm as ever in her chair at the end of the table. He allowed his eyes to linger on her a little longer than etiquette permitted for she was not at all displeasing to look at. Quiet fell over the room, and he thought perhaps he had faltered, but then the empress stood up.

"I believe you have earned yourself one more meal with us Mr. Merrituk. We will discuss it again over lunch tomorrow. I will think about what you have said. In the meantime, please continue to enjoy our hospitality."

Mit Merrituk stood up and bowed. He was unable to keep a charming smile from his face as he straightened. "I look forward to it, Empress."

8
LUMPKIN

Lumpkin, son of Lustor, set his pack down on the ground, and sat next to it. He then pulled off his bright green, pointy hat and tossed it on top of the bag. The hard ground was not comfortable, but he was tired and his legs still appreciated the break, even if his backside did not. His short legs had carried him a long way. He had left a small village on foot, what seemed like days and days ago. But there in front of him, finally, was the former city of Secord.

Lumpkin pulled out a cloth from one of his many pockets, wiped his sweaty forehead and stood up again. The dwarf was short, shorter than most dwarves and a trip of this distance had been taxing on him. Although he would not consider himself old, his body was telling him he was not young anymore, either. Reaching down, he reclaimed his pointy hat and placed it back over his dark brown hair and hoisted up his pack.

After walking a little farther, he entered the ruined city. Fallen buildings and partly still-standing stone walls were all around him as he moved about the city. Night had fallen and the sky grew dark. Lumpkin undid the buttons on his thin dark jacket, revealing an inner layer which was lined with small pockets. Each of those pockets had a vial of liquid in it, causing a clicking sound when he walked. He reached into a pocket and pulled out a vial with a pale-yellow liquid. Undoing the stopper in the vial as he continued to walk, he casually poured the yellow potion onto his boots.

The dwarf continued to walk as he returned the vial to its pocket. After a few more steps, his boots started to glow. With each step they seemed to get brighter and his feet became like drops of sunlight in the darkened city.

Lumpkin considered himself an alchemist of sorts, and his potions could be useful for many things, such as casting a little light into the night. He was a bit of an outcast, however, and most of his dwarven kin considered him quite odd. Whether it was his pointed hat, silly potions, or rambling speech, that caused him to be looked at in such a way, Lumpkin was not sure. Or...maybe it was all three of those things.

A little while later, his portion started to wear off, but even in the failing light he noticed a change in the area around him. The building in front of him, although also in ruin, seemed different somehow. He walked through what was a doorway at one time and looked around. Off to his left the rubble had been cleared away, revealing an entrance underneath the old building.

Lumpkin started to descend the stairs as the brightness of his boots completely faded away. After walking down another flight of stone steps, Lumpkin could see at the limit of his vision, a bit of light coming from further down. Lumpkin continued down, towards the light. Coming to a stone-arch doorway he stepped into a large, brightly lit hall. The hall was filled with books! He had made it to his destination, the great library of Secord.

He continued to walk into the hall, his eyes wide in amazement. He didn't even see the old man sitting at a desk at the other end of the hall, his eyes so distracted by the sight and magnificence of it all. His feet continued to move and his eyes wandered until he finally saw the man, not more than a spear's length away now.

Surprised, Lumpkin just stood there a moment, before deciding to see if any other old men were hiding somewhere and he looked wildly around. Satisfied this was the only one, Lumpkin returned his attention to the man and the desk.

The man seemed not to realize that Lumpkin was standing there, or just chose to ignore him. Stacks of books were on both ends of the desk. The man seemed to be closely studying the leather-bound tome on the desk in front of him. Lumpkin chose to wait to be noticed and after a little while he started rocking back and forth on his toes and heels. Soon he started whistling to himself. A few moments later he realized he was whistling and stopped. He returned his attention back to the man, who was still focused on his book. So Lumpkin waited some more and before he knew it he was rocking and whistling again.

Finally, the man looked up and Lumpkin thought the old man would be startled to see a dwarf in front of him. But he didn't seem surprised at all, just content.

The old man smiled and said, "Well, you have arrived right on time."

Sure that the man certainly couldn't be addressing him with such a statement, Lumpkin slowly turned to see who was behind him. But no one else was here. The old man chuckled and gestured with his hand to the chair on the other side of the table, though Lumpkin could have sworn there wasn't a chair there a moment ago. Sitting down, Lumpkin dropped his pack to the ground beside the chair.

"I do believe I have made a discovery, and so I say again, you are right on time. My name is Zar. And who might you be?" asked the old man.

Still unsure of what was happening, Lumpkin struggled for words, which was unusual for him. Finally, he said, "Lumpkin, son of Lustor."

"Well met, Lumpkin, may I offer you a glass of wine? Flick found it in the cellars, and it is very old, but it is quite sweet." Zar chuckled to himself and poured two glasses of wine from the bottle that had been sitting on a small table behind the man. Giving one to Lumpkin, he sipped from the other.

Realization finally came to Lumpkin. He had said his name was Zar. Zar. The wizard whose name was well known throughout the land after the events of a few years ago. Lumkpin stood up fast in astonishment, almost spilling his wine.

"You are Zar!" he exclaimed. "It is my lucky day, it is. I was coming to this library to find books, books that could help me. But I found you as well. Zar. The wizard. Well this is just amazing! I was coming to the library, did I say that? Anyway, I was coming to the library and here you are, Zar." Lumpkin paused, but just for a second and started speaking again before Zar could say anything. "This is amazing, it is. I think you can help more than books. I had come looking for books." Lumpkin started pacing back and forth in front of the desk and continued mumbling on.

Zar took another drink from his wine glass as he watched the little dwarf pace back and forth and talk to himself. A smile came to the old wizard's face, appreciating the uniqueness of the dwarf in front of him. The pointed hat, nervous energy, and silliness of Lumpkin were not the typical characteristics of a dwarf.

All of a sudden, Lumpkin stopped walking and said, "Wait, you said I had come on time, you did. So, you said that, that I came on time?"

Zar still amused, smiled and said, "I did, twice, and now so have you. Please sit again and I will explain." Zar waited for the dwarf to sit down and once he did, gestured for him to have a drink of his wine. Confident now that the dwarf would listen, he began.

"So, I have been here, in this library, oh, for over a year now. I had visited this library a few years past, with some friends, and enjoyed being around so much knowledge. So I decided to come back and stay here. Flick and I moved in." As if on cue, a small creature raced in from somewhere and now stood on the desk. His movements were so fast and quick that Lumpkin could not follow them. Flick was a longtime friend of Zar. He was even shorter than Lumpkin and had pointed ears and black fur.

"Ah, yes, here he is now," remarked Zar. "Flick, this is Lumpkin. Now, where was I? Oh, moved in. Yes, so we have been here surrounded by so many magnificent stories. At first, I just enjoyed picking up a book or scroll and reading. But then, I took it upon myself to catalog this amazing collection." Zar stopped, and glanced over at Flick who was making motions with his hands. "Yes, yes, of course, we took it upon ourselves," said Zar emphasizing the word *ourselves*. "And just look, Lumpkin, do you see the amount of knowledge around us?"

Lumpkin turned in his chair, again taking in the sight of so many books and scrolls.

Apparently satisfied, Zar continued. "So, as you can imagine, it has been a very long process. But, that brings us to my proclamation earlier. You arrived right on time because I believe I have finally figured something out. For the longest time, everything appeared to be in random places, with no order to them. But tonight as you walked in the door I had a thought. They are not organized by time period, or by writer, nor by subject matter. I had started to think that it was by race. But then as I was reading this large book here, I realized that this book, written by a dwarf, obvious by the language used, was not by other dwarven books on the shelves. And you, a dwarf, walked into a place where no dwarves are. So what if you wrote a book while you were here at the library? Where would that book go? It is really quite simple."

Lumpkin sat at the edge of his seat, listening, but then Zar stopped talking. Lumpkin stared at the wizard, a confused look on his face.

"So, what's the answer my silly dwarf?"

"I don't know, I don't," replied the still confused Lumpkin.

"Why, everything is organized by where it was written!" Zar exclaimed. "I do not know how I did not see it before. But that is why you arrived right on time. You, a dwarf, in a place where other dwarves have not been seen, made it pop into my mind. So I thank you Lumpkin. Finally, now the real work can begin. Don't you agree?"

Lumpkin resisted the urge to turn around again to see if someone else was here. Because why would he agree, what was the work that could begin? Before Lumpkin could voice his question the wizard continued on.

"Now that we know where to look, we can begin our search for more information on what the gate is keeping locked away. We got lucky with our find a few years ago. But now, you and I can plan, search and read," Zar said with confidence and authority that Lumpkin dared not question.

Lumpkin responded as he bobbed up and down in his chair, the vials clinking in his jacket, "May we also try to find books for how to make potions?"

"But of course," responded the kindly wizard.

9
ANOTHER DAY

Jyres returned to the Forest of Malkin, the closest thing to what Jyres could call home. Over the last few years, he had spent more time there than anywhere else, and it was a wonderful place. The elven home was magnificent and still enthralled him just as it did when he had first seen it. The whole elven community lived in structures that were made right into the trees. Lalatco and Elonda had first brought him here after helping him and the human village. Every time he was here, a sense of calm came over him.

As he had suspected, however, Elonda was still away on her journey. He had gone looking for her right away, even though he knew he would be disappointed. After confirming his expectation he headed off in the direction of his home. The elven leader, Malick's nephew, Simamar, had graciously offered Jyres a permanent home, which was located next to Lalatco's and Leah's. Both of the homes were built in and around the same tree.

Jyres climbed the stairs, ascending the elaborate staircase to his residence. He passed a window that looked into Lalatco's and Leah's house, and was surprised to see them both there. They were laughing with each other as they sat at a table.

Jyres continued on until he reached his door and quickly entered. Jyres undid his sword belt and leaned it against the wall, dropped his saddle bag to the floor and collapsed onto his bed. Sleep came quickly to him; the elven home seemed to be the only place that gave him a contented rest.

Descending down the staircase in the morning, Jyres was greeted by a familiar voice.

"Jyres, when did you return?" Leah ran up to him, hugging him tightly and kissing his cheek. She wore an elven morning dress, the color of pale blue. He still hadn't gotten used to seeing her in clothes other than those of a jungle hunter, but he greeted her warmly just the same.

"Just returned last night. It is good to be back. And is married life still treating you well? Or are you ready for another adventure?"

"I have never been better. Lalatco is just getting ready to leave. If you hurry to the stables you may catch him."

"Thank you, and you look lovely," said Jyres as he leaned down and returned her kiss with one of his own on each cheek before hurrying off to the stables. There he found Lalatco just mounting his horse.

"Jyres, I just saw Gerti, and knew you must have come back. How were your travels?"

Jyres grabbed the horse's reins and led it and its rider out of its stall and out of the stables. "All went well. I am surprised to see you still here."

"Yes, a later start than perhaps planned," Lalatco replied with a smile on his face. "Jyres, Leah has made me the happiest I have ever been. It is hard to leave her for longer than I have to. But don't worry, you know me well, and you know that my duty is also a source of my honor and I will not forsake my honor. A Keeper of the Key I shall remain."

"Believe me, Lalatco, I could not be happier for the two of you, my dearest friends. But I didn't realize until now that I also needed to hear of your dedication once again. Thank you for that."

"Take heart, and stick to the plan, as shall I." Lalatco smiled one more time at his friend before taking the reins and trotting the horse towards the east. Jyres watched him go until he lost sight of him amongst the trees.

Sticking to the plan, as they always did, Jyres and Lalatco met up a few days later at an outpost located a day's travel south of the Valley of Dragons. In their plan of revolving key locations, they met at this place twice. Once they had the key, and once they did not. At this particular time, neither of them had the key. Jyres took the opportunity to talk to Lalaltco about the concerns he had over his last meeting with the king.

"Malick all but said he was no longer worried about the creature. I know it is a mistake to underestimate it. I still see it in my dreams, it's mere existence threatening me."

"I can't imagine that is truly the case. Malick may not have been there when the creature escaped, but he knows how important it is." Lalatco stood, his face echoing the thoughts of confusion going through his mind. "Well," he continued, "perhaps we should go and talk with him. We will be direct about our concerns. He respects both of us and will listen."

"Let us go and talk with him right now!" Jyres exclaimed.

"Not now, but soon. We must stick to the plan. You have somewhere to be. And I should return to Leah."

Frustrated, Jyres shook his head. "Fine. The next time we are here, we'll allow time for us to travel together to the Valley. And then we will address the king. Agreed?" Jyres extended his hand to Lalatco.

Lalatco clasped it and pulled Jyres in for a quick hug. Releasing him then, Lalatco smiled, "You have not changed, my friend."

"Should I have?" asked Jyres, unsure of what his friend was saying.

Lalatco chuckled. "No, no. You are always thinking of the task at hand. Your mind is set on the problem, as it always is."

"Don't you remember, when my mind was set on Leah instead of the gate?"

"I do, yes, but who can blame you, I certainly can't." Both laughed at each other, and then Lalatco said, "I must edit my statement. You have grown in confidence. Since defeating Meslar, you have become a more confident man. That is good, just don't let it convince you to go and try to do something without me by your side, all right?"

"Oh, all right," replied Jyres. "I will only do something stupid if you are with me."

Lalatco laughed and shook his head. "Maybe that is not quite what I meant."

"I know." Jyres was nodding his head. "I understand. I look forward to talking with the king. Perhaps my fears are unfounded."

"We can hope. In the meantime, we can continue to do our part."

The two embraced one more time before Lalatco left the small outpost to begin his ride back to the Forest of Malkin and his lovely bride. Jyres, on the other hand, had to go retrieve the key.

Jyres led Gerti away from the outpost, starting his journey toward the cliffs and the home of the dwarves. Vurth's son, Tagro, was the leader of the dwarves now. Although Jyres liked him well enough, it was not the same as seeing his friend with the orange beard. But Tagro would welcome him and offer his hospitality if he chose to stay with the dwarves for a night or two.

Jyres traveled in a northwestern direction, traveling across the plains of Alhazar toward the northern end of the Forest of Malkin. Jyres and Lalatco could have traveled together for a little while before Lalatco split off to enter the forest, but the two Keepers of the Key tried to limit the amount of times they were traveling together, another way to make it hard to track them. If there was anyone tracking them. At this point, King Malick seemed to think otherwise.

As luck would have it, though, Jyres' and Lalatco's paths crossed again later in the day as they both needed to cross the Mitelow River. Jyres had spotted Lalatco's slender frame and after confirming it was him, turned Gerti in that direction. The first time they crossed this river together didn't go so well. Lalatco had almost ended up being washed away by the river, but had been able to save himself. This time, neither of them had trouble crossing, and they said their goodbyes once again as Lalatco went deeper into the forest and Jyres skirted the northern end on his way to the cliffs. This eventually led him to the same outpost he had stopped at on his way to Skystair.

After a short stay at the outpost, he moved on to the cliffs where he was greeted kindly by the dwarves. Choosing to make his stay a quick one, he looked for the first opportunity to leave unnoticed from the dwarves' homes. The cliffs had a waterfall that rushed out and became the Eternal River. The waterfall was also one of the hiding spots for the key.

Jyres made his way out of the tunnels of the dwarves and to the back side of the cliffs and the rushing waterfall. There he found the path that led to the top of the falls. He paused there, watching the river come out of the cliffs and rushing out into the air. The dwarves had tried to find where the river began underneath the cliffs, but had never been able to do so, leading to the name Eternal River. He followed the river just a short way before he found the spot he was looking for.

A small opening had been cut into the rock and there in a small box was the key. Grabbing the small box Jyres held his breath as he opened it. He was relieved to find the key still there and untouched. He picked up the key, stuffed it into his pocket, and returned the box.

Jyres turned and walked back out to the start of the waterfall, watching the water rush out and down. It was a beautiful sight, the water cascading down to the forest floor. Looking out to the north he could see the plateau where Skystair sat. And if he shifted his view to the south, the Forest of Malkin sprawled out across the land. Past the forest were the uncharted lands, the area the elves were exploring for the king. Elonda was out there somewhere.

Another day had passed. Another day and the key was still safe. Another day and the creature still had not been seen. Another day. Time continued on, unchanging, much like the river he stood before. As the river went on, so did time, eternally.

10

THE SHEPHERDS OF THE ISLES

The sky was dark, but the night moon was bright against the darkness. Elonda remained in her hiding spot, watching for any movement across the water. She had decided that helping the yixl against the Shepherds of the Isles was her best option to gain the trust of the scaly creatures. The only issue being that no such option had yet presented itself. This was her third night of watching and listening, but no discernible movements were made by the shepherds.

Elonda was almost disappointed, which made her feel guilty for wanting these creatures to be attacked just so she would be given the opportunity to defend them.

She was surprised her elven friends had not caught up with her yet and wanted to have a level of trust built up before more elves walked into their midst. But for all she knew, her fellow travelers had left her to her decisions and headed for home. Either way, when she returned home with news that she had found life, the elven leader would send word to King Malick. Malick would want to bring them into the kingdom as he had everyone else.

For that to happen, Elonda had to come to some sort of a plan of trust or the yixl would just be scared by Malick's attempts. Malick believed safety came with everyone united together. But that strategy had failed before with the Week of Peace. Who's to say it would not fail again?

It was getting late, and Elonda decided it would be another wasted night at watch. She returned to her small cave, and after discarding her gear, laid down on the hard rock floor. The elves had certainly gotten used to rough sleeping arrangements during their explorations, but this was less than perfect. Pulling her blanket tight around her, Elonda closed her eyes, waiting for sleep to come.

But it didn't.

Her mind was restless, the warrior in her still not satisfied with the current state of affairs. A frustrating sigh escaped her lips as she rolled onto her side.

As she laid there, she took a few deep breaths, calming herself, feeling the world around her. She kept her eyes closed, breathing in a deep and consistent manner. Her mother had taught her early on the needed meditative practices for her wild spirit. She continued to focus on her breathing as a picture of Jyres came into her mind.

Her thoughts quickly turned to wondering where he was and what he was doing. The image in her head changed to one of him standing next to his horse, talking with a group of elves. The last thing she remembered as she drifted off to sleep was his smile cast in her direction.

Finally, Elonda thought to herself, as she spied a small boat creeping ever so slowly towards the shore. Elonda had been lucky, catching its moving silhouette in one of the moonbeams. She had been able to continue to track it as it moved out from an island and approached the shore. Its general direction seemed to be heading towards the rock face that Elonda had had to climb a few days ago.

As had become the routine, there were a couple of yixl not far away from

Elonda as she did her nightly reconnaissance. Elonda motioned to them to stay where they were and put a finger to her lips. Hoping the yixl would oblige, Elonda began to slowly, and quietly, move down the coast line. She chose her moments to move along from rock to boulder as the figures in the boat looked in other directions. Satisfied of her position in relation to the direction of the boat, she huddled behind a boulder large enough to hide her slender shape.

Peeking her head around one side of the boulder she kept a close eye on the boat as it slowly slid onto the sand about a stone's throw from her position. There were three figures in the boat who she assumed were from the group called the Shepherds of the Isles. All of them seemed to be humans, but it was tough to tell in the dark. They appeared to say a few words to each other, before two of them started to walk towards the rocky cliff, leaving the third by the boat. They each carried a wooden club in their hand or on their back.

Elonda chose to observe them a while longer and remained in her hiding spot. She took a quick look at the shepherd by the boat, making sure he had not moved before focusing her attention on the other two. She watched with curiosity as she realized these two were going to attempt what she had done for the yixl a few days before. They each started to climb the rock face in different directions, each going towards a nest. They continued their climb, and she realized it would take them a little while; they appeared to be plenty strong, but lacked the agility that she possessed. This left just one shepherd able to defend against her as the two others were in mid-climb.

She silently crept out from her hiding spot, keeping one hand tightly on the sword on her back to keep it from making any noise as she moved. Her feet made nary a sound as she traversed the distance to the boat. Only when she was a few steps away did the shepherd see her approach. His shocked face looked like that of a male human as he tried to bring his club up to defend himself. But he was too slow. Elonda sprang from the ground and went knee first into the chest of the intruder, who fell to the ground, his club falling from his grasp as Elonda landed on top of him. Her knee was firmly planted in his chest, holding him to the ground.

The shepherd had the wind knocked out of him from the force of the blow. After finally catching his breath, he was about to shout a word of warning to his comrades, but Elonda had drawn her knife and held it to his neck. She raised a finger from her opposite hand to her lips, gesturing for the man to be quiet. He complied, for the moment at least.

Keeping her knife as a constant threat to the man, she proceeded to bind the man's hands and then shoved cloth into his mouth to ensure he could not make any noise. Satisfied with her work, she turned her attention to the others on the rock face. They both were starting their descent, each with an egg stuffed into a pack on their back. Once they reached the bottom and their concentration was no longer solely focused on the climb, they noticed Elonda.

She stood not five arm's lengths in front of them, a menacing shape. The dark of night only added to the effect, as she stood with sword drawn, face determined, and dark clothes that blended in with the night. The two shepherds shared a quick look with each other before reaching for the clubs at their backs.

Elonda's movements were a flurry of gray and dark blue as she engaged them. Even at two on one they were outmatched. Her sword sliced through the air knocking aside a club before it had even been swung. Elonda pivoted on her left foot and jumped, her right foot landing with a solid kick to the face of the shepherd. The shepherd fell backwards into the rock face and landed in agony on the ground.

As she finished her jump kick, her sword parried a swing from the other's club. It was a hard swing and she lost her grip on her sword and it flung against the rocks. A smile came to the face of the bigger of the two combatants.

But, what he didn't know was that he had left himself open to the same move that had downed his friend. He had swung too hard, leaving an opening and Elonda didn't hesitate, sending this one to the ground as well with one kick. Both of the shepherds were on the ground, slowly starting to stand.

Once they finally righted themselves, they realized their attacker was not alone, two more figures in black now stood beside her. Karth and Brigand had come quickly to back her up, even though it appeared she did not need it.

Elonda stood in the main cave alongside Brigand and Karth. The three prisoners sat on the ground, their hands and feet bound. Elonda focused on them. They did indeed appear to be human, as they had looked last night. Elonda did pick up on a few differences though. All three were hairier than any of the humans Elonda had seen. Their arms and legs were covered with brown hair, but not as thick as to be mistaken for fur. All of their noses were quite flat, with sunken eyes, giving their faces a flat appearance. They had muscular arms and legs. Powerful, she had no doubt.

Karth began speaking in the common language. "First, I need to know if you can understand me. Please respond or shake your head to acknowledge." The one in the middle nodded his head, but a mask of confusion was on his face. "So, maybe you do. Say something."

Again it was the one in the middle who reacted and he began to speak. His voice was deep and raspy and it did sound like the common language, but there were differences. Karth, of course, understood perfectly and Elonda and Brigand could follow most of what was being said. "We came for eggs, why do you keep us here?"

"You have done more than just take eggs in the past," replied Karth.

"Defense only, only defense," cried the man who had an earnest look on his face.

"Why do you steal these eggs, this is not your land?"

"We need eggs—needed. We go now, go now." The man motioned with his hands toward the water as he said so.

"No, not yet," replied Karth.

As an aside to Brigand, he said, "Stay watch, I will go talk to the yixl leader. Elonda, why don't you investigate their boat and their things, see if they brought anything else that would shed any light on the situation."

The boat had been brought to the caves and the shepherd's things had also been collected and put there. Elonda approached the boat and found two yixl by the boat sifting through things. She nodded her head when she was standing next to the boat. "May I see?" she asked, gesturing at the boat with her hands as she did so. Each of the yixl held up a broken egg, high inflection clicks issuing from their mouths as they did so.

"Broken?" Elonda said, with a confused look on her face. "Why would they take broken eggs?"

The yixl just stared back at her, unclear of what she was saying. She searched through the rest of the shepherds' things, but didn't see anything else of real use. Feeling more confused than before, she investigated the small wooden boat. The elves had a couple of boats back home as well, but they were seldom used. These seemed similar in construction as she scanned the boat for anything out of place.

Then she noticed something shiny on the bottom of the boat. On closer inspection she realized small pieces of broken eggshells were all over the outside of the boat. Somehow the pieces were used in construction of the bottom of the boat.

Elonda pointed it out to the two yixl still with her at the boat. Curious looks came over their faces. Elonda pointed at the broken egg shells in their hands and then at the bottom of the boat. They both nodded emphatically.

Elonda took one half of the broken egg shells from one of the yixl's hands. She pointed at the eggshell and then at the yixl. The yixl shook his head. He then put the half egg shells together, lining up the cracks.

Once it was back together he pretended to crack it again and pointed at the inside. He then handed the shells back to Elonda with a look of disgust on his face. Elonda smiled, leaped up, shells in hand, and raced back to the main cave.

Elonda found Karth and the yixl leader quickly. They were in mid discussion when she found them, but she interrupted anyway.

"The eggs, the shepherds only use the outer shells," Elonda said, smiling. The two just stared back at her, not understanding.

"Don't you see, Karth? The shepherds only use the outside of the eggs and the yixl only use the inside of the eggs. They are clashing over a commodity they can easily share."

Karth, recognition now clearly seen on his face, said, "You are saying that there is an option for peace, for trade. I will translate and we will see what can be done.

A few days later Elonda was saddled on Wild Spirit for the first time in what seemed like weeks. Elonda could feel the energy and enthusiasm radiating from the horse as they began their journey. It had taken a little work, but the discovery Elonda had made about the different uses of the eggs by the two different races had enabled them to broker a peace between The Shepherds of the Isles and the yixl. Elonda's involvement had also finally earned her the trust of the yixl. Their leader already put that trust on display by sending one of his kin, a yixl named Rutu, with Elonda to meet King Malick. Karth and Brigand also volunteered to go along to act as both translator and independent parties for any diplomatic conversations that would take place.

The four travelers had a long journey ahead of them. Rutu had no experience at all with horses and only after Elonda demonstrated riding the horse and explained there was nothing to worry about did he agree to sit behind Elonda on Wild Spirit. Karth and Brigand were also astride horses, with both horses carrying heavy packs of supplies for the journey.

11
STOVEA

Bram stood on the top of his castle. The big purple gargoyle was deep in thought. He had thought it all had worked out rather well, the human killing Meslar and one creature still escaping from the gate. It had been almost three years now since the creature had escaped the gate, but Bram had not made as much progress with his plan as he would have liked. Shortly after those events from three years ago Bram tried to help the creature obtain the key, but the creature seemed to be missing the abilities needed to do so.

The creature's mind was set on getting the key, but it lacked a strategic mind or the planning capabilities to do it. It had that one purpose, but Bram could not see how it would achieve that goal. Bram had struggled to keep tabs on Jyres while also making sure that the creature didn't get itself into trouble. Bram did not want someone else to interact with the creature and try to use it for their own gain. If anyone was going to capture and exploit the creature's powers, it would be him.

This had led Bram to make a difficult decision. He decided to keep the creature isolated in the castle, and it had been there for a long time now. Although it put their long-term partnership at risk, it would allow Bram to focus on locating the key instead of worrying about the creature. Bram was hopeful that if he delivered the key, the creature would quickly forget its captivity. The act of securing the creature had also produced one more benefit. Bram believed he had discovered at least part of what made these creatures so dangerous and why they had been trapped by the Gate of Fire.

A smile came across the gargoyle's face as he unfurled his wings, leaped into the air, and let the wind lift him higher. Patience, he told himself. He banked hard to the left joining a handful of other gargoyles in the sky. They parted for him, letting their leader take the lead. Already he had sensed the change in the people from the other side of the mountains. Their focus was on their new castle, on expanding their reach, on moving forward. This meant their focus was not on the key or the gate. Soon, very soon, Bram had confidence he would see the opportunity before him to further his plan. He would again take possession of the key. And this time, the gate would be opened wide.

He roared a challenge to the gargoyles with him, tucked his wings in tight and dove downward. The others behind him did the same, trying to match Bram's move. Bram started to pull up and turned hard with the wind, before letting the wind propel him forward. He looked back and saw just two other gargoyles still close behind and in response he went higher and higher. Then, with no warning, he dove straight down, leaving the others far behind.

After slowing his descent just enough, he landed on the castle wall with a crunch. Patience. The time was coming.

✳✳✳✳✳

Merrituk stood in front of the king and his Advisor. King Malick was seated and raised above the floor. The King's Advisor, the dragon Esmeralda, lay comfortably on the ground, her large form taking up much of the available space. Mit still was not used to the dragon and shifted his stance uncomfortably.

"We are glad to see you again," said the dragon, startling Mit. Despite the deepness of the dragon's voice it was pleasant sounding.

"Yes, yes, thank you. It is good to be back. Thank you again, King, for asking Gargan to assist me in my travels," replied Mit. First looking at the beautiful emerald colored dragon before shifting his attention to the king.

"Of course. Please, tell us, was it a productive trip?" Malick's voice remained as kingly as ever, but Mit could tell there was hope in that question. Here he was, at his moment. If he could convince the king that he had indeed found a way to bring Heritage into the kingdom, he would have his spot right alongside the king and the dragon. He would be seen as one of the inner circle.

"I believe that it was, sire." He paused, letting the king's anticipation grow. "They see the benefits of being part of Calridian, but as you know they are a proud people. They would see themselves as equals."

"I have already granted them a spot on the Council of Peace. Their voice will be as important as anyone's."

"Be assured, King, they have been made aware of that fact. I was overly complimentary of their city and how they would be seen as partners. But that is not what will bring them under your banner.

"Human," said the dragon in a frustrated voice, "we are not some distant land you need to banter with. Out with it."

"Very well," Mit cleared his throat. "They wish to see Jyres. He is a hero. He is a human, someone of their race and someone who has brought honor to humans everywhere. They have planned a welcoming celebration, a chance for the empress to meet this hero and to offer him her gratitude. The whole city would be eternally grateful just for the chance to look upon Jyres with their own eyes. I believe that if we bring Jyres to them for a visit, they will join your Kingdom with songs on their lips and joy in their hearts."

"This is great news!" replied Malick. "More progress than we have ever made before with the city of Heritage. Though, Jyres is an important member of this Kingdom and it is rare that he has free time." King Malick's head was racing. A precious few knew about Jyres' and Lalatco's real responsibility. Could he ask Jyres to do this for the kingdom?

"Surley, he could be spared for a little while. Gargan would be more than happy to ferry us back to Heritage. Gargan and Jyres would both very much enjoy each other's company again," Mit replied as he watched the king closely.

Would he go for it? *He will*, Mit thought. *He must. This is what he has been wanting.*

"I will talk this over with Esmeralda. You have honored the kingdom with your service."

After hearing Malick's response, Mit bowed low and upon rising said, "It is my pleasure, sire." He then quickly left the king's presence, a smile on his face. He had succeeded. The king would not turn down this opportunity.

✵✵✵✵✵

A girl silently slipped off of her cot. She knew elves would be near, as they always seemed to be, but she was confident that Rajeem was sleeping. She was always the one who kept the closest eye on her. Ever so carefully the girl took a step towards the outer tent wall. Hearing no one, she took another step, and then another, until she was next to the thick white canvas of the tent wall. She carefully laid on her belly, and little by little slid her body under the tent and out into the night.

Once she was completely out from under the tent, she waited. Then she waited some more. Confident no one had heard her, she stood up and looked around. Seeing no one nearby, she quickly moved across the grassy valley and towards the nearby rocky base of the Alhazar mountains.

Once there she followed her usual path, which brought her to a small hole, just big enough for a girl her age to slip through. Falling the short drop, she landed feet first on the floor. She had entered what she thought of as her private domain. It was a very small cave that she had found not all that long ago. Since then she had escaped to it whenever she could. It wasn't much really, a small cave not even big enough for six people to sit comfortably, but it was hers.

The girl had dark brown skin and she kept her black hair short, to the frustration of the elves who saw to her care. They all seemed to have long flowing hair and saw it as odd that she would choose to wear her hair short and often unkempt. She had remembered being one of the taller girls in her village, but that was when she was eight years old. She was now twelve.

Her mother had brought her to the elves, but she never really understood why. Rajeem had told her that her mother was very sick and wanted the best for her. But she just didn't understand why she was here.

She had not seen her mother since. She had no memory of her father.

Whenever she tried to ask questions, whether it was of Rajeem or even the king, she didn't receive any answers that helped her. The last time that she had asked Malick a question, he had yelled at her and she stomped out of the throne room only to be scolded again by Rajeem for her behavior.

All she wanted to know were things like why her life was so much different than the other girls her age? Was her mother still alive? Did she have a father? Why was she living here instead of the elven forest or the village with other humans? This small cave at least gave her someplace that she could call her own. And do what she wanted to do without being constantly looked after or scolded.

She picked up the blanket that she had snuck into the cave, rolled it up and placed it under her head, and laid down. She stared up at the cave ceiling, which was not really very high. But when she laid down like this, it always gave her the feeling that her little cave was larger than it was. Grabbing a small stone, she threw it against the ceiling watching it ricochet away and land on the ground. She did that a few more times to enjoy the cracking sound the impact of the stone made. Finding a little bigger stone, she threw it again. But this time, it came straight back down towards her. In surprise she threw up her hands and yelled, "stovea", an old elvish word she had heard somewhere.

She then realized nothing had hit her, and she slowly opened one of her eyes, and then the second one. To her absolute amazement, the rock that she had just thrown sat in midair floating just above her hands. It was just floating there like something had caught it and held it. Unsure of what to do, she quickly backed away, pushing backwards on her hands and feet. As soon as she did so, the rock fell and clattered on the ground. The girl looked around still in shock. She slowly reached for the rock, it did not move. Nervously, she picked it up. It felt just like any other rock. She gently tossed it in the air, and it fell back to the floor, hitting the ground and rolling away.

The girl scratched her head in confusion. *What just happened?* She picked up the rock again and threw it one more time at the ceiling. The rock again quickly fell back down and hit the cave floor. What was that word she said? She could not remember. Why couldn't she remember what she said? It had just come to her.

Still in utter confusion, the girl started to climb back out of the cave. Dropping into the cave was the easy part, getting back out had proved to be a little more difficult. She carefully tried to climb back up to the entrance of her cave, but as she did so, she slipped and fell. That same word she had said earlier somehow found its way out of her mouth and as she fell she braced herself for impact.

Only it never came.

Her whole body floated just barely above the cave floor. Then that instant was over, and she rested on the floor. Her surprise started to turn to fear and her breathing became fast and her heart rate increased. Quickly, she climbed to the hole, this time making it out of the cave and she sprinted toward the tent.

12
CYNA

Jyres sat, and waited. Again. Lalatco was later than planned, again. Jyres had tried to remain patient, but it was getting difficult as they had both agreed to go together to talk to the king when they both were back at this outpost.

More days had gone by and more of the same had transpired. The key continued to be safe and moved about the kingdom per Jyres' and Lalatco's detailed plan. No new sightings of the creature Jyres considered as dangerous had been reported and life for most people continued to move on as normal.

Jyres struggled with this new normal, as this ever-present danger stayed in his mind, preventing him from relaxing. Preventing him from seeing his friends with any sort of regularity and interrupting any plans to connect with Elonda. And here he was again. Waiting.

Another few arcs, the adopted way to track the passing of time, passed by and still there was no sign of Lalatco. Jyres' patience also seemed to wane throughout the day, as if the moon's shifting in the sky took his patience farther and farther from him. Determined to move on, Jyres departed, traveling during the night.

Late in the night, as he approached the valley of the dragons from the south, he slowed Gerti to a walk. It was hard to see in the night, which was near its darkest point, but he was certain he had picked someone out in the darkness sitting on an outcropping of rocks. Carefully dismounting, Jyres left Gerti and quietly walked closer to investigate. There he saw a human girl sitting on a rock.

The young girl was just throwing a rock up in the air and then catching it as it came back to her. Jyres watched her for a little while, wondering who she was and what she was doing out here. Although travel had increased quite a bit among the races, it was still odd to see a human sitting alone in the middle of the night and nowhere near the city of Skystair.

As he watched, his curiosity only increased and then skyrocketed as he saw a stone floating in the middle of the air above the girl. She had thrown it up and there it floated above her, not returning all the way to her hand. He stared, unable to tear his eyes from the small stone. How did this happen? Who was this girl? Then he heard someone calling and ducked completely behind a rock as he heard a small stone fall and hit rock before rolling away, making small crackling noises as it did so.

"I am coming," the girl suddenly yelled before running off.

The next day Jyres was still sleeping soundly when a rough hand grabbed his arm. Jyres' eyes flashed open in astonishment, and he started to rise quickly, breathing hard. Then, seeing Vurth was the one there holding his arm, he let himself fall back down to his makeshift bed.

"Vurth, you can't wake someone like that!" he yelled, his heartbeat finally slowing down again.

"Ha! I figured I owed you one!"

"Well, I suppose you did." Jyres chuckled.

"When did you arrive, I didn't see you come last night? We could have had a couple of drinks," the dwarf said, laughing to himself.

"It was very late." After a pause, Jyres looked back up at the dwarf. "Hey, can I ask you a question?"

"Of course." Vurth stroked his beard as if he was already thinking about the question before Jyres had even asked it.

"Last night, I saw a girl—a human—not far from here. Young girl. I found it odd. Any idea who that is?"

"I am sure it was Cyna. She is not content to stay put all the time. Malick, sorry, the king, seems to keep her always within reach." Vurth's hand fell away from his beard and he offered a hand down to Jyres to help him up.

Jyres grabbed it and propped himself up before standing. Jyres then reached for his shirt and pulled it over his head before asking, "Who is she?"

"Ha," Vurth exclaimed. "That is the same question a lot of us have been asking. But we long ago gave up expecting an answer in return."

"I would like to talk with her if I could."

"I am sure that I can arrange it. But may I ask why?"

"Let's just say I, too, used to be a small child who didn't always appreciate my environment."

Later that day, Jyres and the girl sat on a couple of boulders. Not too far away was the elf, Rajeem, well within earshot for an elf.

"So, what is your name?" asked Jyres. The girl did not respond and avoided any eye contact. After a few moments, he tried again. "My name is Jyres. Now maybe you could share yours?" Although she did look at him this time, she did not respond. "I was surprised to see you last night," he continued. Her eyes popped wide, and Jyres gave her an ever-so-slight nod. The girl's eyes shifted toward Rajeem.

Jyres, taking a gamble, stood up from his seat and went to Rajeem asking her to give them some privacy if she wouldn't mind. Reluctantly, Rajeem did so, probably only because he was Jyres and that name seemed to carry a lot of weight. Returning to his boulder, he said. "Let's try again. I am Jyres, and you are?"

This time the girl responded, though not enthusiastically, "My name is Cyna."

Jyres smiled in return. "Cyna, how old are you—thirteen?"

"Twelve." Her voice was only a murmur.

Jyres continued to try and ask easy questions to help her grow more comfortable with the conversation. "How long have you lived with the elves?"

"A long time."

"Okay, I can tell you are afraid of me, but…" The rest of what he was going to say was cut short as Cyna interrupted.

"I am not afraid of you," Cyna said with emphasis on the word not. It was more energy than she had shown in all of her other answers combined. "I know who you are, you're the hero everyone talks about. So go be a hero and leave me alone." She was about to get up and stomp away, but two little words from Jyres stopped her.

"I saw."

Cyna's eyes went wide before she shifted her focus to her feet

Jyres gave her a moment letting his last comment sink in before he continued, "I have some questions about that. But I want you to be comfortable talking with me. I can wait until you are ready."

Silence followed. Then more before she said, "Like, we are just going to sit here until I talk to you?"

Jyres laughed and said, "If you want. I was thinking we would speak again in the future." Jyres shifted on the bolder, so he was completely facing the young girl. "Judging by your reaction to me earlier, I am guessing no one else besides me knows about this. You must have a lot of questions?"

The girl turned to face him, and looked up at him, with tears in her eyes. And with sadness in her voice she was able to say, "That is all I ever have is questions. Questions that nobody answers. Why am I here? Who was my dad? What happened to my mom? Why can I lift rocks?" Cyna's tears continued and she looked down to the ground.

Jyres saw Rajeem walking toward them and he knew his time had run out.

"Well, Cyna, it was a pleasure to meet you. I would love to help you answer some of those questions you have." Jyres paused. "You must know Vurth."

The young girl shook her head yes in response. The tears started to subside.

"Great. I will be here for a couple of days. If you want to talk with me and can't find me, just tell Vurth, okay?"

She shook her head again and wiped away the last of her tears.

"Is everything all right over here?" asked Rajeem in a very stern voice.

Before Jyres could respond, Cyna did. "Yes, Rajeem, everything is fine." Then as she stood up to follow Rajeem, she turned back to Jyres and said, "Thank you."

Jyres stood before the king's raised dais; it currently sat empty. He had a couple of things on his mind that he wanted to discuss with the king. But his confidence in Malick had been shaken. How this next conversation went could either further shake that confidence or restore it. Just then Malick entered the temporary throne room, interrupting Jyres' thoughts.

"Jyres, sorry to keep you waiting. But I am glad you are here. There is something I wanted to discuss with you later today," said Malick as he took his seat on his throne.

"Don't give it a second thought, sire. I am sure you are very busy."

"I always have time for one of my keepers."

Jyres smiled absently before responding. "Sire, there is a matter I would like to discuss with you, as well."

"Very good, go ahead. What is it, Jyres?" asked Malick.

"I had the pleasure of meeting Cyna. I was surprised at first to see her here, then I remembered that I had seen her one other time when I was here. She was leaving your presence as I was waiting to talk with you." Jyres paused, trying to judge any reaction from Malick, but none was there to judge. So he continued, "I was wondering who she is and how she came to be in your service?"

"That is nice of you to have talked with her, but you need not worry yourself about her," replied the king, his tone holding the same noble manner it always did.

"It is not worry, sire, more curiosity."

"I see. Well, either way, it is none of your concern." This time, the king put a little more sternness into his statement.

Jyres realized he was not going to get any more information and didn't want to risk any possibilities of harming his relationship with King Malick. "I understand," was all he said in response.

Thinking the matter was resolved, the king moved on. "Please return, if you will, in one arcs' time, and we will discuss the matter I had referenced earlier."

Jyres gave a slight bow before leaving and, as chance would have it, he bumped into Cyna just as he left the king's presence.

"Cyna, good to see you again," he said.

"Hi, were you talking with the king?" asked Cyna with curiosity.

"I was. I am thinking about taking a walk around the valley. Would you like to join me?" asked Jyres, keeping his voice light and conversational.

"Sure."

They began to walk, taking in the beauty around them. It was another gorgeous day and the valley was full of life, it seemed. Birds sang, and squirrels squeaked, and a family of ducks could be seen entering the river.

Jyres took it all in for a moment before turning to Cyna and asking, "So have you thought much about our conversation?"

"A little," answered Cyna.

"Good. I have as well. I really would like to help you, Cyna, if you would let me."

"How can you help?" Cyna looked up to the taller Jyres, her eyes showing a guarded curiosity.

"Well, I have known two people who have had powers like you. I, at least, know what is possible."

"You do?" she exclaimed, a sudden hope in her voice.

"Yes, one I have come to know very well. He is a very powerful, kind, and thoughtful man." Jyres's mind quickly drifted to Zar. He had not seen him in quite some time. A matter, Jyres hoped to rectify soon.

"What about the other one?" Cyna asked.

"He died a few years ago." A quick memory of his sword movements when he had killed Meslar skipped across Jyres' mind. He shook it away.

"No, the evil wizard! You mean I could end up like him?" asked Cyna, in a quivering voice.

Jyres stopped walking as they approached the waterfall at the end of the valley. Grabbing Cyna by the hand, he knelt down so he was eye level with the girl.

"Cyna, I didn't mean to scare you. I believe you are a delga. A delga is a race just like any other. Humans, elves, dwarves, and dragons. A dragon is only evil if it chooses to be, it is the same with the delga."

The young girl just continued to stare back at him, not responding, but not looking away either.

"I don't know why no one has told you about your past, but I think together we can figure it out. I also think the other man I told you about could help you, so you wouldn't have to be afraid of your power anymore." Jyres held her attention a little longer before he released her hand, and Cyna used the back of it to wipe away a couple of tears.

"I would like that," she said.

Jyres again found himself before King Malick. But this time, Esmeralda and Mit were also present. Jyres didn't know much about

Mit Merrituk. He knew he was from the human village, just as he was, but had little recollection of him. Mit stood not far from him, a smile on his face. *What is he doing here,* Jyres wondered.

"Thank you for coming," started King Malick. "I have brought you here to share some good news. We believe an alliance with Heritage can be formed. This will go a long way in securing Calridian and bringing everyone together under one banner. Mit Merrituk was able to make progress on this during a recent visit to the city. He is confident that a visit from the human hero will finalize the alliance."

It took Jyres a moment to realize that the king was referencing him. Apparently, they believed he was the key to forming the alliance with Heritage. After being silent for a moment, Jyres asked, "How can we be so sure of this?"

Merrituk spoke up. "The people love you, Jyres. They are enthralled with the fellow human who killed Meslar. I assure you, if you come to the city of Heritage, you will unite the city with our kingdom."

"I am happy for this progress, sire. I am." Jyres had to be careful of how he proceeded, as Mit did not know that Jyres was a Keeper of the Key and Jyres didn't want to say something that would reveal that very thing. "But, you know, sire, that my other duties prevent me from performing this task for you."

The mighty dragon was the next to speak. "We are aware of this. A different solution will have to be made in your absence."

Jyres did not like this at all. The king's recent disregard for the mysterious creature and its ramifications for the protection of the key continued to astound Jyres. "I must insist that I am needed here," he said.

"What is more important than this alliance?" asked Mit. "Don't you see, your king asks this of you? This is the next step in the strengthening of the kingdom."

If you only knew, Jyres thought.

"Will you not do this, Jyres? I thought you would be excited for the opportunity to see the city of Heritage. I will also arrange for

Gargan to be an escort for you. I am sure you would be happy to see him again," said Malick.

Jyres's mind was still uneasy, but he was worried that he would not have a choice. *It would be nice to see Gargan again,* he thought. "Very well. But I have two requests."

"Go on," said Malick, who was at least open to listening to the requests.

"First, I will request a private audience with you, King, to discuss the performance of my other duties while I am away. And second—" Jyres paused, unsure if this next request would work. "I ask that Cyna accompany me."

A look of confusion crossed Mit's face, he had no idea who Cyna was. The dragon Esmeralda let a sly smile cross her big face. Jyres was unsure of what that meant. The king, on the other hand, was frowning, not happy with the request.

"Why would I grant that? She would only be a hindrance to you."

"I disagree. I think a visit to the great city of Heritage would do wonders for Cyna. She would get to see the world and some of her own race. I would not see her as a hindrance at all. In fact, just the opposite. I am sure many in Heritage would like to meet not just one human, but two humans from our Kingdom."

"Be that as it may, I..."

Jyres cut the king off before he could finish. "Sire, you know what you are asking me to do." Jyres' voice took on a serious tone. "It is not my wish at all to go on this adventure. But I do as my King asks. I only ask that he grant my request in return."

"Very well," replied Malick, whose voice became as stern as Jyres had ever heard it. "Rajeem will accompany her. You both will see to Cyna's care and her safe return."

13
LALATCO DELAYED

Lalatco had just finished readying his horse to leave the elven home. He wore his customary long-sleeve green shirt and dark green pants. He knew he was going to be late to meet Jyres again, but the arrival of Elonda's searching party had delayed him. The party had returned. Without Elonda. Lalatco had waited to leave in hopes that Elonda would show up before he left the forest. Unfortunately that had not been the case. Now he was going to have to deliver some worrisome news to Jyres.

His thoughts were interrupted when he heard a commotion. Not far off he could hear excited voices as they traveled through the trees. Lalatco, wondering what all the commotion was about, left his horse in the stables and went to investigate.

There, to his delighted surprise, he saw Elonda! Not just Elonda, but two humans as well. And a creature he had never seen before. He ran up to her, with a smile reaching almost ear to ear. They gave each other a quick hug.

"Where have you been?" he asked as they began to walk toward the main complex, with all the others and curious elves following along. "We have been very worried about you ever since your party returned without you."

"I have been busy," she said as she motioned to the knights and Rutu. "Lalatco, I am sure you remember Brigand and Karth. This here is Rutu."

Lalatco shook hands with the former knights before looking down and smiling at Rutu. "Elonda, you are always full of surprises."

Elonda and her fellow travelers were escorted to the throne room where the elven leader and nephew of the king, Simamar, awaited them. Lalatco had to wait outside as did the other elves who had followed the group. Excited conversation broke out among the elves as they waited outside the throne room. Lalatco heard whispers.

"What does this mean?"

"Did you see that creature?

"It looked like a giant lizard." Lalatco smiled to himself, not at all surprised by Elonda's actions, her results, and the reactions they caused.

Inside the throne room, Elonda bowed before Simamar.

"You have returned. The reports of your actions were distressing," said Simamar in a voice that showed frustration. He stood, allowing his uncle's old dark green robe to fall about him. "We feared we would not see you again." His voice softened a little as he said, "But we are glad that these fears were unfounded."

"I do apologize for my actions and any fear they caused. But I ask you to focus on the results. I bring before you a new race. They are the yixl." Elonda stepped back a bit and gestured to Rutu. "This is Rutu."

Rutu stepped forward, touching both hands to the top of his head before spreading his arms out wide and speaking in his own language.

"If I may," said Karth. "He brings greetings from his kin and leader, and thanks you for the help one of your own offered to his people"

Simamar studied the creature and tried to keep his face neutral as he replied, "We are honored to have you in our presence. I am pleased that Elonda was able to offer assistance and that she has brought you here today."

Elonda observed the conversation as they continued to exchange pleasantries and Karth did the translations. She could tell how excited Simamar was. He was not hiding it all that well. He knew what this could mean for him and his people. He had been following his King's orders to explore the land and she had delivered success for him. Malick would be very impressed by his nephew. Malick would now hope to expand the kingdom to this new race and would have Simamar to thank for it.

With the initial conversations over, and their visitors shown to their lodgings, Elonda wanted nothing more than to return to her home. But she knew Lalatco would be waiting for her to talk more. She left the throne room and did find Lalatco waiting for her. She filled him in on everything that had happened and tried to learn all she could about how Jyres was doing.

Finally, she fell onto her bed, exhausted. But she was surprised that sleep did not find her immediately. Her mind was still working through all that had happened and now would happen. She was sure that Simamar would want to bring this news to the king himself. And if that was the case, what did that mean for her? Would she be asked to go along? Would she be sent out to explore again?

Or maybe. Just maybe. She would get to see Jyres. With that thought, she drifted off to sleep.

*****

Jyres and King Malick sat alone, the quiet like a wall between them. Neither had really made any progress in convincing the other that their idea to keep the key safe was the correct option. Jyres insisted that it be left with Lalatco, while the king said that he would keep it until a better option presented itself.

Jyres tried again. "Sire, Lalatco is the only option."

"No, it is the only option you will consider."

"For three years you have entrusted the safety of the key with two people. I dare not keep the key with me as I travel to Heritage. Lalatco should continue to keep the key safe as he always has. I see no reason for any other action. Let the Keepers of the Key continue to do their duty."

"As I have said, the sooner this trip begins the better. And we do not know with certainty where Lalatco is, as you yourself have admitted. If we wait for Lalatco the trip could be delayed longer than necessary," said Malick, though his words seemed to lack conviction.

"I understand. But I will not leave until he and I are able to meet and plan for my being gone." Even the king didn't know if Jyres had the key right now or not and Jyres would give no indication. Jyres would not budge on this issue. The king's lack of concern about the creature only cemented Jyres' position even more. Jyres tried to think of other ways to stress to Malick his strong opinion on the matter as he waited for the king's response.

"Very well," said the king, finally agreeing to Jyres' demands.

Jyres bowed before taking his leave and venturing outside into the cool air. Jyres let out a long breath, trying to release the tension that he could still feel after that conversation. He was thankful that King Malick had finally given in, because he had run out of talking points. But Jyres knew he had just spent any favors the king felt he owed him. Going forward, the king would be less inclined to give into him on any future matters after what had just transpired.

Jyres closed his eyes and threw his hands up in front of his face as a gust of wind surprised him and bits of dirt flew at and around him. But then the wind was gone. And he realized that the mighty dragon Crimson's wings had caused the gust as he landed. Jyres smiled at the red creature who returned the smile before walking by him.

"Impressive creatures," said Mit, coming to stand alongside Jyres.

"Yes, they certainly are."

"May I ask, Jyres, why have you not picked a last name?" said Mit, changing the subject. "Most of the humans have now."

"I don't know, it just doesn't really mean anything to me I guess."

"Why, what do you mean? The family name can mean what you want it to mean. The elves for example see great honor to be part of a certain family. So much so they often get recruited or gathered into a family group. That's why all the elves right now wish to become part of the family of Malkin and many elves in the family group aren't actually related. Lalatco for instance, not related by blood to the Malkins is known as a Malkin because he was recruited to that family at an early age."

Jyres nodded in response, wondering how Mit knew that tidbit of information about Lalatco. Jyres returned his attention to Mit.

"Or the dwarves," Mit was saying. "All of their focus is on the head of the family. That is why you often hear about Tagro, son of Vurth. Not just Tagro, but Tagro, son of Vurth. The delga, I am told, some have family names, but others often take on a descriptive name, like Demorous the Fierce for example. This is most likely due to the uniqueness of each individual delga. Some humans now take great pride in their chosen name. Take mine for example. I was trying to come up with a name that was both unique and memorable. A name that people would not forget." Mit paused, leaving empty space in between his comments in case Jyres wanted to respond. Not hearing anything, Mit continued, "Did you know that the humans of Heritage all have last names and can trace their families' history back generations?"

"No, I did not know that," replied Jyres, with little interest in the conversation.

"I find it fascinating," continued Mit. "They must even have records before the great war. How amazing would it be if there were humans from Heritage who had followed the dragons to this part of the world? Just think of it."

Jyres didn't know how to respond to that and Mit patted Jyres on the shoulder before leaving him alone with his thoughts. Jyres surprised himself when his mind did start thinking about that last statement Mit had made. The humans that made the trip to Tomackus obviously came from somewhere on the other side of the mountains and Heritage was certainly the most likely point of origin.

It was well known which 13 delga came across the mountains, and the elves had fairly accurate records of their own people as well. Of course, the delga and elves had the benefit of the fact that many of them who made that trip across the mountains were still alive today. A reminder of the gift of long life for the delga and immortality for the elves. The humans had no such gift and, as such, their history was lost with those who died long ago.

Jyres pushed those thoughts away, instead preferring to focus on the here and now. Where would Lalatco be? Why was he late again? Why didn't they meet at the outpost so they could talk with Malick as they had agreed? And now he had to go to Heritage, which left the protection of the key solely in Lalatco's hands. He only hoped that Lalatco would be up to the task.

14
A Dragon Pericarp and a Reunion

Zar and Lumpkin sat quietly, each at their own desk in the library. Zar was continuing to catalog and Lumpkin was studying a book full of recipes, remedies, and potions. He had come across it as he helped Zar with his cataloging project. He was currently looking at a page with an illustration that looked like an acorn or something similar, that had been enlarged.

Lumpkin reached down to his pack laying next to the desk and pulled out a small orb with a striking orange color. Lumpkin set it on the table next to the book. The orb looked almost like a crystal with different shades of orange being reflected, depending upon the way the light hit the orb. Lumpkin returned his attention to the book in front of him, before moments later reaching down to his pack again and pulling out a container of different ingredients. He opened the handmade wooden container. Inside, the container was divided into small sections, allowing Lumpkin to keep his ingredients separate.

He carefully pulled out the desired ingredients and set them in a small bowl. Then, taking a hardened wooden spoon, he started to mash the garlic cloves, dried worms, and plums together. Very carefully, he added water into the bowl until he had just the right amount and stirred it all together. Then, he took out three empty vials from his jacket and undid the stoppers. He poured the concoction into the vials, careful not to make them overflow. Leaving them uncapped, he returned to the book.

He quietly practiced reciting the words written on the page. After a few times he picked up the orange orb in one hand and the vials in the other. Then, loudly, he repeated the words from the book. At first there was nothing, then a wave of energy ran through him, leaving the orb and traveling through him into the vials. The vials now contained a dark purple liquid.

He talked excitedly to himself as he placed the stoppers back in the vials and cleaned up his table. He then placed a small pebble in the middle of the table. Taking one of the vials, he brought it close to his face and examined it before placing it next to the pebble. For a moment he just stood there, staring at the two items.

"Well, what are you waiting for? Go on," said Zar.

The voice scared Lumpkin who in his excitement had forgotten all about the kind old man. "Yes, yes," he said, before picking up the vial of purple liquid and undoing the stopper. He then brought his face down to the desk, his eyes level with the pebble. Slowly, he tipped the vial until just one drop dropped from it on to the pebble. He stepped back, as if he were in danger being so close. Nothing happened. The dwarf started to scratch his chin in confusion before the pebble shifted. Then it did again. And then it started to grow.

The pebble continued to get larger until it was half the size of the desk. Lumpkin started jumping up and down in excitement. "Worked. It worked. How exciting!"

Zar smiled at the jubilant dwarf and said, "It certainly did. Do you know why?"

That question stopped Lumpkin mid celebration. He furrowed his brow in confusion. He opened his mouth to speak, but then closed it again, unsure of what to say.

"Do you know what it is you hold in your hand?" asked Zar.

Poor Lumpkin was not sure what hand the old man was referring to. And his head shifted from one side to the other, gazing at both the orange orb and the vial. Zar pointed at the orb in Lumpkin's left hand. Lumpkin turned his face toward it again as if in deep thought.

"I think it is a stone of power. Delga Stone. Yes." Lumpkin said in a way that made it sound more like a question than a statement.

"You are correct, it is an item of power. But it is not a Delga Stone. That, my friend, is a Dragon Pericarp."

Lumpkin's eyes went wide as he stared at the orange translucent orb in his hand. "But, works, works like a stone. But... what's a Dragon Par...what did you call it?"

"Dragon Pericarp. It possesses many of the same qualities as a Delga Stone. It is a common mistake. But it has a different purpose that far outweighs that for which you are using it."

Lumpkin didn't know what to say, or what to do. He just stood there, staring at the now all-of-a-sudden unfamiliar object in his hand. After a moment, Zar stood up and helped the dwarf return the Dragon Pericarp to his pouch and clean up from his potion making. Then, the enlarged pebble shrank back down to its original size.

"How did you become the owner of such a rare item?" asked Zar after returning to his chair.

"I traded for it. Traded with a dwarf, who thought it was a pretty item. Pretty."

"Interesting. How long have you had it in your possession?"

The dwarf started to become more unnerved by the questioning. "Not long, not long," he eventually blurted out.

"Sorry, I will let you be," said the wizard, returning his attention to his own affairs.

"What now? Now what?" stammered the dwarf.

"Now we wait," replied Zar.

*****

Jyres woke up refreshed and feeling ready for whatever the day may bring. He let out a yawn and stretched before looking up and almost screaming in surprise. There, to his astonishment, stood Lalatco.

Jyres was about to start asking where he had been, but he didn't get the chance.

"Before you say anything, I am sorry. I know I messed with our timing. Again. But withhold your judgment for a moment." Lalatco paused, unsure of which news to share first.

"I am withholding," Jyres began, "And?"

"I have some news." Lalatco decided he would save the best for last. "A new race has been discovered by the elves. They live far to the south. They are called the yixl. And, if what the elves report is to be believed, they live on the border of a body of water where water is all you can see for as far as your eyes can see."

"That is news! Wow, I did not expect to hear that," said Jyres, his tone revealing his wonderment at this discovery. "Who was credited with the find?"

"Take one guess," said Lalatco, who had a half smile and gave Jyres a sideways glance.

Jyres smiled back, "Elonda."

"Who else," chuckled Lalatco. The elves are on their way right now with a yixl to see the king. It won't be long until they arrive."

"Well, that just changed my day, I am sure." Jyres shrugged and stood up before walking over to shake Lalaltco's hand. "Oh, I am sure it has," Lalatco couldn't resist letting a rather large smile take shape on his face.

"What, what else do you know?" asked Jyres.

"She is coming with them."

Jyres could not stand still. The anticipation of seeing Elonda for the first time in what felt like ages was making his stomach go topsy turvey and his arms were covered in goosebumps. Jyres paced back and forth as Lalatco stood close by. They awaited the arrival of the elven entourage. They stood at the entrance to the valley, a little offset from the king and his welcoming party, which included his Advisor, Esmeralda, and his Captain of the Guard, Vurth. King Malick had even decided to wear his crown on this occasion, marking it as a special one.

Jyres finally convinced his body to stop moving and stood by Lalatco. Lalatco gave him a small nod and half smile. Jyres returned the smile and turned his attention to the east. They didn't have to wait long before the first of the travelers could be seen in the distance.

Lalatco, sensing the turmoil in his friend, rested his hand on Jyres' shoulder. That small gesture made all the difference. Jyres let out a deep breath and relaxed.

As the group approached, those gathered searched the group for signs of this new creature that had been discovered. Jyres, however, scanned the crowd looking for Elonda. It just so happened they were next to each other. An unexpected yet welcomed feeling of warmth rushed through Jyres at the sight of Elonda. Her beautiful black hair flowed behind her revealing her blue eyes and fair soft features.

Elonda and the yixl dismounted Wild Spirit, and a hush came over the crowd as Simamar, Elonda, the yixl, and two humans Jyres did not recognize approached the king. They all, except the yixl, kneeled before him. The yixl stepped forward, touching both hands to the top of his head before spreading his arms out wide.

Malick bowed to the yixl in return before saying to the others, "Rise, and accept my most gracious welcome. I am pleased to greet a member of the yixl. And a special thank you to Simamar, for he has brought the yixl here to the Kingdom of Calridian."

Simamar, Malick's nephew, approached and the king kissed each of his cheeks in greeting. More of the same followed as those close to the king engaged in traditional greetings and fellowship. Jyres said a silent thank you to Lalatco, whose grip on Jyres shoulder continued to keep him steady, much like a horse who was tethered, but needed to be for its own good. Finally, with the formalities accomplished, the group started to disperse and Lalatco let go of Jyres.

Jyres was about to go straight toward Elonda to welcome her, but he didn't have to. She was running. Straight to him. His heart leaped in his chest as she collided into him, wrapping him in a tight embrace. Neither would let go, they just stood there, wrapped in a hug that said I missed you. Finally, they let go, and both started laughing, a moment of pure joy.

Elonda grabbed his hand, practically crushing it with her insistence, "Come here, you have to meet Rutu."

Jyres let her lead him away to the yixl, who Jyres assumed was Rutu. He was standing with the two humans dressed in black, whom Jyres had not recognized.

"Jyres, this is Rutu. Rutu, this is Jyres, a dear friend of mine."

One of the humans started to say something, and it took a moment before Jyres realized that the man was translating what Elonda had said. Then the creature responded to him before the human turned back to Jyres.

"He is pleased to meet you. He is happy to meet someone who is a friend of Elonda. She has been so kind to him during this journey."

Jyres smiled at that and was then officially introduced to Karth and Brigand, two knights, who, not that long ago, had wanted him dead. Jyres had only seen former knights on rare occasions since the death of Meslar. And whenever he did, he had to remind himself that Meslar had been the real enemy, and he himself was the one who said the knights should be allowed to do as they please.

Everyone was then ushered toward the tents in the valley and assigned areas where they could rest and leave their belongings.

Afterward, Elonda and Jyres found each other and went for a walk, before stopping by the waterfall at the end of the valley.

"So, I hear you have quite the story to tell," said Jyres.

"Maybe I do," she laughed. "Another time perhaps. Tell me about you. It has been so long, you must have stories to share."

Jyres smiled, a sad smile. "Not really, I guess. If I am to be honest, it has been a struggle."

"Lalatco told me some of it, I think, but I wanted to hear it from you."

He smiled, "You are here, and seeing you has brought me joy. Let's focus on that tonight."

"That sounds like a wonderful idea," said Elonda who rested her head on his shoulder.

Jyres put one arm around her and held her close. Together they looked up at the waterfall and mountains beyond. They didn't talk. Just stood in each other's arms in comfortable silence.

Jyres, Elonda, Lalatco, Leah and Vurth all sat on empty barrels in a corner of the tent they had staked their claim to. The five of them had not been together in some time, and joy and laughter filled every space of the tent. Vurth spun tall tales that sent the four listeners into fits of laughter and one such tale even sent Elonda to the ground she was laughing so hard.

"You don't know how good this feels to be surrounded by my friends again," said Jyres.

"Well, of course, we do, you hobgoblin, we are here, too!" said Vurth, the closest he would get to being sentimental.

"Look at us, together again," said Leah while brushing back her beautiful blonde, revealing a smile that couldn't have been more genuine.

"The world hasn't gotten so big that it should keep us apart," replied Lalatco, sharing a smile with each of them.

"Well, it did just get bigger. You're welcome," said Elonda with mock arrogance and a dramatic bow.

That sent everyone into laughter again. A sound that carried across the way to where a girl stood listening, with a tear rolling down her face. Cyna listened intently, absorbing every laugh and every shout of joy, wondering if this is what families did. Is this what she had been missing out on? Because if so, she wanted it. More than anything.

15
DEPARTURES

Bram stood high on a mountain ridge, looking down into the valley. There in the valley was where he assumed the key now waited. There was a big gathering in the valley tonight, and Jyres was there. Although Bram had no idea if Jyres still had the key, in Bram's mind, Jyres was the link to it. If he didn't have it, he would know where it was or, in the worst case, someone one who did know where it was.

Jyres' movements had proven difficult to track. He was, of course, helped by the fact that Bram could only track him at night. But still, even without that it still would have been difficult. Jyres never seemed to stay in one place for too long. Bram was beginning to think that was by design, but hadn't been able to put together any sort of pattern or purpose. Given enough time, perhaps he could put together some sort of pattern. But time was something that Bram was running out of.

Despite all the past movements, Jyres seemed to be content in the valley for now. He had stayed there longer than he usually stayed in one place, and to Bram that meant something was up. Perhaps his time had arrived. He knew where Jyres was, and Bram dared to hope that Jyres would remain in this place long enough for Bram to take action. If not now, when?

No time to waste. Bram launched himself into the air and rode the wind currents toward his castle. Time to gather his forces, and, in a few nights' time, descend upon the valley. Then capture Jyres, claim the key, gain the creature's trust again and unlock the Gate of Fire.

*****

With the castle's occupants asleep, a man clad in dark gray silk, completely covered except for around his eyes, crept silently about. As he stuck tight to the wall, he was all but indistinguishable, even in the daylight, not that anyone was expecting him. The stone gargoyles looked down from the castle's walls and towers with frozen expressions.

He had been here before, a few years ago. This time was different. He was here for a different purpose. But those few days spent here came back to him as he moved into the castle. He followed his memory and intuition and they brought him to his destination. There in a cell, in the deepest part of the castle, sat the creature. The creature turned toward him, its face hard to read in its gelatinous exterior. The man in gray studied it for a moment, unsure of his next action now that he was here. But that thought quickly left him and the man stepped up to the bars.

"Do you have a name?" the man asked. The creature did not reply and the man was unsure of what that meant. Could the creature not understand or did it just choose not to answer? So he tried again. "What do people call you?"

"The horde," it said, its speech a little garbled.

"Fair enough. Would you like to get out of this cell?"

"Very...much...so."

"I could do that," replied the man.

"Why...do that...you...try and use....horde...like them." The creature almost spitting the words out as if they disgusted him.

"Maybe. But mostly to remind others who I am."

"What...you...called?"

"They call me the Silver Shadow."

*****

The Valley of the Dragons was a hub of activity. King Malick's ultimate goal was in sight. He had personally prepared and signed two letters offering both the City of Heritage and the yixl a spot on the Council of Peace and membership in the Kingdom of Calridian. Included with each letter was an invitation to the first official gathering of the Council of Peace, which would transpire on the Day of Two Moons. A day in early fall when both moons shine equally bright in the sky. An event that only happened once a year. This would also be the day that Serenity Castle would be officially opened.

Assuming these invitations were accepted, his Council of Peace would grow to 13 members, the king, Advisor, and Captain of the Guard being three of those members. The other members would come from the different areas of the kingdom, which was now being divided into regions. Those regions included Tomackus, which had representatives from Castle Mystic, Skystair and the dwarven cliffs. Alhazar, with its representatives Simamar and Ogla. Ogla was an orc, one who had been able to keep control over the orcs and goblins in the mountains.

Then there were the regions from the old world, which were being divided into three new regions. One region was Secord, receiving the name because of the once great city. Small towns in the area would elect one representative for the Council.

The second region from the old world was called The Stone Way. It received this name due to the mountain pass and the castles in the region. Gargan would be a representative along with a representative of the small towns in the area, just like the Secord region.

The third region was named Heritage and the empress would be the representative. This was the obvious choice, but also one more tool Mit Merrituk had at his disposal in convincing the great city to join the alliance. Finally, the last member of the Council would be a member from the yixl, representing what was being called the Coastal Region.

Travelers prepared to head both to the east and to the west to deliver the letters of alliance and invitation. Lalatco and Jyres finally took an opportunity to talk with King Malick about their concerns revolving around the creature. The conversation evolved into discussions about the key while Jyres was in Heritage. By the end of the conversation Jyres and Lalatco felt a little better about their fears, knowing that the king was not dismissing the creature outright. But it was still obvious that it was not at the forefront of his mind.

With that conversation and King Malick and Jyres having come to somewhat of an agreement earlier, that meant that Jyres would head to the west. The party to go with him had been agreed upon. Jyres, Mit, Rajeem, and Cyna. They would also be accompanied by a few of the King's Envoys before meeting up with Gargan and a few gargoyles, who would accompany them the rest of the way. Elonda would head to the east along with Rutu, Karth, Brigand, and a handful of elves.

Again, their duties would pull Jyres and Elonda apart. Not what either of them had wanted, but it was what they both expected. Although they didn't talk about it much, Jyres was pretty sure Elonda had come to realize that he and Lalatco were heavily involved with the protection of the key. He was sure others suspected their duties as well, but the less others knew, the better for the protection of the key. Although he would have liked to talk to her about his concerns when it came to the key, it was also nice to know he didn't have to explain his travels to her. And it was the same with her. Elonda didn't need to tell him how busy she was being kept by Simamar.

They both knew full well what was keeping them apart for such long periods.

But they had embraced their few days with each other and enjoyed them to the fullest. When they were able, they would enjoy time with just each other, but they fully enjoyed interactions with their friends as well. Elonda and Cyna had hit it off right away, and Jyres was happy to see that. This gave him another way to be able to connect with Cyna, which he hoped to do while on their trip to Heritage.

Jyres wasn't sure where this desire to help Cyna had come from and why it was rather strong. It could be that he remembered what it was like to grow up without parents. Or perhaps it was that he knew what it was like to be afraid of those who saw themselves as superior. But Jyres did not think that either of those suspicions were correct. It was somehow connected to Meslar. When he saw what Cyna did, his mind went to Meslar and all the things he had seen him do. Was it fear? Fear of another Meslar that was the true motivation? No, that didn't sound right either. Hopefully, this answer would come as he spent more time with her over the next few weeks.

As the preparations for the groups' departures came closer to completion, the goodbyes and well wishes began. To Lalatco, Jyres entrusted the key. Something that was harder for him then he had ever expected. It had basically been part of his reason for living over the last three years. And now he was giving up that responsibility for a short time. Plus, Lalatco hadn't really instilled confidence of late when it came to the priority of protecting the key. But, once he had given Lalatco the key, they clasped hands before pulling each other in for a hug.

Leah left him with a kiss on the cheek, which Vurth offered as well. Jyres was quick to decline and they both got a good laugh from that. Finally, he said goodbye to Elonda. They said little, letting their eyes do the talking. Then a kiss, and an embrace that Jyres tried to hold onto in his heart before they departed.

*****

Bram had arrived back at his castle only to find that the creature known as the horde had somehow escaped. This left him furious. Now he had to find the creature again, and capture him, a process that was not easy the first time. His plan to assault the valley with his gargoyles would have to wait. Even though Jyres had finally seemed to stop in one place, finding the creature before someone else learned of what the creature could do was the first priority.

Bram thought the gargoyle's trait of turning into stone had always been a blessing and a curse. Their stone bodies kept them safe and rejuvenated them. But it also left them often unaware of their surroundings and the events occurring during their dormancy. Only on rare occasions could a gargoyle's slumber be disturbed, so as they slept, someone had helped the horde. Or the horde had somehow helped itself. Another setback, another delay to his overall plans.

Bram had already sent out his gargoyles to search for the creature. It was only a matter of time. He would have to continue to be patient. It had been three years since this creature had emerged from the gate, and a few more days or weeks would not prevent the inevitable. He would be in control of everything, because he would be the wielder of the horde.

16
HERITAGE

The lights of the city of Heritage came into view. Its wooden walls contained the city in a protected ring. The palace stood tall above the city, in roughly what was the middle of the city. Jyres paused for a moment, taking this sight in for the first time. The city was large, much larger than Skystair, and its clay palace was more impressive than anything Skystair had to call its own. Jyres admitted to himself that he was excited to see it up close.

Mit went on ahead, as Jyres, Cyna, and Rajeem waited outside the city with Gargan, two other gargoyles, and the horses. Cyna had seemed uneasy around the gargoyles when they had first started their journey. But she seemed less afraid as time went on. Currently, she stood with Rajeem, who was talking to her about something. But Jyres could tell Rajeem had lost the attention of the young girl.

Gargan, standing next to Jyres, said, "What do you know of Mit?"

"I don't know him that well. The king seems to value him. Why do you ask?"

The big gargoyle made a raspy sound that Jyres took to mean that Gargan was either unsatisfied with the answer or concerned. He then said, "I have accompanied him to this city once before. For some reason I feel like this time is different. Something...something has changed."

Jyres considered his words for a moment. "I suppose something has changed. This time I am along and he thinks that will help finalize the alliance with Heritage. I am sure that is all it is." Jyres smiled up at Gargan, remembering the first time they had met. Gargan had scooped him up and brought him to the Cliffs of Catastrophe before the Knights of Enchantment could catch him. "You are always looking out for me, and I appreciate that more than you know."

"You, Jyres, are my friend. The first human that I could really call as such. And for that I am thankful."

Early the next day, palace guards led Mit, Jyres, Cyna, and Rajeem to the palace. The empress had requested they come directly to the palace to avoid the city finding out they were there before the planned announcements. In order for this to happen, the guards had met Jyres and the others outside the city just before the sun came up and led them through the back streets of Heritage before the city awoke. The gargoyles declined to stay in the palace and Gargan told Jyres where in the city he could find him.

Upon reaching the palace, they were shown to rooms that were prepared for them. Cyna and Rajeem shared a room, and Mit and Jyres each received their own. Soon after they were settled, Mit and Jyres were brought before the empress.

Jyres allowed Mit to do the talking, bowed when appropriate and confirmed what Mit said when needed. Jyres took the time to appreciate what was around him. He was in a city, a human city. A city of more humans than he had ever met in a lifetime. He realized as Mit and the empress talked, that she had a speech pattern a little different from his, as did the Palace Official when he spoke. The empress' face rarely changed or gave away her feelings and it left Jyres unsure of her. Either she was very guarded in her responses, or lacked the enthusiasm that others of her age often displayed.

After the meeting, Jyres and Mit were shown back to their rooms and then met in Mit's room where they went over the days' plans.

"First, you will have a tour of the palace. The Palace Official will be here one arc from now and he will show us some of the other parts of the palace. Then, we are invited to lunch with the empress."

"I would like Cyna to accompany us on the tour," Jyres said. "I think she would enjoy seeing the palace."

"I am sure that can be arranged," replied Mit in a frustrated tone. "I still don't know why we brought her along."

"You don't need to know why," responded Jyres.

Mit gave him a sidelong glance before continuing. "The lunch will be private, as we will discuss important business. Then, tomorrow you will be introduced to all the people from Heritage, who will gather around the palace to hear the news they have been invited to hear."

"Which is what, exactly?"

"A surprise, of course! The people will love it that you have come and that they will see you in person. Trust me. I was here before. You are a human, like them, and one they are dying to meet. After that, a few select members of Heritage have been invited to meet you face to face. And that is it."

"It doesn't sound too painful. What about the formal agreement of alliance with the Kingdom of Calridian?"

"That will come in a few days, after word of your arrival has taken the whole city by storm and word of how great it is to have you in the city of Heritage comes back and reaches the empress' ears. We need the city to embrace you and be thankful that their empress saw fit to bring you here. Then we will have an alliance."

Before long it was time for their tour, and Mit, Jyres, Cyna, and Rajeem were shown around by the Palace Official. Although the Palace Official lacked a charismatic personality, he made up for it with his intellect. He did seem to know all there was to know about the palace. Jyres found himself asking a lot of questions, and although Cyna didn't ask any herself, she seemed to be very interested in the Official's answers.

The more Jyres learned about the city and its people, the more he wondered how it would feel to be able to know his history. Whether it was his family's history or the history of the small human village, now turned into Skystair, he wondered how that would impact his life. If he knew his ancestors were from this small town, or that village, or even Heritage, would that matter? *On some level it must. Look at Heritage and how much pride they take in the history of this city and its people.* But if he had known the history of his human village, would he still have sought to change the fortune of the humans in Tomackus? Or would he have tried to do something earlier?

With all the questions popping up in Jyres' head, he knew that yes, had he known more about his family and history, it would have absolutely had an impact on him. For better or worse, he could not say.

"Yes, here we are," said the Palace Official as the group walked up to a tapestry hanging from on the wall. "This is a family crest, and as you can tell it is very old. This particular family line can be traced back for centuries, and is believed to be one of the founding families of the City of Heritage."

"Centuries?" Jyres repeated in amazement.

"Yes, it is quite extraordinary," replied the Palace Official in the same monotone voice he had been using throughout the tour.

The group continued to take in the tapestry, appreciating the intricate detail in its design. Before long the Palace Official said, "That brings us to the end of the tour. I can show you back to the rooms if you like."

Surprising everyone, as she had not said anything throughout the tour, Cyna said quietly, "How do you know all of the things you have told us?"

The Palace Official, unsure he understood the question, gave a sidelong glance at Jyres.

"I think she means, how do you keep track of everything that has happened, and how do you learn about it," replied Jyres, trying to help the Palace Official with any confusion.

"Oh, a very good question. The city of Heritage has long held its history and significant events in that history as very important. We can thank the founders of Heritage for that. As such, we have many, many records of years gone by. There was a time as well when many of our documents were copied and sent to the library in Secord. All of our young people are also taught the history of Heritage. We continue the practice of recording events and saving them in our records room to this day. For example, your visit Jyres, will be recorded and any notable events documented for the future citizens of Heritage."

"Can I see it?" asked Cyna, her voice a little louder than last time.

"See what?" replied the official.

"The records room."

"I am sorry, but we only allow a select few into the room itself," said the official whose tone of voice didn't seem to match the statement. Apparently, not concerned at all for Cyna's feelings.

Disappointment flashed across Cyna's face, and Jyres quickly said, "Well, perhaps we could just stand on the outside and get a glimpse?"

"I suppose that couldn't hurt anything. Very well, follow me."

For some reason Jyres had assumed they would go down stairs to arrive at the records room. But to his surprise they had to go up a couple of flights of stairs. Upon reaching the room, the official stopped the group outside the door. "Now, we will just look, we will not enter." The official then withdrew a key from his pocket and unlatched the wooden door and swung it open. The door creaked as he did, a high-pitched sound that made Cyna flinch.

Light from the hallway filtered in through the door revealing the area closest to them. The room seemed very large, and a table was set in the middle and shelves of books and scrolls along the outside. There were two more doorways that presumably led to more rooms like this one.

"The table is used by our scribes to record events, and anyone wishing to view the records held here must be approved. Our scribes also inspect each book that leaves and returns to the records room."

Cyna stood on her tiptoes as if trying to see further into the room or through the darkness at the back of the room. Jyres smiled at her interest and allowed the Palace Official to continue talking without interruption.

Later in the day, after returning to their rooms, Jyres stopped by Cyna and Rajeem's room and was able to talk with Cyna without Rajeem's interference. Perhaps a sign that Rajeem was growing more comfortable with Jyres, or, maybe she knew Jyres would find ways to talk with Cyna anyway.

"I have been doing a lot of thinking since our tour today," Jyres said. "And I was remembering how you were telling me you had so many questions. Questions that no one could answer."

Cyna shook her head in response, showing she was paying attention.

"And, I kind of have some of those same questions now," continued Jyres. "I wonder where I come from. Did my family have a family crest? You know things like that."

"I know. The tour was a lot of fun today," replied the young girl. "I wish I had a records room that would tell me about who I am." The girl looked down at her hands, as if something she said was wrong.

"You know what," replied Jyres. "I do, too." Jyres paused, thinking about what it would be like to have a library of information at your fingertips. Then he moved past it quickly and continued. "But I hope that you are comfortable enough with me now that we could talk about your past a little bit. I thought if you told me anything you could remember about your village when you were there, maybe I'd know something that could be helpful. When you were eight, I would have still been in the desert village, you know."

"What kind of things could I tell you?" asked Cyna, clearly interested.

"You told me before that you don't remember your father, what about your mother?"

Cyna's face took on the classic features of sadness as she thought of her mom. "She was so pretty. She had hair like mine. She was so nice and always took care of me. It feels so long ago now, I am scared that I will forget her."

"I can see that she meant a great deal to you, you won't forget her. What was her name?"

Cyna looked down for a moment before looking back up, with a few tears in her eyes. "Celeyna. Her name was Celeyna."

Jyres tried to hide any signs of sadness and recognition in his response. For he recognized the name, and it was the name he had suspected he would hear. "I knew Celeyna," he said. "She had dark skin like you, wore her hair short as you do now."

"You knew my mom?" Cyna asked with excitement.

"I did. Not really well, but it was a small village. I remember her having a daughter. But I don't think you and I ever talked to each other."

"What else do you remember?"

"Well, Cyna. This may be hard for you to hear, and that perhaps is why no one has told you. As Rajeem told you, your mom was sick. I don't remember her taking you to the elves. But I do remember when the disease got worse." Jyres could see tears forming in Cyna's eyes already, but knew she deserved to know. "Your mom died, Cyna. I assume not long after you were brought here."

Cyna had an initial burst of tears, but they seem to subside quickly, to Jyres' surprise. She then started to shake her head. "I know. They never really told me, but somehow I knew."

"I am sorry," said Jyres who put his arm around the young girl.

Cyna rested her head on his shoulder. "Thank you for telling me. I miss her, but at least I know for sure now. I know that I am on my own."

17

No More Waiting for Lumpkin or the Silver Shadow

Zar got up slowly from his chair. His energy had begun to wane over recent months, the initial surge of energy he had from being back in the old library must have been wearing off. But he had been making a lot of progress thanks to the help of Flick and Lumpkin. He felt as if they were getting closer to the information he sought. Cataloging had been going well since Lumpkin's arrival had spurred his discovery of the current organization of the library. It was only a matter of time now.

Zar began the long walk to where his bed was. As he was walking, he heard an exclamation from Lumpkin. Zar shifted his gaze in that direction and saw Lumpkin running toward him with the Dragon Pericarp. Zar stood and waited for him, resting on his cane. As the dwarf came closer to him, Zar realized what was happening and what had caused the dwarf to shout. The Dragon Pericarp was pulsing with light.

"What, the dragon thing, it, what," stuttered Lumpkin.

"I had told you we would just have to wait, my dear dwarf. It appears the wait is over," replied Zar in a matter of fact tone.

Lumpkin stared up at the wizard with wide eyes. Then looked back at the item in his hand, pulsing in different shades of orange, but in a predictable pattern. Completely unsure of what to do, Lumpkin didn't move a muscle, afraid of doing something to the Dragon Pericarp.

"Come, follow me. And bring that with you," said Zar. "Flick," he then called, "where are you? Come." Then to Lumpkin he said, "Flick won't want to miss this."

Lumpkin, not knowing what "this" was, had no choice but to follow Zar. They walked to the end of the long row of shelves and slowly started to ascend the steps. Somewhere along the way Flick joined them. The three of them soon exited the underground library to emerge into the light of midday.

Zar stood quietly, gazing up into the sky. Flick and Lumpkin looked at each other with bemused expressions before looking up to the sky as well. Their watchfulness was rewarded a short time later, as two creatures could be seen flying in their direction. Lumpkin hopped up and down excitedly, then realized he was still holding the pulsing crystal in his hands and stopped.

As the creatures drew closer, their outlines clearly indicated they were indeed dragons. Lumpkin's excitement started to change to worry, as he was beginning to wonder if the dragons were what Zar had said they were waiting for.

The dragons landed in a clearing amidst the city ruins with both a ferocity and grace that only a dragon can demonstrate. The dragons then worked their way over and through the ruins to where Zar and his helpers waited. Flick and Lumpkin both retreated to hide behind Zar. They then peaked their heads around him as the dragons approached.

"Esmeralda, Crimson, the sight of you in flight never gets old," commented Zar. "I have missed that, being tucked away in my library."

"Zar," replied Esmeralda in her deep yet womanly tone. "Why am I not surprised to see you here at the end of our flight?"

A chuckle escaped the old man's lips as he shrugged his shoulders. Lumpkin had never been this close to the dragons before and made no move to leave his spot from behind the wizard.

"Where is it?" asked Crimson

"My friend here, Lumpkin, son of Lustor," said Zar, motioning to Lumpkin, "happens to have it."

Crimson took another step closer to them, and as he did so, Lumpkin fell to the ground, clutching his precious crystal. Crimson lowered his large head to the ground, just hovering over the frightened dwarf.

Zar smiled. "Come now, there is nothing to worry about. The eccentric dwarf will allow you to have it with no need for threatening. It is yours to have after all."

Lumpkin glanced up at the wizard, who nodded. Then Lumpkin stood up and held up the pulsing orange Dragon Pericarp. He looked away and closed his eyes as he did so, then opened one eye, curious enough to not be completely afraid. The dragon reached out with its front claw and snatched it from Lumpkin. He then brought it to Esmeralda and the two shared a glance at each other.

Flick and Lumpkin stood in shock not knowing what to think of it all. But not Zar. Zar knew what this meant and what passed between the two dragons at that moment.

Esmeralda turned her attention to Lumpkin. "We thank you, dwarf. We had thought all hope was lost. You can't possibly understand what this means!"

Esmeralda and Crimson, in unison, pointed their heads upwards and blew out a stream of fire into the sky. Then, with one last look at Zar, they jumped into the air and flew toward the west.

Lumpkin turned toward the wizard. "What happened? Now, what happened now?"

"Somehow, beyond all possible likelihood, you, a most peculiar fellow, were in possession of the last Dragon Pericarp. They were thought to all have been destroyed or lost forever after the War of Ages." Zar smiled at Lumpkin, who was waiting for more information. "They are the last two dragons in existence. And they had believed that there was no way to change that. Because there were no Dragon Pericarps. You see, without a Dragon Pericarp no new dragons can be born. But now, now there is hope for them. It really is quite extraordinary!"

"But, potions, used it for my potions."

"That's right you did. But, it will now serve the purpose it was meant to serve. Don't worry, I have a plan for you, too."

****

The Silver Shadow stood on an overlook. Watching. The creature referred to as the horde was below him, milling about. The two of them had some trouble communicating with each other and it was slowing down the process. The creature's vocabulary seemed to be limited, and it didn't always understand the Silver Shadow's intent. Intent. That was a word that had a whole new meaning to him now. For so many years, the Silver Shadow's intent didn't matter, it was non-existent.

The Silver Shadow had been one of the Knights of Enchantment. Knights in service to the wizard Meslar. Little did they know that Meslar was slowly taking over their minds. And before long, they were not truly themselves anymore. And during that process, their powers had dwindled as well. Now, since the defeat of Meslar, the knights were themselves again. They were delga who could access their powers again and they could have a will of their own once more.

At first the 11 former knights had stayed together, but soon some of them went their separate ways. And what a relief it was. To be away from the castle and any reminders of what Meslar had done was like a needed salve on a fresh burn. The Silver Shadow felt free. Free to make his own choices, have his own intentions. And to use his delga power, which provided him a near invisibility when used effectively. His ability allowed him to blend into the shadows. A skill that he had perfected in the years leading up to his and the others' escape from the War of Ages over the mountains to the new world.

Now that he had his power back, the question was what was he going to do with it. He felt like he had to prove himself again: to the other delga, the world and even to himself. Freeing the creature called the horde was just the first step in that. He was a powerful delga. Yet the fact that he and the other knights had failed in so many ways a few years ago, ate at him like a disease. But it was proof of what Meslar had really done to them.

The Silver Shadow in the old world, before Meslar's deception, was seen as a skilled warrior and assassin who was dominant and powerful. The delga and humans had often used him leading up to the great war to take care of someone whom they had decided needed to be done away with. What they didn't know was that he had often done the same for the dragons.

Those failings from a few years ago needed to be rectified. The knights had been bested by Jyres, Lalatco and others. And the Silver Shadow, for one, would not sit around pretending that was okay. As it stood, Jyres and his friends were seen as the heroes so they had prestige and respect tied to their names. Right now the only thing tied to a delga was the memory of Meslar...and failure. He would see to it that people would know the name the Silver Shadow again.

A delga wizard was seen as the most powerful delga, and so received all the attention. But all delga were gifted with different talents, being a wizard was just one of the possible delga abilities. The Silver Shadow knew that his ability and some of those of his former fellow knights were powerful in their own right. What better way to show how powerful a delga like him could be than making up for lost battles? A rematch. Show the world that Jyres was just a man, a human. The Silver Shadow smiled behind his gray silk mask. He already had a plan forming in the back of his mind. The name the Silver Shadow would be respected and feared as it once was.

18
ARMANT

This was it. The moment had come. Mit looked himself over one last time. He was dressed in the finest clothes he owned. He wore a fine silk vest of the color purple over a lighter colored purple shirt. He wore a chain around his neck with a small vial containing the healing salve hanging from the chain. It was a reminder of how he had started his ascent. Nodding his approval, he stepped out of his room and knocked on Jyres' door.

"Jyres, it is time to be going," Mit said from outside his room. "We do not want to be late."

A moment later, Jyres stepped out of his room, wearing the same usual well-worn clothes. A brown vest and tan shirt. Mit frowned at him, but decided to let it go. "Well, then, follow me."

Mit led Jyres through the palace toward the balcony that overlooked the palace grounds where many citizens would be packed shoulder to shoulder as they awaited the promised surprise. The Palace Official stood next to the empress and palace guards lined the hallways. Rajeem and Cyna were already there as well.

"Excellent," said the Palace Official. "When the moment arrives you will join the empress and I on the balcony," the official motioned toward the balcony as he talked. "You will know when to come out."

Jyres merely nodded in return and the Palace Official stepped through the curtain and out onto the balcony. "Citizens of Heritage thank you for coming," shouted the Palace Official. "You are here to witness a special occasion. But first, I present to you the one who has made this day possible, your empress, Empress Constance Octavia."

Mit could hear the crowd cheering and clapping and shifted his attention to the young empress. The empress was wearing the same simple gown she had been wearing on the day they had first met. The empress pressed her hands down her dress to smooth out wrinkles that weren't there to begin with. Then putting on a forced smile, she stepped out on the balcony.

Mit listened carefully to the crowd as they first grew louder and soon softer as if they had been instructed to quiet down. Then he heard the empress in a loud, calm, smooth voice say, "Today is a great day for this city. In its long history, many days can be pointed to as days that made Heritage what it is today. And today might be another one of those days. My people, today I have the honor of presenting to you a hero. Not just any hero, but a human. And not just any human, but one who has roots in this great city."

Mit's eyes roamed the faces of those standing around. Jyres' face was one of pure shock. The young girl, Cyna, looked as though she might cry. Whether that was out of grief or joy, he could not say. Then Jyres eyes locked with his, a question behind that gaze. Mit threw up his arms in a gesture that said, "I don't know, either."

Outside, the empress continued, "That is right. Jyres, the Hero of humans is now Jyres Armant. He is part of one of the most storied families in the history of Heritage. Citizens of Heritage, I present to you, Jyres Armant, Hero of Heritage!"

The crowd erupted in applause. But Jyres was frozen with shock. *How could this be? How could they know this?* Those and more questions swirled about his head as Mit encouraged him to go out on the balcony. Still he didn't move. Cyna came over and gave him a hug, tears falling down her cheeks as the crowd continued its cheers. Finally, Mit came over and grabbed Jyres by the arm and led him out onto the balcony.

If possible, the crowd got even louder as Jyres stepped out onto the balcony to stand beside the empress. His vision was filled with people, who were standing shoulder to shoulder, filling up the whole space in front of the palace and spilling over to side roads and alleys.

The Palace Official held up his hands for silence, and finally the noise from the huge crowd lessened. "Jyres Armant will be with us all week," shouted the official. "He is here to give thanks to this city and to broker a friendship with the new world." A murmur pulsed throughout the crowd at the mention of this. After a few moments, he spoke again, "Jyres the Hero of Heritage, believes this to be beneficial to all." The Palace Official then turned and gestured to Jyres.

Jyres stepped forward to the forefront of the balcony. He again surveyed the crowd, astonished by the number of people. He had never seen so many humans in one place. That they were all here to see him left him speechless. The crowd was gazing at him expectantly, waiting for him to speak. He decided to start with that thought.

"Seeing you all here today," Jyres began, "brings great joy to my heart. I have never seen so many humans in one place before. By now most of you have heard my story. A story that started because I wanted my people, our people, to be in a better place than we were on the other side of the mountain." Jyres paused again, trying to collect his thoughts. "I see now that Heritage is already there. I am humbled to be able to call it my city. And I know, with Heritage at the lead, humans in the new world city of Skystair can learn how to get there, too." Finished speaking, Jyres waved and bowed to the crowd.

The crowd, once again, erupted in cheers. They either were already forgetting about the suggested friendship with the new world or agreeing with Jyres that Heritage could again lead all humans to a better place. Jyres backed away and retreated quickly into the palace. He rested his head against the cool brick and closed his eyes.

Jyres just didn't know what to think, or what to do next. Somehow, he was a son of the great city of Heritage. Something that seemed to drop from out of the sky right into his lap. All of a sudden he had a history. He shook his head, let out a long breath and opened his eyes, but his mind still seemed unsettled. Then a small hand grabbed his, and he looked down to see Cyna holding onto his hand with her own. He smiled at her and his mind slowed down for just a moment. Just enough to understand. He was Jyres Armant, Hero of Heritage.

Jyres didn't have time to focus on that to long and was ushered into a room to meet with a few select members of the Heritage elite. After, Jyres retreated to his room. He flopped on the bed and tried to relax. Although his legs appreciated the rest, relaxation didn't come. What had just happened? Jyres took a deep breath trying to clear his mind and slow his thoughts. But laying on the bed didn't seem to accomplish anything. A short while went by and he was up again, pacing and wondering what was the first thing he should do. Then he remembered the family crest that he had seen on the tour. That's it. A place to start. He could find out what the crest for the Armant family was.

It didn't take long before his request to the Palace Official had been granted and Mit was knocking at the door with a book in hand, a weathered leather-bound tome that was simply called "Families of Heritage." Thanking Mit, he took the book and hastened down the hall to find Cyna. Finding her in her room, the two of them opened the book and gazed at the first page. The first couple of pages were a table of contents of sorts, with names of different families written in an elaborate script.

Jyres' heart began to beat faster as he read through the names until finding Armant. Looking over at Cyna, he realized she had found the name as well. He thought to ask how she had learned to read at a young age, something that he had not been able to do until his teens, but then realized that the educated elves had properly taught her how to read in who knows how many languages. They smiled at each other and Jyres turned to the appropriate page.

In bold script across the top of the page was the word Armant. Just below the name was a beautiful rendering of a family crest. The Armant family crest was a picture of two criss-crossed sickles with a bird in between the handles. Jyres was not exactly sure what type of bird it was, but it was a bright blue color. He enjoyed the detail of the artist's work for a moment before looking over at Cyna.

"What are those?" she asked.

"Those are called sickles. Farmers use them for a variety of purposes. Mainly, a farmer would hold onto the handle and then use the curved blade to cut wheat or whatever they were growing. So, apparently the Armants were farmers."

Looking further down the page Jyres read out loud the small paragraph that was there. "The Armant family is one of the eight families that founded the city of Heritage. Chester Armant was vital to the initial growth of the city. His knowledge of farming immediately produced food that was used to feed the city and trade with neighboring towns."

"Well," Jyres said as he leaned back in his chair. "Chester, I like that name."

Cyna smiled and said, "Can I look at more pictures?"

"Of course," said Jyres, who slid the book closer to Cyna.

Jyres felt satisfied. He had accomplished one thing at least since he was completely set off kilter with the news of his ancestry. His mind immediately wanted to take him to the next question. But no. One would be enough for today.

That night Jyres left the palace and walked toward the town proper, seeking to find Gargan and tell him of the news. He soon found it a challenge to get very far as many who saw him wanted to talk with him. At first, Jyres didn't mind, but an arc later and he was wishing he could go back to not being popular. Finally, Jyres made it to where the gargoyles were staying, a rundown stable off the beaten path. Gargan and three other gargoyles were there and they greeted him when he arrived.

"You seemed to have caused something of a stir, your name is on the wind," said Gargan.

"So you heard the news then?" asked Jyres.

"What news?" asked Gargan in his usual flat, deep tone.

"My family is from this city!" Jyres extended his arms out wide as if gesturing to the city.

"What are you talking about, you have lived in Tomackus all your life."

"Yes, but originally, my ancestors came from here."

"I see," said Gargan, unimpressed.

"Don't you understand? I know where I come from, that I have a past, a family that had a home, a life possibly better than what most humans of Skystair have currently experienced." Jyres watched for a reaction from his large friend, anything that would show he was understanding Jyres' feelings.

"I don't understand, you want to live in Heritage now?" questioned the big gargoyle, scratching his chin as he did so.

"No, well, I don't know...oh forget it." Jyres sighed, swatting his hand in the air in front of him as if pushing the subject away.

"Sorry, perhaps I don't understand, as our gargoyle clan has been in the same region for ages. But don't sell yourself short. Perhaps they are different from here, but the humans from Tomackus are resilient."

"Well, the news will go a long way in solidifying the alliance, which is what the king wanted accomplished."

"That is good," replied Gargan before pausing and adding, "but I sense that you are not at ease."

"Just a lot to think about. I will be fine."

As they stood in comfortable silence, many forms began to pass by overhead.

"Gargoyles," said Gargan, in a voice that Jyres knew meant they were not of his clan.

"There are a lot of them," replied Jyres.

"Yes, there are. We must see what they are about."

"Be careful," called Jyres as the four gargoyles began their pursuit.

19
HIDE AND SEEK

Jyres and Cyna were paging through the book of family crests again in the middle of the day when Cyna stopped and leaned back.

"Jyres, can I ask you something?" she asked.

"Sure, anything."

"Well, remember," she started quietly, "when we talked by the waterfall and you said you wanted to help me, you know with my lifting the rocks?"

"Yes, of course, I do." Jyres smiled back.

"Well," she said, growing a little louder. "I was wondering when, or um, how you are going to do that." The girl looked up at Jyres expectantly.

Jyres smiled down at her. "As soon as this business is done and Mit has finished what he needs to finish, you and I are going to visit that old friend I told you about."

"Really!" Cyna almost jumped up and down in excitement, but contained herself.

"Yes, really. I also anticipate that will be happening soon. In the meantime, I requested another book or two on the family of Armant. Figured we had so much fun reading this one together, we might as well see how they knew I am from here. In fact, why don't you walk down to the records room and see what the holdup is."

"Okay," replied Cyna with a strong nod of the head.

Once she had gone, Jyres went back to his room in search of Mit to try and get an update on the alliance talks with the city.

Cyna walked around the palace taking the long way to the records room only because she liked the tapestries better. The shorter way was so dull. A couple of people said "hello" to her as she passed by. The people here had been very nice to her. She hardly ever saw any humans, and she enjoyed the chance to observe them. She had talked to a few, but for the most part she just watched at a distance.

She turned at the corner and into the hallway of the records room. To her surprise the door was left ajar. She approached the door and gave a gentle knock. Not hearing any response, she pushed the door open a little farther and said, "Hello, anyone here?" Still no response, so she pushed the door the rest of the way open. She took a few steps into the room and, looking around, realized that no one was here. That seemed odd to her. She remembered the Palace Official talking about how important this room and it staying locked was. And here it stood, open, with no one here.

She looked around at all the books and wanted to reach out and touch each of them. But she knew that she should wait and come back when someone was here. As she retreated to the door she heard a voice in the hallway.

"I know, but the request has been made," a man's voice said.

Cyna panicked. What would they do if they found her here? She quickly ran into one of the adjacent rooms, which was dark. She hid in a corner and waited as two voices became louder as they entered the room.

"But I don't understand what you want me to do?" It was a different voice than she had heard before.

The first voice responded, and this time, listening closely, she was almost certain the voice belonged to Mit. "Listen, I don't mean to confuse you. He is asking to see how we know that he is from here."

Jyres, they were talking about Jyres.

The voice that sounded like Mit continued. "So we need to provide that."

"I am telling you that we can't provide that," replied the other man, his voice rising in pitch.

"And I am telling you. That you can and you will."

After a few moments, she heard retreating footsteps and the closing of a door. She still dared not move, unsure of whether they both left or just one. Her answer was found just a moment later because she could hear someone mumbling under his breath and rummaging through something. *So*, she thought to herself, *I am not going anywhere for a little while.*

She took the time to review everything she had heard and commit it to memory. She wanted to make sure she could remember everything just as she heard it. Because to her it sounded like they had made it up. Mit and the others. They had lied to Jyres and the people of Heritage.

Why, why would they do that? Jyres thought he had a family now, but he didn't. Not from Heritage.

This would crush him; he had been so excited to find out. She had been so excited for him, because she knew what it was like to not know anything about your past. But it looked like that had all been made up.

She had to tell him, she had to get out of here. But how could she now? If they knew she had heard what they said, what would they do to her? She would just have to wait. Hide and wait.

*****

Gargan and his gargoyles had tracked the other gargoyles they had seen last night, but it did not lead them anywhere. This night, however, was a different story. As he and three of his fellow gargoyles flew, they could pick out individuals on the ground in the distance. As they grew closer, Gargan realized that there were gargoyles and two other individuals. Gargan circled the area one time, taking in the surroundings.

Bram and five other gargoyles had encircled a man and a creature. Not just any creature, the creature. Gargan didn't know what that meant. But he knew that whatever Bram's intentions were with the creature, they would be in his own interest and not that of others. With that in mind, he led his gargoyles to ground, landing in the circle by the man and the creature.

"Gargan," an angry Bram yelled. "Leave. You have no stake here." The big purple gargoyle stared at Gargan, his face full of contempt.

"The whole world has a stake in this, when it comes to his creature," replied Gargan.

"I will deal with you later. Right now, I need to deal with this one," said Bram, pointing at the man dressed all in gray. "He is a trespasser."

"Who are you?" asked Gargan, looking at the man.

"Bram, Gargan, I am the Silver Shadow. I was only trespassing to right a wrong. You had this creature in a prison."

So that is why the creature had not been seen for so long. Bram had been keeping him captive. Gargan did not respond, unsure of how this was going to play out.

"You know nothing. I am helping the creature. You have done nothing that helps it," shouted an angry Bram.

As if in response, the creature reached out to the nearest gargoyle, which happened to be one that was with Gargan. When the creature touched the gargoyle, a painful roar echoed from his lips. In response his body quickly turned to stone, a defense mechanism against the creature.

Gargan roared in anger, and the man calling himself the Silver Shadow disappeared. Then chaos ensued. Gargoyles attacked gargoyles. And the creature started to leave the area. Gargan meant to follow, but then Bram was on him. Their claws met, each trying to overpower the other to the ground.

When that didn't work, Bram released Gargan and planted a powerful punch across Gagan's face. Gargan dodged the next punch before landing a punch squarely in Bram's torso. Then he quickly spun and landed his elbow on the side of Bram's head, sending him to the ground. He pounced onto Bram, but Bram was ready for him and used his strength to redirect him.

They circled each other. This battle was a long time in the making. They had always been at odds with each other. But since the events of three years ago, their animosity towards each other had grown even more.

"You have interfered with my plans for the last time, Gargan," growled the purple gargoyle.

Looking Bram straight in the eyes, and with all certainty, Gargan replied. "I believe it is time for your clan to find a new leader."

Bram's response was to charge him at full speed, Gargan waited until the last moment, then darted to the side and used Bram's own momentum against him, pushing him to the ground as he went past. Bram wasn't content to stay on the ground and twisted around using his wings to keep Gargan from gaining any advantage.

"They need someone who can lead them in this new age," continued Gargan as he took one step to his left.

"I will be dead before I let you or anyone else lead my clan," roared Bram in defiance. "A new age is here, one that will see the gargoyles as the rulers of the land. Join us, or be left behind."

"I think we will never see eye to eye." Not waiting for a response, Gargan launched another attack, flapping out his wing at Bram to disguise his punch, which landed smack across Bram's face.

The two continued to battle, as did the other gargoyles around them, while the creature and the Silver Shadow slunk away. Bram had the numbers on Gargan and eventually they started to overpower Gargan and his friends. Slowly Gargan was able to regroup his gargoyles, standing in a circle around their friend who was still in stone form after being touched by the creature. Gargan, breathing hard, could see his fellow gargoyles were laboring as well. But he also knew that the sun was coming soon.

"Well," he said to Bram and his allies, "it seems that you have won this round."

"This round?" scoffed Bram. "There will be no second round. I have won this fight. And you will surrender."

"I believe we had already established that neither of us would give in to the other, that includes surrender." A half smile formed on Gargan's face, for he knew what was coming.

"Very well, we will finish where you stand," replied Bram.

"Not tonight you won't," replied Gargan, allowing the half smile to turn into a smirk.

The gargoyles started to charge at Gargan and his friends, but before they could strike every gargoyle was turned into stone as the first rays of sunlight lit up the battleground.

20
HERO?

Cyna had stayed hidden so long that she had fallen asleep. Her eyes slowly blinked open and it took her a moment before she remembered where she was. Once she did, the adrenaline quickly woke her fully. She listened carefully. She didn't hear a sound. Very quietly, she moved away from her hiding spot and toward the main room. Glancing out of the doorway and finding the room empty she quickly made for the door.

Cyna slowly turned the door knob and opened the door. She grimaced and inadvertently jumped as if the creaking door inflicted some pain on her. Seeing that the hallway was clear, she closed the door and took off running, almost running right into a woman as she turned a corner. "Sorry," she yelled as she continued on.

Cyna opened the door to Jyres' room with a flurry. "Jyres, Jyres!" she called in between gasping breaths.

"Cyna! Where have you been? Everyone is so worried about you!" Jyres ran over to her, wrapping her in a hug.

"Jyres, I need…" Cyna was still breathing hard from her run through the palace.

"It's okay, you're okay now," said Jyres, misunderstanding. He hugged her again. "Guess what," he said, "whatever you said must have worked, Mit brought some more documents for us to look over."

"But that's just it," Cyna said, her breathing more under control. Pushing away from Jyres so she could look up at him. She continued, "It's all a lie. They made it up. All of it." Tears started to fall down her cheeks and Cyna quickly wiped them away.

"What are you talking about?" asked Jyres.

"Last night, I heard them, they didn't know I was there. Mit was talking to someone who said they couldn't prove it. They couldn't prove you were from here."

"But they brought things to me this morning," Jyres said, motioning to the table.

"I know what I heard. I repeated it over and over in my head," Cyan replied, fighting through the lump in her throat.

"But why would they do that?" asked Jyres in confusion. A moment later he answered his own question. "They need to unite the people under one banner. I was their way to do that. Now the city thinks I am their hero, and thinks that their empress discovered the truth and brought me here."

Cyna didn't respond at first, just looked up at him and said with a sad tone, "I am sorry."

"You? What are you sorry for? You didn't do anything wrong." Jyres put his hands on her shoulders. He calmed the turmoil inside him and focused on the girl in front of him. "Now, you stay here. I will let Rajeem know that you are here. She has been worried. Then I am going to go talk to Mit and straighten this whole thing out. After that, we are leaving as soon as possible. We will go find Zar and start learning more about you. Sound good?"

Cyna just nodded in response and Jyres left the room.

Jyres stormed into Mit's room. Mit looked up from whatever he held in his hands.

"Jyres," said Mit, seemingly unconcerned by Jyres' current mood. "Great news, I have it right here. Heritage has signed the alliance. It is done." Mit raised one arm into the air in triumph.

"Is it true?" asked Jyres with an edge to his voice he hadn't even tried to hide.

"Well, of course, it is true. I hold it right here in my hands," said Mit as he lowered his arm and held out the signed scroll with both hands.

"Not that. Is it true?" he said again.

"Speak plainly, Jyres," said Mit, feigning as if he didn't understand while he rolled up the scroll.

"It was all a lie. Wasn't it? The family name, the Hero of Heritage, all made up. Just like those documents you gave me this morning." Jyres was teetering on the edge of rage as he looked at the man in front of him.

"Look, you are obviously upset about something, let's talk when you have calmed down." Mit placed the scroll on the desk before turning back toward Jyres.

Jyres crossed the rest of the room and brought himself right in the face of Mit.

"Tell me," said Jyres in a tone that left no room for anything else.

"It is a lie," Mit finally admitted. "All of it. But it worked, the alliance was signed."

"Why didn't you tell me, instead of leading me along," Jyres yelled.

"Would you have gone along with it? We had to get this done." Mit pointed back at the scroll as he talked. "And it is done."

Jyres turned his back and walked a couple of steps, before turning around to look at Mit again. "I was excited, I was happy to be from here. You gave that all to me, and now it is gone as quickly as it came."

"Maybe you are from here, you don't know," responded Mit.

"Exactly," screamed Jyres. "I don't know. And you told me I did." Jyres turned to leave, this time for good.

"You mustn't tell anyone, Jyres. This has to stay our little secret," pleaded Mit.

"I don't care, Mit. Do what you have to do. I am going to see an old friend."

****

All of the gargoyles awoke at the same time, the stone melting away. Gargan and those from his clan immediately began running toward the nearby trees. One of his gargoyles, who had true wings, took to the air immediately. Those gargoyles that chased them and that could fly with their wings were in the air, while the rest were on all fours.

Once they made it to the tree line, the gargoyles quickly climbed the trees and then leapt into the air, gliding on the wind and into the sky. Gargoyles from both clans filled the skies, banking and grabbing at each other. Gargan swung by one enemy knocking him to the side and allowing his friend to fly by. Then he called to the others and they turned away.

The chase was on. Bram and his fellow gargoyles wouldn't let them go quite so easily. The gargoyles banked and weaved, matching each other in a battle of flying proficiency. When Bram or others of his clan got close enough to their prey, they would lash out with a claw or tail. But Gargan and his gargoyles would dodge or bat them away, doing all they could to stay ahead of their pursuers. Gargan led the way and his clan members trusted him, following his lead and matching his dangerous flight maneuvers. The mad flight continued on, with Gargan's clan staying just enough ahead of their nemeses.

As the night wore on, Bram realized Gargan was slowly leading him toward Gargan's castle, where Bram would be greatly outnumbered. Cursing under his breath, he finally called a stop to the chase. Gargan had escaped, this time.

****

Very late in the night, in fact, it was almost morning, there was a knocking sound. Jyres heard it a second time, and then a third before he realized the knocking was real and not a dream. Slipping out of his bed Jyres walked towards the knocking, realizing it was coming from the window. The window was really just an opening in the side wall with wooden shutters. Jyres' eyes adjusted to the darkness and he realized Gargan was hanging on the outside wall of the palace, looking in through the open shutters.

"Gargan, there you are," Jyres said with a yawn, "I looked for you at the stables; you were not there.

"Yes, we had a bit of trouble," frustration clearly evident in his voice.

"So have I. You go first."

"We saw the creature. Bram has been keeping him as a prisoner. But someone named the Silver Shadow has freed him."

"The creature—he is back? We must do something!" exclaimed Jyres.

"We ended up battling and fleeing from Bram and his gargoyles. I do not know what happened to the creature. At least we delayed whatever Bram had planned with the creature." Gargan paused, turning his head to the side as if in thought, before turning back to Jyres. "What was your trouble?"

"Nothing as concerning as that, but remember what I told you about being from here? I guess it was all made up. A deception. To ensure the people would be comfortable with joining the new kingdom. Mit is happy to have the treaty signed, and isn't bothered by the actions needed to get it accomplished."

"To me it doesn't change anything, you are from the village."

Jyres shrugged it off. "Tell me more about the creature. Where were you when you saw him?" Jyres asked urgently.

"We were not far from here," replied Gargan. "Near the trees at the base of the mountains."

"Great, let's go and investigate now."

"We can't, the sun is almost upon us. I must return to the stables, we will talk more on this." Then Gargan released his hold on the wall and jumped into the air, gliding on the winds toward the stables.

Jyres couldn't fall back asleep. His mind was focusing on the events of the day and it was increasing his anger and frustration as he laid in bed. Finally, he gave up and got dressed. He began pacing the room as his anger threatened to get the better of him. Images of Mit played in his mind. Mit had given him a hope that he didn't know he had. Once he thought he was from Heritage, so many questions that were hidden under the surface popped up, now they had a chance to be answered. And just as quickly, he learned they would never be answered.

So here he was, in a great human city, but still not linked to any of them. Much like his feelings about the human city of Skystair. Or the elven forest, for that matter. He had his home there. But he had no family there. Who was he really? A human with no home? A "hero" with no place to call his own?

Yes, he had friends, those that he could count on. But could he? Lalatco had a family now. Vurth a job that kept him busy and tied to the Valley of the Dragons. Gargan didn't understand. He had always had his clan. And Elonda, well they hardly got to see each other. The king kept everyone busy.

Jyres's frustration made him clench his fists when he thought of Malick. The king who so easily discounted the creature and the threat it could potentially be. But the creature had been seen again. If Jyres did not act now, he might lose any chance to. What if the creature goes into hiding or goes after the key? Or does who knows what?

Jyres stopped pacing. Took a breath. *That's it,* he thought. Jyres rubbing his chin as he thought. He knew that he needed to track the creature and watch what it does. Maybe if he followed it, he could warn someone before it did something terrible. Or maybe he could witness something that would prove to the king how dangerous it could be. No one else had time to help him. No one else would even care that he was gone. No time like the present.

Jyres strapped on his sword belt and descended the stairs to the stables. Finding Gerti, he informed the stable hand that he would be taking her for a ride. After preparing and securing the saddle, he mounted his horse and started to trot away from the stables.

The morning's early light was bright after spending so much time in the palace with its many dark hallways. Jyres was glad to be outside again and happy to be trotting along with Gerti. Jyres' face was set with determined action. He would find the creature, perhaps even end the threat.

Three arcs later, Jyres' determination had started to waver, wondering if he would be able to find the creature's trail on his own. Perhaps this wasn't such a great idea after all. But as luck would have it, Jyres soon found his determination restored as he caught a glimpse of the creature in the long grass ahead. Quietly, Jyres dismounted, leaving Gerti by the trees.

Slowly, Jyres crept closer to the creature, using the long grass to hide him. He pictured himself like a sabretooth on the hunt. Just like the one who had almost caught him all those days ago. Once he was a bit closer, he stayed motionless for a while observing the creature. The creature also stood motionless, seeming to stare at something far in the distance.

Jyres continued to wait patiently, telling himself that observation was what was needed. After what seemed like forever, when all Jyres was doing was sitting in the grass getting insect bites, the creature still had not moved. Finally, Jyres let his impatience get the better of him and slowly started to approach, with his hand wrapped around the hilt of his sword.

Jyres had only gone a few steps before he heard someone say, "That's far enough." Appearing from seemingly out of nowhere, a man stood with a sword drawn and pointed at Jyres' neck. Jyres didn't move. The man moved to face Jyres, his sword stayed in the same dangerous position as he did so. Once facing each other, the man gave a slight nod.

"Jyres, I am so glad you decided to join us. I am the Silver Shadow."

"What do you want," asked Jyres in an impatient voice as he glanced over at the creature to make sure it was not advancing on him as well.

"Right to it? No small talk?" The Silver Shadow's voice was calm and conversational as he spoke.

"I have no need to talk with you, my business is with that creature."

"Well, I have business with you, and seeing how I have the advantage at the moment, you will just have to talk anyway."

"What business do you have with me?" asked Jyres.

"Jyres, the one who completed the prophecy. The one who bested the knights and Meslar, and now Jyres the Hero of Heritage." The Silver Shadow mocked Jyres with his tone and gestures as he spoke. Turning more serious he went on. "I need to prove to you, myself, and everyone else that there is only one reason you and your friends were able to beat us. And that reason is that we were not ourselves."

"Everyone knows that Meslar controlled your minds. We have told people that, we let all the knights do as they please."

"But no one knows how truly gifted we can be. After this, they will," said the Silver Shadow with a wicked smile. The Silver Shadow then lowered his slender sword. "On guard," he yelled. "Just you and me." He then took up a ready position, his sword held out in front of him and his knees bent.

Left with no other options, Jyres brandished his own sword and slowly advanced.

The Silver Shadow struck first. His attacks were quick and precise and Jyres struggled to fend him off initially. But then he fell in step with the attacks and the swords clanged off each other in a steady rhythm. The sounds of clanging swords echoed around them as the creature watched the two exchange blows. The Silver Shadow sidestepped instead of parrying Jyres' swing and caught Jyres arm with the end of his own blade. The blade drew blood, but it was a superficial wound.

The two swordsmen continued their dance, but Jyres grew tired and could not breach the other man's defenses. The Silver Shadow sensed Jyres' discomfort and pushed the attack. Jyres' defense grew wild and desperate. Jyres swung his sword down low and blocked a stab from his opponent, but the block left him unbalanced and with his free hand the Silver Shadow punched him across the face sending him to the ground. Before Jyres could recover the Silver Shadow stood over him, his sword pointed at Jyres neck for the second time.

"That was nothing," said the former knight. "I could have ended you much earlier." The Silver Shadow's smirk was everything Jyres would have suspected. All arrogance and superiority.

"I believe you," is all Jyres managed to say in response between his gasping breaths.

"Now to leave my mark."

Before Jyres could think of what that meant, in two quick motions the Silver Shadow cut thin lines on the inside of Jyres' wrist. Jyres screamed in pain, dropping his sword and clutching his wrist with his right hand. After a moment, Jyres pulled his hand away, dripping with blood, to see lines in the shape of two Ss on his wrist. Jyres quickly grasped his wrist again and closed his eyes to block out the pain. After a moment, he looked back up at the man still looking down at him, and then glanced at the creature still watching.

Looking back at the Silver Shadow, Jyres asked, "Now what?"

"I am done with you." The Silver Shadow backed away and the creature approached.

The creature, a gelatinous being, slowly walked over and stared down at Jyres. "Key," it said.

"I don't have it," replied Jyres, holding his hands out wide to emphasize the point.

"Key," it said again, undeterred.

"I don't have it," Jyres screamed back.

The Silver Shadow came forward again and roughly searched Jyres as he laid on the ground. Finding nothing, the Silver Shadow shook his head at the creature.

"Where...Key...?" asked the creature.

"I am not telling you anything," replied Jyres, who slowly backed away from the creature, using his legs to push himself across the ground.

The creature looked at the Silver Shadow, who only shrugged. The creature then returned its gaze to Jyres, who had crawled away a bit more.

Jyres found it hard to read the creature's expressions, but whatever it was feeling it wasn't good. Jyres, in a moment of desperation, reached for his sword and lunged forward impaling the creature's leg with his sword. The creature looked down at the sword as his leg seemed to retract into itself. Jyres watched as it retracted right over the blade, leaving the blade in midair. The leg then returned, away from the blade. Jyres stood there in shock, unsure of what to do.

The creature reached out and grabbed Jyres' arm. Immediately, pain shot through his entire body, and he collapsed to the ground. He cried out as the pain worsened, traveling to every part and fiber in his body that could sense pain. It became hard to breathe and his heart pounded in his chest at an astounding rate.

"You might need him," Jyres heard someone say. And suddenly the pain was gone. But Jyres couldn't move, couldn't breathe, and the last thought that came to him was, *I am not a hero either*.

21
DISCOVERIES

Lumpkin laid on his desk, miserable. He missed his dragon pleather, or whatever the old man had called it. Here he was with all this knowledge around him, and no power to use it. No more potions to be made. He absently tapped the desk with his hands which were lying flat, palms down. Then he gave a sigh of exasperation, before turning his head to the other side.

"Now, my dear Lumpkin. Did I not tell you all would be well? Come. Come. Follow me." Zar led the way, leaning heavily on his cane.

Lumpkin was just curious enough to force himself up from the desk and follow the old wizard. He was only half paying attention to where he was going and almost ran right into Zar. Zar had stopped. Lumpkin looked up and the old man was offering something to him. Lumpkin reached out for the object before he even realized what it was. It was a staff. At the end of the staff sat a purple gem.

Lumpkin's mood began to lighten as he realized what had just happened. A new stone had come into his possession. The wizard had just handed over a delga stone. And it was such a pretty purple! But before he made a mistake again, Lumpkin thought he should ask the wizard to be sure.

"Delga Stone? Delga Stone this time?"

"Yes, yes. It is. And it is yours if you want it."

Lumpkin took the staff, placed the end on the ground and looked up. The staff was bigger than he was.

"I suppose we will have to do something about that part." The wizard chuckled. "Now, remember. You are not a delga. So you cannot overreach yourself. I am thinking you have already learned your limits, and that is why you have resorted to potions. But magic can be dangerous for those in whom it is not ingrained in."

Lumpkin looked up at the purple gem and smiled widely. He was completely unaware that this was the staff of the wizard, Meslar, who had so briefly been able to open the gate three years ago. Lumpkin was happy again, so perhaps it was for the best that he didn't know the stone's legacy.

"Now, come along. I have a feeling today is going to be a big day for us."

Zar was proven right. Their cataloging and searching of the library produced many promising books that day that might shed more light on the subject of the gate. So Zar and Lumpkin sat down to read. Some books were in languages that Lumpkin could not read, but he helped go through the ones that he could. The first book was maybe the most boring book he had to read yet, and he had fallen asleep at least once. It was a book that went through, in painstaking detail, the lives of a certain kind of rodent. After a little while, Lumpkin deemed it not helpful and not what they were looking for. He then reached for the next book.

Zar had picked this particular book to be read, as this one was written by a delga during the time period that Zar had been looking for. As Lumpkin read the beginning, he realized it was almost like reading a timeline. It seemed like a summary of certain blocks of time. So, interested, he read on.

Finally, he read a line that said, "This brings us to the purpose of the Gate of Fire. The horde." Lumpkin carefully read it again, double checking the elaborate script of the writer. Then he hastily put the book down and ran over to where Zar was reading.

"Gate. Mentioned, yes, Gate!" said the excited dwarf.

"Good, very good. Let's have a look," said Zar, putting the scroll he was reading aside.

Lumpkin retrieved the book and brought it over so Zar didn't have to get up and move, something that was starting to prove difficult for the wizard. Lumpkin pointed at the page and Zar began to read out loud.

"This brings us to the purpose of the Gate of Fire. The horde. At this point in the age there arose an enemy so vile, so evil, that something extreme had to be done to save us from the horde. No one seems to know where the horde came from. Only that they came. Like a swarm of locusts. And every town they went to they left nothing behind, but death."

Zar paused his reading and looked at Lumpkin. "We have found the enemy," Zar said.

****

Cyna started to realize what she had done to Jyres when she had been stuck in the library all night. It had only been four arcs, and she was already worried. No one seemed to know where he was. Which Cyna found odd. How does someone as popular as Jyres just disappear? Even though a fear continued to grow inside her, she did not let herself lose hope. And she spent the whole day searching the palace and asking anyone she could think of if they had seen Jyres.

Feeling defeated as the day drew on, she decided to head to the palace's stables. Once there she walked amongst the horses, patting them and talking to a few of them. Then she realized that Gerti was no longer in a stall. Running up to a boy who was there, she asked, "That horse on the end of the row, where did it go?"

"Oh, a man left this morning, saying he was taking it for a ride. I haven't seen him or the horse since."

A knot started to form in her stomach and Cyna almost yelled at the poor boy in response. "When? How early?"

The boy almost backed away from her, unsure of how to react. "Um, I was barely awake. It was so early."

Cyna took off running out of the stables and down the main path. She was beyond worried now. Here she thought she had found someone who could help her, and truly listen to her, and just like that he was gone. She turned the corner and kept running. Kept running. Finally, she found the out-of-the-way path she was searching for, which took her to the old rundown stables.

She ran inside huffing and puffing, putting her hands on her knees and breathing hard before she looked around. Four gargoyles stood in their stone forms waiting to be awakened from their slumber. Almost on cue, the last of the sun disappeared and the gargoyles roared to life. The first time she had seen this, she had been afraid. But not anymore. Now she marveled at it.

"Gargan," she cried as soon as she thought he could hear her. "Cyna, what is it," said the gargoyle once he had fully awakened.

"Jyres," she stammered, "he is gone."

"Gone, what do you mean gone?"

Cyna started to pace back and forth in front of the big gargoyle. "I can't find him anywhere, and his horse is gone, too."

"I think, I know why. We must hurry!" said Gargan in a voice that showed concern. Gargan then scooped up Cyna in one arm and climbed to the top of the stable using his free hand and his feet. Then, holding her in front of him like a small child, he and the other gargoyles took to the air.

A small gasp escaped Cyna when they started to fly. This had occurred a few times on the way to Heritage, something Jyres had encouraged her to try. He seemed to get a lot of enjoyment from being in the sky with Gargan. But being in the air still took her breath away. Humans weren't meant to fly. She regained her composure after a moment.

"Is he going to be okay?" she asked, a question filled with hope and worry.

"I do not know," Gargan replied.

A reply that made Cyna feel so weak that she would have fallen to her knees had she not already been cradled in Gargan's arms. Gargan must have sensed the distress in her because he tried to calm her.

"We must not give up hope. He is resilient. Like his people."

Cyna wiped tears away from her eyes and looked up at Gargan. She wondered what it would have been like the first time Jyres had met him. She had been scared the first time she met Gargan, and she had the benefit of Jyres telling her the whole time that he was a friend. Jyres would have not had any idea who or what it was when they had first met.

Then she thought about what Gargan had just said. "Like his people." Gargan thought he had people already. Why didn't Jyres think like that? Why had Heritage been such an exciting thing to him then? She had seen it the same way he had. The way she would want to see it. She wanted to know a family, to know what happened to her. So she had thought Jyres would need the same thing. But maybe he didn't.

"His people?" she asked, looking up at Gargan's clearly defined facial features.

"Yes. When I first met him, he led his people away from danger. Then, to keep them safe, he left them so Meslar would not hurt them. I think he has forgotten what he did for them. He protected them just like I would my clan."

"I don't have any people," she said.

"You have Jyres," Gargan replied matter of factly, as if it was something well known.

Gargan and the gargoyles reached the area in which Gargan had last seen the creature. Gargan instructed his gargoyles to spread out and the four of them flew low over the land scanning for any sign of

Jyres or the creature. They continued to investigate, moving on to the adjacent areas once the first area was properly searched.

"Gargan!" Cyna shouted. "Look!"

Gargan turned his head to where Cyna was pointing and saw someone lying face down in the long grass. He landed quickly and set Cyna down. As soon as he did so, she ran to the man. When she reached him, she called out.

"It is him!" Cyna looked down, grabbing Jyres by the shoulders. "Jyres, are you okay? Jyres!" She turned back to Gargan and through her tears she said, "He is not answering me."

Gargan approached and bent down close to him as the other gargoyles landed nearby. Gargan gently picked him up and that is when Cyna realized he was or had been bleeding.

"Oh no!" She screamed. "Gargan, he is bleeding."

"It is only on his hands and arms," he said, glancing him over and starting to fear a little himself.

"Is he alive?" Cyna asked in desperation, the tears coming like a river from her eyes.

"I do not know. We must hurry."

Another gargoyle scooped up Cyna and before long they were all in the air again.

Cyna focused on Jyres, now cradled in Gargan's arms as she had been only moments before. The gargoyle carrying her was to Gargan's right and she was close enough that she could see Jyres' face. His eyes were closed and his mouth was closed, and he showed no signs of life.

And all Cyna could do was watch.

Gargan had said they must hurry. But she didn't know what that meant. She didn't know where they were going, how far it was, or if any of it mattered. Was it already too late? Gargan had just said that she had Jyres. Gargan had seen Jyres as her family. But now, maybe she was back to not having anybody.

22
ALIVE?

Zar and Lumpkin had taken a break from reading and were sitting with Flick around a table and eating. They were chatting as they ate, enjoying each other's company when they heard an unnatural loud yell reverberating off the walls throughout the library.

"Zar!" And a moment later, "Zar!"

All three of them looked at each other for a moment before rising to their feet and heading toward the noise. Flick raced out ahead of them to investigate. Just a short time later he came racing back, talking excitedly. As usual, Lumpkin couldn't pick up on what Flick was saying, but Zar did.

"My goodness!" Zar exclaimed. "Lead them to us! Hurry!" And Flick was gone again in a flash. "Lumpkin, go get all of your vials and your staff. Hurry now, hurry!"

Lumpkin didn't need any more encouragement. Even though he didn't know what was going on, he knew Zar needed him and so he went. Lumpkin rushed back towards the study after retrieving his things. Only to find gargoyles rushing down the stairs with humans in tow. Lumpkin had never seen gargoyles up close before, and it took him a moment to recover and follow them where Flick was leading them to.

Zar had cleaned off the top of a table and the biggest gargoyle laid a body on top of the table. Lumpkin rushed past the gargoyles and the crying girl to stand next to the wizard. The man on the table had blood on his hands and arms, but otherwise looked uninjured. Lumpkin did not know who he was, but he seemed important to everyone else in the room.

"Where did you find him?" Zar said.

"I believe he tried to go after the creature," said the biggest gargoyle in the group.

"The creature!" yelled Zar, fear now coming into his eyes.

Zar started to examine the man who was laid on the table. He looked him over, at first looking for any wounds. He only found the strange mark on his wrist, which had stopped bleeding. He then put his ear as close as possible to the man.

"Whatever injury he sustained is internal. He is alive, though perhaps not for long," said Zar. "Lumpkin, hand me a vial, the potion we just made yesterday, hurry."

Lumpkin dug into one of his many pockets, and withdrew a red vial and offered it to Zar.

"That's the one. Hopefully it will buy us the time we need." Taking the vial, Zar uncorked the stopper and gently poured the red liquid into the man's mouth. "Stay with us, Jyres," said the old man. "We are here."

A feeling of astonishment rose in Lumpkin's chest. Jyres? This was Jyres, the man who had saved the world! What had happened to put him in such a state? So many questions entered his mind, even as he tried to process his amazement at seeing Jyres in person, though it appeared to be in dire circumstances.

"Now, Lumpkin, we must work together. He is barely breathing. Hold your staff over him, concentrate, and repeat after me."

Zar then held out his hands, and Lumpkin held out his staff with the purple Delga Stone. Together with the combined powers of the delga wizard and the delga stone they began a spell. Lumpkin was not even sure of the true nature of the spell, and he hadn't tried to use a stone in this manner ever before! But he did exactly what Zar did. And one after the other, they continued to chant their spell in the ancient language.

Cyna and the gargoyles looked on, powerless to help and fearing they were too late. For as the wizard and dwarf continued their chant, they did not perceive any difference in Jyres' appearance. Their fears only increased as time continued to go by. Cyna fell to her knees, unable to bear the emotions flying around inside her.

Suddenly, all of the chanting stopped. And all eyes turned toward Jyres, who gasped briefly, and then there was silence. But, Jyres' chest began to noticeably rise and fall. No one spoke, unsure of what just happened.

Zar collapsed back on his chair, the spell exhausting him. "Well," he said. "I do believe he will stay with us. Any longer and he would have been too far gone. You did well my friends getting him here. And you too, Lumpkin, I could not have done it alone."

Cyna started to weep, and Gargan noticeably relaxed.

"It is okay, child," said Zar, reaching a hand out to pat her shoulder. "He is resting now. As should we all. But first, Gargan, please take him to a bed where he can be more comfortable." Pointing to the dwarf he said, "Lumpkin, show him the way."

Jyres slept for many arcs, and it was not until later that next day that he awoke. He was in a dimly lit room, and he was lying on a bed. He saw Cyna sleeping on a chair next to the bed, but the rest of the room seemed to be empty. Jyres couldn't place where he was exactly. He let out a sigh and tried to sit up, before deciding he wasn't ready for that yet.

It took him a moment to recall what had happened. He had tried to hurt the creature. Only it didn't work, and as soon as the creature touched him he felt pain. A pain like he had never felt before. After that, he didn't remember anything. He had no idea where he was or how he got here. What was Cyna doing here? He figured all would be explained to him. He drifted off to sleep again. The next time he woke up, Cyna was awake, standing over him.

"Jyres!" she exclaimed. "He is awake! Zar, he is awake."

As Jyres started to take in his surroundings again, the old wizard entered the room.

"Hello, young man. I knew you would wake up. How are you feeling?"

"Zar?" Jyres asked, his voice coming in a croak.

"Yes, it is me. Cyna is here, too. Cyna, please fetch some water for Jyres." Once she had gone, he said, "That one has not left your side."

"Where am I?"

"A great question. You are in the library in the old city of Secord. You have been here before, I am sure you will remember." Cyna returned and handed the small clay cup to Zar. "Thank you, my dear. Now, let me talk with him for a moment. I will call you shortly." Zar waited until the reluctant Cyna stepped out of the room again. "Here is some water, let's try a sip shall we?" Zar helped Jyres bring the cup to his lips and take a drink.

"How did I get here?" asked Jyres, voice not as raspy as before.

"Gargan and Cyna found you and brought you here right away. Had they not found you, I fear you would be dead. Lumpkin and I then healed you with magic."

"Lumpkin?" Jyres had never heard that name before and even though he had a headache and wasn't feeling all that well, he was pretty sure he would remember such a unique name.

"Oh, he is a most delightful dwarf. You will meet him soon enough," said Zar, waiving the question away for now.

"Well, thank you, I think," said Jyres.

"Tell me, how did you receive that wound on your wrist?"

Jyres raised his left wrist to look at it. A scar with an SS was now on his wrist. "The Silver Shadow. He beat me in a duel, then left that mark for me."

"The Silver Shadow. Well that is disappointing news. But that doesn't explain why you were barely able to breathe. How did that happen?"

"The creature, he touched me and all I felt was pain." Jyres grimaced at the memory of it.

"The horde," said Zar quietly.

"What was that?" asked Jyres, who had been unable to make out what the wizard had said.

"We have been busy at the library," said Zar, motioning to the area around him. "The horde. That is what the creatures from the gate are called. And it appears they were blocked off from this world for good reason. They would leave death in their wake." Zar paused and shifted his focus back to Jyres. "And now that you have experienced their touch, it seems easy to understand how. They can hurt or kill with a touch. Most likely, the longer they hold onto someone, the more lethal. A member of Gargan's clan was also touched by the creature. The gargoyle immediately turned to stone. Thankfully, the stone form seems to protect them from permanent damage by the creature."

"And you can't harm them, either," said Jyres, his voice already growing weak. "My sword did nothing to it." The memory of his failed attack on the creature was still fresh in his mind.

"All the more reason for the gate it would seem. Now, rest some more. When you awake again, you can try something to eat. And you will talk with Cyna as well. She is so happy that you are okay." Zar patted him on the arm, slowly rose from his chair, and left the room.

Cyna was waiting in the room again when Jyres woke up later that night.

"Hey, kid," said Jyres to get her attention.

Cyna shot up from her chair and stood next to the bed. "Jyres, I am so glad you are okay."

"Me, too, and it sounds like I have you and Gargan to thank for that. Thank you for coming after me."

Cyna leaned over and gave him a hug. "What were you doing by yourself?"

"Doing exactly what Lalatco told me not to do," said Jyres. Seeing Cyna's confused expression he chuckled and went on. "I acted rashly. I was frustrated, alone, and did not make a good decision."

"Why do you feel you are alone?"

"Because I am, Cyna." Jyres gestured with arms out to the side. "I don't have a place to call my own, I don't have a family."

"I think you…and me for that matter, are wrong on that one. We both got so excited about you being part of Heritage. But something Gargan said has stuck with me."

"Why do I get the feeling you are going to teach me a lesson? Shouldn't it be the other way around?" Jyres had a half smile on his face and winked at Cyna.

Cyna smiled and said, "Well, he said you are resilient like your people. He sees your people as the humans of Skystair."

"Okay, I can see that."

"But, I remember sitting outside the tent in the Valley of the Dragons before we left for Heritage. And you and Vurth, Elonda, Leah, and Lalatco were all laughing and having so much fun. And…" Cyna faltered, unsure if she should continue.

"Go ahead, keep going," encouraged Jyres, already knowing what she was saying. What he knew, but didn't admit to himself.

"And, well, that's what I wanted. Family." Cyna unconsciously placed her hand over her heart as she talked. "You already have it, Jyres. People that care for you and enjoy being with you. Gargan, for example, would do, and has done, so much for you, and, well you know."

Jyres was a little choked up listening to Cyna. "I *do* know. Thank you for reminding me of it." He cleared his throat. "I just forgot. With how very little I get to see everyone it is hard. And then, with the chance to be from the great city of Heritage, I just felt so out of place when that was taken from me. So I had to try to be the one thing that I knew that I was, a hero. And I failed at that too. You know why I failed?"

Cyna just shook her head no.

"Because I tried to do it alone. You and Gargan are right. I am from Skystair, and I have a family, a family of heroes." After a moment of silence, Jyres said, "You taught me enough for today, what about you?"

"What about me?" asked Cyna.

"Who are you?

"I still don't know."

"Well, let's see if Zar can help us with that."

23
SANDS

Another day went by and Jyres seemed to have made a complete recovery. During the last few days Gargan had been busy, quickly organizing his gargoyles and those who were a part of the King's Envoys to send messages to the king and to help escort Mit back to Alhazar. They hadn't sent detailed messages, for fear of any interference from the Silver Shadow, Bram or anyone else. The details would have to wait until Jyres and Cyna were ready to return to the Valley.

At the moment, Jyres sat at a table with Cyna and Zar. Jyres had just gotten done explaining to Zar what he had seen Cyna do. Cyna then shared the experience she had had in her cave when she had first discovered her powers. Zar sat quietly, listening to both of them. "So, anyway, I thought that she might be a delga," said Jyres, "and I convinced Malick to let her come with me to Heritage. Then I had planned to visit you, Zar, just not in the way that it happened," said Jyres with a half smile.

"Well, it would certainly seem that Cyna is a delga," replied Zar. Turning to Cyna, he said, "Tell me child, who are your parents?"

In response, Cyna dropped her head and stared at the floor. "I have not seen my mother since I was eight. We lived in the village.

The elves told me my mom was sick. Jyres confirmed for me that she died from that sickness. I do not know my father."

A pained look swept across Jyres' face as he rested his hand on Cyna's shoulder. "She has been with Malick and the elves for a while now. No one will tell her—or me, for that matter—why she is there or if they know more about her father. I knew a little of her mother. She was human, I am confident she was not a delga."

"I am sorry, dear Cyna, I did not know," replied the kind old wizard.

"It doesn't make any sense, why is this information so secret?" asked a frustrated Jyres.

Zar sat thoughtfully for a moment, and Cyna lifted her head again expectantly. "Well, for some reason Malick has kept this a secret. Cyna, has anyone else seen you use your newfound abilities?"

She shook her head. "Just Jyres," she replied.

"Then, he already knew you were a delga or could potentially be one. It makes sense in a way, after what happened a few years ago he didn't want people to know that you were a delga. I trust he was trying to keep you safe dear, and that he had good intentions."

"How would he have known? How does anyone know?" asked Jyres.

Zar chuckled. "It is really quite simple. A delga is a race, just like humans or elves. Every delga has some sort of power in them. It has always been so. Some are wizards, some are stronger than the average man, some are more intelligent, and so on. I knew a delga who could turn into a dog. It didn't seem all that helpful to him, but he could do it."

"But you said, could potentially be one, what does that mean?" Jyres still hadn't wrapped his head around what Zar was saying.

"Well, sometimes one parent is a delga and one is not. So sometimes the child is a delga and sometimes it is not. So, I think Malick knew who the father was, and knew there was a chance that Cyna was a delga, and somewhere along the way she would develop a power. And it appears that Cyna has the ability to be a delga wizard. Like me."

"So I guess we have to badger Malick until he tells us who the father is," said Jyres, glancing at Cyna.

"I think I can do better than that," replied Zar.

"You do?" asked Cyna, suddenly very hopeful.

"Yes, Cyna, if you are willing. There is a spell I know that only works with two delga wizards. All that you need to do is put your hands in mine, close your eyes, and try to stay calm."

"Will it hurt?"

"No, no. You may be a bit uncomfortable, but with this spell I can look at a moment in time in your memories. The longer I look, the more uncomfortable you can become, but in this case I know exactly what I am looking for."

"Okay," replied a nervous Cyna.

"Are you sure about this?" asked Jyres. "We can wait and talk to Malick. Or, remember, you may not like the answer. Just like I didn't like when I found out the lie Mit told."

"No, I want to know." Cyna's statement was confident.

"Very well," said Zar. "Now place your hands in mine and close your eyes."

Cyna did as she was told and let out a deep breath. Zar held her hands and closed his eyes. He mumbled something that Jyres couldn't hear and then went silent. Jyres watched over the next few agonizing moments and nothing happened. Worrying that something would go wrong, he tried hard not to pace back and forth. Then he saw Cyna wince, and he was about to protest, but before he could do anything Zar released her hands and leaned back. Cyna opened her eyes and withdrew her hands, her breath shaky and palms sweaty.

"Well," said Jyres with a tone of voice that showed worry with a small amount of hope.

"It was successful," said Zar in a way that was not overly cheerful. "But I fear you may not like what you hear."

"Tell me," she said, reaching over to grab Jyres' hand as she said so.

"I am sorry to say that your father died. He is no longer with us," said Zar in a soft voice.

A tear ran down Cyna's cheek as she gripped Jyres' hand tighter. "It is that Meslar, isn't it?" she asked, her voice shaky and sorrowful.

"No, dear, you are not Meslar's daughter, or my granddaughter, which that would have made you. Although, I would have loved to have a granddaughter as beautiful and kind as you."

That made Cyna smile and she wiped a tear away from her face.

"Your father was a delga named Lemont. Often known as Lemont the Lost. He died in the battle by the gate three years ago."

"Lemont," said Jyres, genuinely surprised. Lemont the Lost had been one of the Knights of Enchantment and the only knight who lost his life in that battle. "I am sorry Cyna, I really don't know much about him."

Cyna didn't know what to say or what to think, as she sniffled and held Jyres hand.

"I don't know much about him either, I am afraid," said Zar. "But I can tell you this. The memory I saw was of him holding you, a little baby, tight to his chest. A smile was wide on his face. We know Meslar had complete control of the knights in the years leading up to the battle." Zar reached over and squeezed her arm. "But don't worry about that, don't worry about what other people may say about the knights or about your father. Hold on to that memory I saw, of a loving father holding his baby girl."

After a few quiet moments went by, Cyna thanked Zar and retreated to her temporary room in the library.

"Thank you for that, Zar," said Jyres.

"You are welcome, I am glad I was able to give her that much." The wizard had both his hands on his cane, and rested his chin on them.

"What does this mean for her? Her being a delga and Lemont's child?"

"It doesn't mean anything. She is a 12-year-old delga girl, that is all."

Jyres shook his head. "Malick is afraid of her—or *for* her. It means something."

The wizard lifted his head, but left his hands on his cane. "Malick is scared of delga now. You have said it yourself that he keeps track of the knights. And unfortunately, the Silver Shadow will only heighten Malick's concern. But Cyna will not harm anyone just because she is a delga."

"But she needs someone who can help her, train her. You must show her how to be a delga wizard."

Zar chuckled and waved his hand as if pushing the statement away. "She doesn't need me. She needs you."

"Me?" asked Jyres. "I don't know anything about being a delga."

"Why does her being a delga need to change anything for her? Hmm?"

Jyres was having flashbacks to his conversations with Zar from three years ago when they talked about prophecies and heroes. The wizard always seemed to know what was going on in Jyres' head. And he just had to ask the right question or point out the right thing to lead Jyres to arrive at the only possible solution.

Jyres smiled. "What are your driving at, you haven't gotten me there yet."

"What answers have you both been seeking? What is it that has brought you together?"

"History, family, a place in the world," answered Jyres, who was finally understanding. "And that is still what she needs, delga or not. She needs a family. And we know that both her father and mother are gone."

"Correct. She needs you," Zar said again.

Later on Jyres found Cyna reading a book in a corner of the library. "Hey, I have been looking for you," said Jyres. "I wanted to check in on you." Jyres had a realization after talking with Zar.

And that realization was why he gravitated to Cyna. And it wasn't one of his earlier theories, it was because he knew she was lonely. Something that he also had been experiencing as of late.

Cyna shrugged and continued to read.

"I am sorry that you finally learned who your father is, only to find out that he died. We have both been through a few things lately, huh?" Cyna just shook her head yes, and he continued. "So, here is what I am thinking. Did you know that the humans of Skystair started using last names?"

Cyna put her book down and shook her head no.

"Well, we are both from the human village, right? And seeing as how you don't have a last name and I don't have a last name, I figured we could pick one."

"Okay," Cyna said, unsure of this idea. "But what would I choose, or what would your name be? How would we decide?"

"Well, I thought you and I could pick the same name. Become a family." A family they both needed. That's why they had connected and been drawn to each other. It had nothing to do with her being a delga. It was about being there for each other. Like his friends had been there for him, as Cyna had reminded him earlier.

Cyna's eyes lit up immediately. "Do you mean it? Like, you would be my dad?"

Jyres laughed. "Yes, I mean it. I was thinking more like a brother. How about it, sis?"

Cyna leaped up and put her arms around him and again tears came from her eyes, but this time tears of joy. After a few moments, the tears turned into laughter, a laugh that comes from that feeling of joy and contentment in an incredible moment in time.

"So," Jyres said. "Jyres and Cyna. Jyres and Cyna…what?"

"I don't care," said Cyna, still wiping away tears and holding back laughs, "just as long as it is the same as yours."

"Let's see. We are both from the village, but from the village before it was Skystair. Oh, I've got it. Sands. Jyres Sands and Cyna Sands."

"I like it. But why Sands?" Cyna's face was scrunched up in confusion.

"You know, like a sand dune, or like in the desert where the village used to be."

Cyna laughed. "Well, that's stupid, but it still sounds nice."

"Gee, thanks, sis."

"You're welcome, brother."

Jyres, Zar, and Gargan sat together, the books of knowledge surrounding them. The conversation had just hit a lull. Gargan, who had been sitting on the floor, no library chair could have supported him, stood up and paced the room, seemingly in deep thought.

"Well, let's focus on what we do know," said Zar, breaking the silence. "We now know that this creature and the others like him still held at bay by the gate are known as the horde. And it appears they were put there for good reason. Both of you have had experience with the horde now, and know what a touch from it can do. Which means, we all owe Jyres another debt of gratitude. If more of those creatures had escaped three years ago...." Zar's voice trailed off.

"We should send word to King Malick," said Jyres.

"Some of my gargoyles who are also part of the King's Envoys should have arrived in the valley by now and told the king that we have been delayed and to be on their guard. Gargoyles are also escorting Mit and Cyna's watcher to the valley." Gargan stopped moving and continued talking. "We can give them full details when we arrive."

"What if that is too late?" asked Jyres. "The Silver Shadow, the horde, and Bram are out there right now. All three of them could be planning something, or advancing on our homes, and we wouldn't be able to do anything about it!"

"The Key?" asked Gargan.

"Right," said Jyres. "We have to assume that it is in danger."

"But from who?" asked Zar. "Does the horde make its move? Does the Silver Shadow have some hidden agenda? Or does Bram know where the key is? Are any of them working together?" Zar let his questions sink in before he continued his train of thought. "No matter what the answers are to those questions, I believe that we will need to learn more about the horde and the Gate of Fire. Lumpkin, Flick, and I are now making great progress, and I think that the three of us should continue to research so that we can learn all there is to know about these creatures and the gate."

"Agreed," said Gargan sternly.

"What happens if we run into the creature again, we can't defend ourselves." Jyres was starting to let his frustration get the better of him and his tone did not hide the fact. "There might be nothing we can do."

"All the more reason for me to search for answers," replied Zar in a calm voice.

Jyres, let out a sigh. "All right. What do we do in the meantime?"

"Protect the key," said Gargan.

"Agreed. Then it might be helpful if you knew where it was," said Jyres.

Zar cut in before Gargan could answer. "The key has been safe for three years, due at least in part, to the fact that no one knows anything about where it is. Perhaps you should keep it that way until absolutely necessary."

24
PREPARATIONS

The castle was complete. Malick and Vurth stood outside gazing up at the completed structure. The stone castle was large, but the mountains still seem to dwarf the building, somehow making it less impressive. The castle was situated towards the end of the valley, but on the eastern side of the valley. The waterfall rushed out of the mountains just to the west of the castle and flowed into the Mitelow River. The castle had one tower in the back left corner of the castle, which meant it was close enough for the spray from the waterfall to dampen the tower.

With the mountains as a backdrop behind and to the east of the castle and the waterfall and river to the west, Vurth had thought it a very defensible position as well. Though if they ever had to retreat for some reason, the only option would be to somehow make it to the mountain pass. This would involve climbing rocks and slipping through tight spaces, making an attack from that direction illogical.

The front gate stood large and menacing and the stone archway above the gate was flat and wide. The front gate, Great Hall, and Throne Room were constructed in a way to allow dragons to enter, to lay, and to exit comfortably. Most of the rest of the castle, such as the upper levels, would not accommodate their size.

"Excellent work, Captain!" said King Malick. "I am very pleased, as all the people of Calridian will be.

"Thank you, sire. I am glad we were able to complete it before the Day of Two Moons. It will make a great setting for the first meeting of the Council of Peace."

"Yes, it will," Malick agreed. "I wish I knew where the dragons headed off to. I would very much like to hear their opinion on the completed castle." Malick changed his focus to the sky as if looking for the dragons. "They will be back soon enough. We know better than to interfere with the plans of the dragons," huffed the dwarf, who paused before changing the subject. "Any word from the delegations you sent to Heritage and the yixl?"

"Yes, gargoyles from the King's Envoys have continued to relay messages. I know that both delegations arrived safely. But it still takes a gargoyle a while to reach the coastal regions, so I won't have news of whether the alliance was accepted for a few days. I have not heard from Heritage lately, which concerns me."

"Oh, I am sure Jyres will have those folks in Heritage as friends in no time. Your Council of Peace will be complete, don't you doubt."

As if in answer to their questions, Mit and Rajeem could now be seen entering the valley.

"Well, it looks like we will have our answer. But I wonder where Jyres and Cyna are?" mused the king.

After some moments of silence went by, Vurth excused himself, entered the castle and took the first flight of stairs up to the Captain's quarters.

As he entered his quarters, his thoughts remained on the castle. It had been a long process building the castle, but overall, Vurth was very happy with what they had been able to accomplish. Now all of his workers, mostly dwarves, had earned a break. He knew it wouldn't be long before the king asked for more roads or paths to be established, but he had sent his workers away before any new tasks could be assigned.

Vurth flopped down on his cot, tired. But his mind still went over things on his task list. Even though there was still plenty to do, the completion of the castle was like a huge weight lifted off his shoulders. The pure size of the project had taken so much of his time. Now he and the king could put more focus on the protection of the kingdom.

From what did the kingdom need protection was the question. That last three years had gone by relatively uneventfully. But Vurth was not so naive to think that meant there was nothing to be worried about. He went over the threats in his mind. The creature was still out there somewhere, threat number one. Bram and his clan of gargoyles, threat number two. Orcs and goblins could always become a problem so that was threat number three. Although Ogla, the most outspoken of those creatures, did seem to have them under control for the moment.

After a few more moments went by, and no more threats popped into his mind, he drifted off to sleep. A sleep that provided more rest to the hard-working dwarf than any other sleep in recent memory.

King Malick met with Mit Merrituk and Rajeem in his new Throne Room. The Throne Room had yet to be decorated, so it seemed dark and cold, but Malick knew that would come in time. His throne he sat on was an elaborate stone seat with intricate markings and designs made in the stone work. So far, the vague remarks Rajeem and Mit made about Jyres and Cyna were not overly encouraging. It sounded as if the gargoyles who had escorted Merrituk and Rajeem most of the way home were being purposely tight lipped on the subject.

"But they are safe to our knowledge?" asked Malick with a hint of concern.

"Yes, sire, they are and will be joining us soon," answered Mit.

"Very well. Rajeem, you are excused." After the elf had left, the king smiled at Mit. "Please tell me more about Heritage. How were you able to obtain their support?"

Mit looked back at the king, struggling to keep a neutral face. He was unsure of how much to tell. He wanted to secure his place of importance, but if he told the truth, would the king approve of his methods? If he stuck with the story of Jyres being from Heritage would Jyres or that girl, Cyna, tell the king otherwise? Still unsure of how to proceed, but knowing the king was waiting for a response, he started talking.

"It was not easy. I am not sure if the new empress made it harder or gave us the opportunity. She was very hard to read. But in the end, Jyres made the difference."

"How so? Something he said or did in the city?"

"No, actually..." Mit paused for a second, before steeling himself for the next sentence. "It turns out that Jyres is from Heritage, in a manner of speaking. The records of Heritage were able to trace his line to the Armant family. A historic family in the city. Heritage now refers to him as the Hero of Heritage. He didn't take to the news with much excitement, and I don't think he will claim the Armant name, but it was what helped secure Heritage as part of the alliance."

Well, I said it, Mit thought. For better or for worse, his decision was made. A decision that could prove costly in the future perhaps, but for now, it might be just the thing the king needed to hear.

"That is extraordinary," said Malick softly, as if in amazement. After a moment he said, "What made them think to look into his history?"

"Well, I encouraged them, sire. I thought it was worth looking into."

"Well done. Well done. I wonder why Jyres didn't appreciate the news?"

Mit made sure to not allow any sort of inflection in his voice during his response. "I could only guess, sire."

"Well, in response to your excellent work, I do believe I have an excellent role for you. We will talk more, after the Day of the Two Moons.

"Very good, sire." After saying this, Mit bowed before leaving the throne room. And he couldn't help but smile.

Vurth had just received word from Malick that both Heritage and the yixl had agreed to the alliance and had been added to the Kingdom of Calridian. They also received a vague message that Jyres would be delayed and to be on their guard. Vurth, unsure of what to be on the lookout for, had added a few more soldiers to the guarding of the castle guard detail as a precaution.

All efforts now pointed to the Day of the Two Moons. Preparations were underway for what promised to be a monumental occasion. Vurth was a little on edge now, however, after receiving the message and he began to plan on how he was going to protect everyone at Serenity Castle during the events that were to come. With representatives coming from all over for the first meeting of the Council of Peace, the safety of everyone involved was of the utmost importance. They couldn't allow the Council of Peace to be interrupted by something that was, well, unpeaceful.

Vurth also had to start planning for multiple scenarios. The dragons had not returned yet, and everything seemed to be easier when a dragon was around. Okay, not everything, but everything involving protection of the castle. Malick had grown increasingly frustrated with the dragon's disappearances and worried they would not return before the Day of Two Moons. Vurth himself had also started to wonder what the dragons were up to. But be that as it may, he directed his actions to the task at hand. For the Day of Two Moons was not that far away.

*****

Bram stood on one of his castle's walls. Frustration boiled inside him. He had gone after the creature again, only to be interrupted once more by Gargan. Gargan, just the name agitated Bram. Gargan had been his enemy for too long now. Sooner or later one of them would achieve a permanent victory over the other. Bram had earned his leadership of his clan by besting the former leader of the clan in combat. Gargoyles in the clan responded as expected, accepting him as their leader based on his power and strength. Perhaps whoever won this fight between himself and Gargan would gain the respect of both clans. Bram put that thought in the back of his mind for another time. He had to focus on the present.

Bram's gargoyles had continued to search for the creature, but every time they picked up the trail, the trail would go cold by the time Bram could react. This is what was ultimately causing his frustration. The horde had somehow successfully avoided him now since being freed. Bram had thought that by now he would be in control of the world with his horde army. But he wasn't. He didn't have the horde creature in his grasp or the key. Something had to change. Something had to change now. He felt as if time was slipping by him. His time. It was his time to rule, and he would not let it pass by.

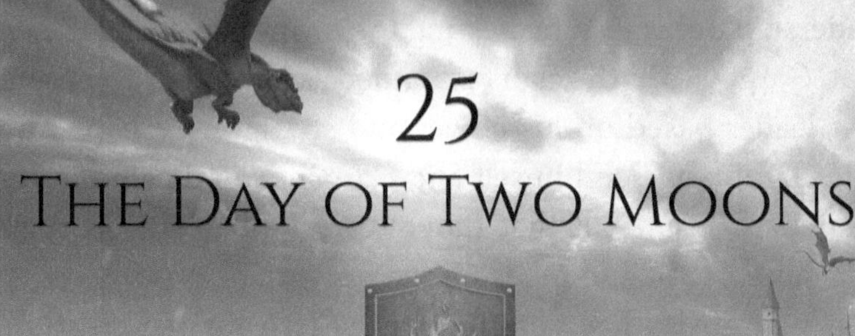

25
THE DAY OF TWO MOONS

Many races from across the land came to see the newly built castle and the representatives who would participate in the first meeting of the Council of Peace had also started to arrive. Vurth stood on the castle wall just above the front gate observing those travelers that had started to file into the valley. Some people had already arrived at the castle in the last few days, including Jyres, Cyna, Lalatco, and Leah to name a few. The dragons had still not returned from their unknown adventure, but Malick vowed to not allow that to dampen his spirits on this big day.

The Day of Two Moons had indeed arrived, Vurth thought to himself as a group of humans from Skystair huddled together in excited conversation just outside the castle's entrance. Farther down the valley, Vurth spotted the representative from Castle Mystic: Lord Kapel on a stallion, flanked by both Demorous and Felix. A smile crossed the dwarf's face as he recalled the times he and Demorous had faced off against one another in the past. Of all the members of the Council of Peace, Malick was most worried about the former knight, Lord Kapel.

Vurth decided to welcome them and headed down to the front gate. Upon their arrival the dwarf bellowed a welcome. "Welcome to Serenity Castle, mighty warriors!"

Lord Kapel dismounted from his horse and approached the Captain of the Guard. "Thank you, Captain Vurth. How kind of you to welcome us yourself." The two then shook hands before Felix and Demourus also extended their hands to Vurth. Vurth shook each one, locking eyes with Demorous as he did so.

"No need to worry, Vurth. Let us leave the past in the past," said Demorous.

"I like the sound of that," Vurth replied.

More and more guests arrived as the morning went on. Most of the members of the Council of Peace had arrived as well. The representatives from both the Secord Region and Skystair had arrived early this morning. The two representatives for the Stone Way had already arrived yesterday. Gargan was one of those representatives.

The empress from Heritage had just arrived with a large escort of her people, as had Simamar. Vurth could see Ogla coming down the valley, as usual, the others giving the orc his space. So that just left three more members who had yet to arrive. Esmeralda, whose arrival, in Vurths' mind was unlikely at best, was one of those three. Tagro, his own son who now led the dwarves had yet to arrive as had the representative from the yixl.

Vurth tried not to grow too frustrated with the delayed arrival of his son. A father always wanted his son to succeed and to lead with honor. But success was a tricky subject when it came to the dwarves. A dwarf was known as a "son of" or "daughter of" until their own success was perceived as greater than their father's or mother's. Vurth had not been called Vurth, son of Rand, in a long time. How long would it be until Tagro had outdone his father? Vurth chuckled at the thought, unsure of what he wanted the answer to be. But either way, he couldn't stand it if his son arrived late. But thankfully, the frustration did not last long, as Tagro had arrived before lunch was even served. The two embraced each other for a long moment before slapping each other on the shoulder.

Tagro would have been the spitting image of his father, with his same orange beard and slightly smaller stature. But Tagro kept his beard much shorter and tied small beads into it, differentiating himself from his father. He was also now in what was considered the prime age for a dwarf, while his father had started to show his age a bit.

Finally, the delegation from the Coastal Region arrived. Rutu, the yixl was among them, as were Elonda, Karth, and Brigand. This was the moment many were waiting for, as word of these newly discovered creatures had spread to all the lands. The gathered guests looked upon them with curiosity and the children with awe as the delegation approached the front gate.

Both Vurth and Tagro were still at the front gate and they greeted the newcomers. Elonda gave them both a greeting that was cordial enough before quickly asking, "Is Jyres here?"

"Don't worry lass, he is here." Vurth chuckled in amusement.

The meetings were set to begin when the two moons would be at their brightest in the sky. This would happen just as the sun went down. Then the Night Moon would brighten, and for this one day, the Day Moon would stay bright as well. With the two moons both bright, the stars would shine and create an unbelievable night sky. The meeting would take place in the throne room and 12 of the 13 members of the Council of Peace would be in attendance. Karth had also been asked to attend the meeting to serve as translator.

Once the appointed time had come and the Council had gathered in the Throne Room, Malick, with his silver crown making an appearance once again, began their first meeting.

"Thank you so much for coming," started King Malick. "I am honored to have you all here for the first gathering of the Council of Peace. We are short but one, Esmeralda, my Advisor, has left on an urgent errand and has yet to return. The first order of business, I believe, is to introduce ourselves to one another. I know some of you have not traveled extensively throughout the land and have not met everyone here." The king paused, and Karth translated for Rutu.

The king and Vurth started by introducing themselves before the king asked the others to introduce themselves by region. Simamar and Ogla both did so, representing Alhazar. Next came Lord Kapel, Tagro, and the Warden of Skystair, Shepherd Rowland from the region of Tomackus. Shepherd was one of the men Jyres had asked to lead the people when Jyres had decided to follow Elonda and Lalatco to the elven forest three years ago. Shepherd was tall, dark skinned, and had a gray beard and a bald head. His voice was rough, as though he always had pebbles stuck in the back of his throat.

The representative of the towns near Secord went next. The representative was a light-skinned human female. She was quite short, and slender, with short red hair. She happened to be sitting next to Gargan, which made her seem all the more petite. But she spoke loudly and with confidence before motioning to Gargan to go next. Gargan was one representative of the area being referred to as the Stone Way. An older, white-haired man was the other. He represented the small towns in the area. And he, in fact, was from the small town that Zar had led Jyres and the others through on their way to Secord those few years ago.

The last two to introduce themselves were perhaps the most intriguing members of the Council of Peace. The empress from Heritage talked next. She was very reserved in her comments and appearance, perhaps disappointing the others who were expecting her to try to command the room. But it was just as well, for all eyes quickly turned to Rutu. Rutu of the yixl, the newly discovered race. Rutu began speaking in his native language and after he was finished Karth translated it for the group.

"Very good," replied Malick. "I welcome you all once again. We will meet over the next few arcs and tomorrow night as well. I have some topics already planned, but feel free to bring up things you wish to discuss. We are all equal here. Each of you has a voice at this table and is a voice for your region. The very first thing I would like to do, well, I think I will just show you." Malick then turned around and pulled on a long piece of braided cord hanging against the wall. As he did so, a large tapestry unrolled from the ceiling. The tapestry hung right behind the throne. It was a large and very colorful depiction of the Kingdom of Calridian.

A round of applause broke out among the group as they beheld the beautiful sight. The colors and details and workmanship were extraordinary. Malick then took a slight bow, before saying, "I cannot take all the credit. For this is the work of the elves. We have Simamar and his artists and explorers to thank for this magnificent piece of artwork.

More applause came from the group. The king acknowledged the applause then proceeded to point out specific features of the map. Many of the members of the Council had never left their corner of the kingdom, and Malick thought it was important that everyone understood the geographical regions. After a while, and feeling confident that the Council had an understanding, he moved on to the next topic.

"I believe the next topic to be discussed should be our collective plans for the future of the kingdom. What we have started, the Council, the regions, the castle, is just the beginning. Vurth and I will share our ideas in time, but first let the Council hear your voice and your ideas."

Jyres and Elonda walked hand in hand, just outside the entrance to the valley. Cyna, Lalatco, and Leah were just ahead of them. Jyres stopped for a moment and looked up to the sky. Both moons shone brightly, casting moonbeams across the plains. He cast his gaze to Elonda, who also stood looking into the sky. A sky that was only seen once a year, on the Day of the Two Moons. Their eyes locked then and Jyres smiled, his excitement and contentment being reflected in Elonda's eyes, as well. They held each other's gaze, getting lost in each other's eyes like a star lost in a field of bright stars.

Finally, the moment passed, and Jyres returned his view to the sky.

Cyna ran over to them just then. "I love this day so much," she said.

"The Day of Two Moons is always special," replied Elonda.

"But it's not just that," said Cyna, wrapping two arms around Jyres and resting her head on his shoulder.

"No, it's not," Jyres replied before smiling at Elonda and then Cyna in turn.

"So," said Lalatco as he and Leah walked over to where the others were standing. The others turned to watch them walk over, and Lalatco's hair seemed to sparkle in the moonlight. His naturally white hair that so often took on a reflection of the colors around him. "Jyres. Do you wish you were in that meeting going on right now?"

"No, do you?"

"Not at all. We are right where we are supposed to be."

The five of them stood there a long time, looking up at the sky and just enjoying the moment. The calm. The closeness.

As they were standing, Lalatco, whose renown as a singer was almost as great as his status as a warrior, began to sing. His voice started out quietly and built as he went on.

A world is cast in the evenings moons' light
Its many men and creatures all take a pause
To look up and see such a night sky

The day of two moons lights up the night
The day of two moons for all to enjoy

The stars in the sky seem to shout
For they shine so so bright
Just one time a year do they create this sight

The day of two moons lights up the night
The day of two moons for all to enjoy

Love will flourish under this sky
All beings, all life will all take part
The day of two moons, celebrate

The song, so pretty and sang so well, left tears in the eyes of all those nearby. Leah wrapped her arms around Lalatco's waist. Jyres smiled at the sight and put one arm around both Elonda and Cyna. They all looked at each other for a moment, and smiled. After a while they started to walk back toward the castle and were soon met by Vurth and his son, Tagro.

"There you are, I was wondering where you got off to," said Vurth as they fell in step with the group and walked back toward the castle gate.

"How was the meeting?" asked Jyres.

Vurth made a humph sound and then, "A lot of talking. This region needs this, this person wants that. By the end, I just wanted to close my eyes or have a brew, whichever one could be made to happen first."

Leah snickered. "It couldn't have been all bad."

"You're welcome to take my spot. You might have a better temperament for that sort of thing."

Leah smiled, and the others laughed, taking joy in their friend's misery.

As they drew near the castle a loud roar ripped through the calm. It startled the whole group, and Cyna grabbed Elonda's hand.

"What in tarnation was that!" exclaimed Vurth.

"It didn't come from the castle, it came from the end of the valley," replied Lalatco. "I can see figures in the moonlight, but I cannot make out who or what they are."

"Neither can I," said Elonda, the only other one with them that would have a chance of seeing something of significance at that distance.

"Quick, everyone inside, lest we find something coming that we don't want to find. Hurry!" called Vurth.

They all hurried to the gate, as did the few others who had ventured outside the castle. Vurth and Tagro each stood at one side of the gate as the rest of them rushed inside. Vurth and Tagro were about to follow, when a torch burst to life in the middle of the valley. The closer the figures came, the more they began to take shape. There, coming towards them, was what looked like...bears? Four of them?

Tagro and Vurth both drew their axes and started to back up into the castle. The last time father and son had seen a bear, it had been a black donosin. They had fought it off long enough and escaped its clutches. But that had been one bear, albeit a rare and powerful one. They didn't stand a chance against four of them, no matter what kind of bear it was.

Suddenly, a voice came out of the darkness. "We mean you no harm."

A human's voice, Vurth thought. "What is going on here?" he whispered.

The figures were closer now, and their shapes more defined. A human was riding one of the bears, the bear in the lead, with three more alongside.

"Who are you and why are you here?" Vurth called out. The bears continued to get closer and Vurth's heart pounded in his chest. *What are you doing?* his mind called. *Get inside, close the gate.*

"You once knew me as Bartholomew the Bold," the voice said in response. The man held up his hand and the bears stopped moving as he jumped down from the back of the bear. He approached the two dwarves, his hands held out high and wide away from his body.

When he was still more than a few steps away, Vurth called out again, "That is close enough. Now why have you come?"

"I have made contact with the donosin, as you can see." Bartholomew was dressed from head to toe in furs and animal skin. His sword was on his back and he wore a necklace made of bones.

"What?" Tagro laughed. "What spell have you cast upon them to get them to listen to you? Just like Melsar and the thars." The thars were a race of wild, tall, and fanged creatures that Meslar had used to form an army.

"There has been no spell I assure you. I call myself the Wanderer now. For I have cast off my life with Meslar and returned to my path of old, before I was a knight."

Vurth scoffed. "You looked better as a knight."

The Wanderer smiled. "I see how I could look different to you. I am at one with nature. I have a power that lets me feel the land around me, the animals, the life, the ground itself."

Unsure of what he was supposed to do with this man calling himself the Wanderer, Vurth looked to his son. His son shrugged and Vurth rolled his eyes at him.

"Well, whatever you are, or whatever you are called, you can't enter my castle with four bears at your back."

"They are the black donosin. Do you not know their history, their knowledge?"

"Ha! I know that the last time I saw one it tried to eat me!"

"For now they will wait outside, and you may take me to see whomever it is you need me to see, fair enough?"

"Aye."

The Wanderer turned toward the bears for just a moment before following the dwarves into the castle, and the gate closed behind them.

26
THE BLACK DONOSIN

"I don't understand," said King Malick. "You can talk to the animals?"

The Wanderer stood in front of the king, who had Vurth to his left. Lord Kapel, who had been asked by the king to join them, was there as well. Vurth had positioned guards throughout the Throne Room.

"It is not like speaking, as we are doing right now. More of a passing of emotion. But rest assured the black donosins outside mean you no harm."

"As Vurth already shared, the last time we met a black donosin it certainly seemed to mean harm to us." Malick was unsure of this turn of events. He knew the old tales of the black donosin better than most, but it still seemed surreal to have four of them right outside his front gate.

There was a pause in the conversation as the king considered the man in front of him. "Lord Kapel," said Malick.

"Yes, sire?" Lord Kapel had waited off to the side, biding his time until he was needed. Now he came and stood in front of the king as well. Lord Kapel's hair was a dark gray color and it was combed straight back. He was a tall, stick of a man, all arms and legs, but they were well defined by muscle.

"Do you vouch for this man? Is he who he says he is?"

"I do," Lord Kapel replied. His voice was a little higher than perhaps the average man, but it still held its authority when he spoke. "This is indeed Bartholomew the Bold, a delga, and former Knight of Enchantment."

"And what do you have to say about his abilities? Is he a danger to us?"

"The abilities that he speaks of are the same that he demonstrated in his earlier life. As you know, my king, Meslar had his hold on us, even me. But delga are no longer a race you should fear."

"But aren't they?" Malick stood up, his form intimidating on the raised dais. His voice grew in strength and showed his anger. Malick, who was known for his calm demeanor and royal timbre, seemed to be showing his frustration. "Then what do you say about the Silver Shadow?"

Lord Kapel, shook his head, a look of confusion on his face. "Sorry, sire, but I am not aware of that of which you speak."

"He has caused trouble," replied the king. His temporary anger now under control, his tone returned to its kingly state. Not wanting to share more than he had to, he chose to keep the kind of trouble to himself and returned to his chair.

"King, if I may," said the Wanderer, stepping forward.

The king nodded and gestured for him to continue.

"We do not know what trouble our former brother, the Silver Shadow, has caused you. But I do know this. I am the Wanderer. No longer a knight, no longer do I carry an evil sword. I have traveled to this valley because I have heard of your will to unite the lands under one banner. I believe for that to happen, you need to listen to the world around you. The elves I knew from many moons ago always did this. You should look to your ancestors' ways. You, too, shall feel what the ground, the trees and animals are saying. Right now they call to you, to be included in your united kingdom."

The Wanderer went to one knee before the king. "The black donosin have heard the call of the world around them. I have brought them here, not to sow discord, but to unite." Then, still on one knee, the Wanderer sang. When he sang, the emotion in his voice was immediately felt by those in the throne room who felt as if it came from somewhere else. It was as if the walls of the castle sang.

There is a tale so broad and bold
Of a race that is from of old
They once were alike to those who speak

They were the leaders of the land
For others they would take a stand
Never have they been considered weak

But they seemed to fade as the years past
Could it be that they were not meant to last
For when is the last time someone got a peek

There will be a time when they return
The ability to speak no longer a concern
For the black donosin you will seek

"Rise," said the king. "You have spoken and sung eloquently, friend. Another trait that is appreciated by the elves. I give my permission for you to accompany one of the black donosin to the Council of Peace tomorrow night. This will be a matter for the whole Kingdom to decide. We will meet in the Great Hall at sunset. Until then, I request that you and the black donosin wait in the valley."

"Thank you, sire," said the Wanderer.

The Council of Peace had gathered together again, this time at one end of the Great Hall. King Malick had thought it wise for the citizens of the kingdom to be able to observe the council. Meeting in the Great Hall instead of the Throne Room, however, did create more issues for Vurth.

Vurth had his guards stationed throughout the hall, some of them creating a border so onlookers could only see from a respectful distance. With the hall being so large that distance kept them out of ear shot. But even though all they could do was look on, many citizens took that opportunity and filled the Great Hall.

Almost everyone from the Council was already gathered. They just waited on Gargan and the Wanderer and the black donosin. Gargan had yet to awaken from his stone form and Malick had given the Wanderer strict instructions on when he could appear before the council. Side conversations popped up among the council members as they waited.

"How do you feel the meeting went yesterday?" asked Shepherd, leaning over toward Lord Kapel.

"It is what I had expected. It will take some time for us all to grow comfortable in each other's presence." Lord Kapel and Shepherd knew each other fairly well. Castle Mystic and Skystair were relatively close to each other and the two leaders had met with each other on occasion. "I anticipate today's conversations to be more productive."

"Agreed," commented Shepherd in his rough voice. "But, will the arrival of this Wanderer slow progress down again."

"Perhaps. But I see it as something that could spur conversation and perhaps present opportunities that will be beneficial for the kingdom."

As if on cue, startled noises from the onlookers broke into the conversation as the Wanderer and a black donosin entered the

Great hall. The gathered people went silent as the bear and man walked toward those waiting for them. All that could be heard was the constant pat, pat of the bear's feet hitting the stone floor. Before they had made it halfway to the end of the hall, Gargan also entered the hall.

The king rose from his chair and the others followed his lead. Malick knew these first few moments of this meeting would be interesting and perhaps critical. He was also somewhat concerned. He now had three delgas in the room…and a bear. He had specifically set up the time when the bear would enter, knowing that when Gargan came in, he would be right behind the bear. He figured of all those gathered at the castle, Gargan would be the one most able to fight off a bear if it came to that. And the delgas were a whole different matter. He still had not allowed himself to completely trust the delga after the events of a few years ago. And the Silver Shadow only heightened that concern.

Finally, the bear and the Wanderer reached the circle of Council members. The bear stood on his hind legs and gave one quick roar before walking to the open space in the circle. The Wanderer followed quietly. Gargan then took his place as well and the meeting began.

"Welcome to the black donosin and the Wanderer," said King Malick. "The Wanderer has tried to explain to me the importance of bringing the black donosin into our fold. So this will be the first topic of the evening."

"Well, I don't see what there is to discuss," said the empress. "We have seen them from time to time near Heritage. They are bears, animals, what value do they bring to this alliance."

"I have had to fight one," said Tagro, son of Vurth, in a loud voice. "I tend to agree with the empress."

"All creatures and races have a place, a purpose," responded Gargan.

"But we have no way of communicating," said another.

These types of comments kept going back and forth amongst the group. Meanwhile the bear laid down, as if not aware, or not caring, of what was happening around the circle.

"If I may," said the Wanderer, and the king nodded his head, giving his approval for the Wanderer to continue. "I can communicate on a different level with animals and the land. Not with words, but with feelings. But I am able to do so with the black donosin even more so. I believe it to be this way, because of what the stories of old tell us." The Wanderer paused, as if expecting to be interrupted or questioned, but no one said anything, so he continued. "The black donosin are an ancient race. I am sure you all have heard something of them."

The great bear next to the speaker raised his head as if knowing he was being talked about.

"Although much has been lost to time itself, we know that at one time the black donosin had the ability to speak, to communicate with other races. If you doubt me, as I see some of you do by the look on your faces, you need only send messengers to the great city of Heritage. The empress herself has admitted to knowing the race and seeing them near Heritage. I don't doubt for a moment that their records show interactions with the black donosin."

The empress, looking simple and yet so beautiful, reacted to the gazes cast in her direction. "It is true. Heritage took care to document important events throughout its history, and it is clear that the people were able to communicate at some level with the black donosin, for there are records of trade with the bears."

"Thank you," said Malick, nodding to the empress. "Even if we agree they could speak with us in the past, that does not change the present. The black donosin has sat here today," said the king, motioning toward the bear, "and although I am pleasantly surprised with its demeanor, it has not communicated with us."

"I understand, my king," said the Wanderer. "That is my point. I have been able to communicate, to understand, what the great bear is feeling throughout this conversation, and on a much deeper level than with other animals. And I think, given time, with the aid of myself and Karth, and if welcomed, they will again be able to communicate with us."

The members of the council remained silent for a while. Lord Kapel eventually was the one to break the silence. "I think the Wanderer is right. But I say that in a manner of looking at his point on a grander scale. The king has made it clear, to achieve true peace, we must remain united. And fend off any danger together. In this way, we will more clearly identify our enemies and be best able to combat them if necessary. Bram, for example, has not shown any interest in joining us and has chosen to remain on the outside. The black donosin, at the very least, know we are united, and their presence here shows they represent no threat. I see no reason not to make a seat available on this Council when the time comes. We may have no idea of when or if that will happen. But let us leave that open."

Lord Kapel as a delga was known to have an intelligence far beyond that of a normal man, and no one around the circle seemed to want to dispute what he said. Many were nodding their heads in agreement.

"Very well," said Malick. "Wanderer, the black donosin are welcome here to this Council of Peace in the future at a time that has yet to present itself."

"Thank you." The Wanderer bowed low to the king and with a gesture to the great bear beside him, the two left the Great Hall.

As Lord Kapel had predicted, the appearance of and discussion surrounding the black donosin seemed to spur action from the group. The night before, the group struggled to see eye to eye or to even agree which topic to cover in more detail. This time, the topic of trade was introduced and all of the members seemed to invest themselves into the conversation. For trade to be a success between the regions, two main obstacles were discussed: organization and safe paths for trade.

Ensuring safety fell to Vurth, and both he and Gargan seemed to steer the conversation and make progress. Vurth shared with the whole group how they had been using outposts and the King's Envoys for different purposes, and they could be an integral part of trade. Gargan talked about the importance of the individual regions helping protect the most traveled paths for trade.

The group also agreed that one person should be put in charge of helping the regions begin the process of trading. Skystair was really the only place that was actively trading, and every representative saw the benefits of it. This led to Mit Merrituk being nominated as the person to help facilitate trade, as he had done such an impressive job for the city of Skystair. Although Gargan expressed his disapproval, the others seemed to support the idea. To them, Mit had proven the ability to do that which now needed to be done on a grander scale.

The meeting came to a conclusion and everyone seemed to be in good spirits, including Malick, who was starting to see his vision come together.

27
A Sound in the Night

Vurth climbed the stairs and emerged onto the overlook above the castle gate. Two dwarven guards stood there, along with Demorous. Vurth nodded to all three of them and took a quick scan of the area. The two torches on the wall were lit. Vurth walked to the end of the lookout and looked to the back tower, and saw a torch burning there as well. Everything seemed in order, and he returned to stand by the others, overlooking the valley.

"So, Demorous, to what do we owe the pleasure?"

Demorous turned to the side to look at the dwarf. Demorous was a large man, both in height and muscle. He turned his head, shaved as always, to face the dwarf. "Boredom," he replied in a tone that matched the comment.

"Ha!" exclaimed Vurth, trying not to stare at the large man's crooked nose as he replied. "Nothing exciting these days for the knights?"

"There are no knights anymore, just former knights."

"Be that as it may, I find it hard to believe that Demorous the Fierce is just sitting on his fat rump, twiddling his thumbs!"

It was Demorous' turn to laugh, and he playfully punched the dwarf in the shoulder for his comment. "I help Lord Kapel run the castle. For he truly is Lord of the castle now. We have been bringing in those who were in need. Slowly, but surely, Castle Mystic is increasing in population. Myself and Felix find those who are out of luck and bring them to the castle, it will produce results in time. But for now, it is at least a home for those who need it."

"Aye, I heard that. It is a good thing you are doing. Perhaps you want to have some bears live in the castle?" Vurth still couldn't believe the events of the day, shaking his head. "The bear just sat there, we talked about it, and it did not bare its teeth once. I tell you, that is not what I was expecting."

"I do find that hard to believe, but you are not the first to tell it to me. Everyone is talking about the black donosin."

"As they should, as they should."

They both fell silent. And everything seemed too silent. Vurth peered into the darkness, shook his head, and let out a frustrated growl. "It is darker than the inside of a boot out here! Next thing I am going to do is build watchtowers at the beginning of this valley."

Vurth turned to try and find the back tower in the dark, and realized the torch in the tower was no longer lit. "Something is amiss. Rust," he said to the young dwarf next to him, "sound the alarm."

The dwarf named Rust ran to the small stairway that led to a small chamber just behind their lookout where a large bronze horn sat. But just as the dwarf reached the stairway a massive figure emerged from the shadows, and with one swing of its arm the dwarf went flying backward. The figure stepped forward into the light and Bram the large purple gargoyle was revealed. He smiled wickedly.

Vurth looked around the castle and saw gargoyles descending from the sky. They were under attack and they needed to sound the alarm! Vurth and Demorous glanced at each other, and at once charged the big gargoyle. Bram swung his left arm at the dwarf, but Vurth ducked, letting the swing go high. Demorous wasn't quite able to avoid Bram's wing which Bram used to bat the big man away and Demorous stumbled forward. Vurth charged right into Bram, but wasn't sure if he even moved the big gargoyle.

Meanwhile, the other dwarf who had been standing watch raced for the small stairway. Bram saw him going that way and started to react. But Demorous was there, grabbing onto his arm and, amazingly, he was able to pull him back. Bram swung his left arm down at him, but Demorous crossed his arms in front of his body and braced himself for the contact. His delga-gifted strength rewarded him, and he withstood the blow. Vurth, wishing he had his ax, pulled out a knife from his belt underneath his long beard and plunged it into Bram's foot. Bram screamed in agony before kicking the dwarf hard across the floor.

The other dwarf had made it to the stairway, sneaking past the distracted Bram. Reaching the giant horn, he quickly blew with all his might.

Jyres, lay in bed, half asleep. Cyna was close by, sound asleep on her cot. He had never fallen into a deep sleep and as he lay there, half in a dream and half aware, a sound like the rush of wind through a cave exploded through the air. Jyres was awake immediately, and the sound came again. A horn, a deep, loud horn. Cyna awoke with the second horn blast.

Jyres quickly slapped on his sword belt and rushed to Cyna. "Cyna, come on, we have to go."

"What's going on?" she asked.

"I don't know, but we have to move," said Jyres as he grabbed her hand and led her to the door.

Jyres and Cyna left the room and ran into the hallway. People all up and down the hall were doing the same thing, entering the hallway wondering what was going on. Jyres led Cyna down the hallway where Elonda, Leah, and Lalatco had already found each other.

"What's going on?" asked Jyres. As if in response, someone yelled from down the hallway, "We are under attack! Gargoyles!"

"Bram," said Jyres. "He knows everyone is here, and is after the key."

"Is it safe?" asked Elonda.

Jyres and Lalatco locked eyes before Lalatco responded. "I have it."

"So what's the plan? Can we fight them off?" asked Leah.

"They have the element of surprise on us. We are not organized for a defense of this magnitude. Stealth is the only way," said Elonda in a voice that left little room to disagree with the statement.

"Stealth, yes," said Jyres. "But also diversion. He will assume I have the key." Jyres pointed at himself, and took a deep breath. "They will come after me first. So Lalatco keeps the key and tries to sneak away."

"What about you?" said Elonda, with tears threatening at the corners of her eyes.

Jyres pulled her close. "I need to find Gargan. He can help fight them off." He took Cyna's hand and put it in Elonda's. "You two protect each other, and get somewhere safe." The sounds of fighting now started to fill the castle.

"We're out of time," said Lalatco, grabbing Leah's hand.

"Good luck to all of us," said Elonda.

They all locked eyes with each other, knowing the other knew exactly what they were thinking. Family always knew. Then, they were moving. All in opposite directions.

Jyres made his way to the upper levels of the castle and it didn't take him long before he found the enemy. An elven guard was thrown across the hall and landed in front of him. Jyres looked up at the gray gargoyle. It had fangs protruding from its mouth and claws the size of a dragon's.

Jyres retreated the way he came and ran to the nearest stairway. He pounded up the stairs and emerged on a small terrace, with no other way to go. The gargoyle followed him up the stairs. He charged Jyres, his fangs dripping with saliva. Jyres pulled out his sword and rolled to his left avoiding the gargoyle's first charge.

The gargoyle rethought his approach and came slowly this time. Jyres waited, shifting his weight on his feet, prepared to strike. The gargoyle struck down at Jyres with both arms and Jyres swiped the air above him with his sword. The sword sliced shallowly into one of the gargoyle's arms, but the gargoyle's second hand came down, swiping his claws across Jyres' arm. Jyres backed up a step and swung again, beating the gargoyle back.

Then another pair of gargoyles swooped down toward him and Jyres dove to his left, avoiding the new enemies. But the gray gargoyle charged at that moment. Jyres tried to recover quickly, but as he got up the gargoyle plowed into him, knocking him off of the castle. Jyres lost his sword as he fell. He was in a free fall, on his way to certain death. Visions of Elonda flashed through his mind. Was this really it? Death from falling. He closed his eyes, and curled into a ball, but the impact never came. Finally, he opened his eyes, and he was in the safety of Gargan's grasp.

"Gargan! Nice catch!" Jyres exclaimed, his heartbeat still threatening to burst out of his chest. Jyres repositioned himself and climbed onto the back of his gargoyle friend. Silently, he tried to process what just happened. He could have died, should have been dead. He absently patted Gargan on the shoulder and let out a long breath.

"Okay," he said, focusing again on the task at hand. "We need to draw their attention away from the castle and the others. The more gargoyles we draw to us, the more lives we save. Any ideas on how to do that?"

Gargan let the wind fill his wings and he rose far above the castle. Then he shouted in a voice that sounded like it was coming from the mountains themselves, "Bram, where are you?" Immediately, they had the attention of many gargoyles. Jyres raised his hand high in the air as if he had something above his head. And Gargan yelled again. "We have what you want, come find it!"

Many gargoyles around Gargan and Jyres, those in the sky and some on the castle walls, watched as their leader, Bram, sped towards the would-be heroes. The gargoyles joined their leader in the sky, taking up positions to the side and behind Bram.

"Well, here we go," said Jyres as Gargan sped off towards the north.

Elonda held tight to Cyna's hand as she led her through the castle. They slowly moved about, careful to avoid the battles that were going on. Elonda would have liked nothing better than to be charging into battle, but Jyres had given her Cyna to protect. Her goal was to keep her safe, no matter what. Elonda had thought about staying put in their room in the castle, but the sounds of battle had grown too close and they decided to move on. She was slowly working her way to the front gate. The gargoyles had most likely attacked from above and would not have concentrated on the front gate.

Elonda and Cyna continued to move cautiously, growing ever closer to the gate. Finally, they reached it. From a side hallway they looked out. The gate was open. Two gargoyles were in combat with a couple of elves on the interior of the gate. The combat, in effect, blocked their exit.

Elonda armed herself with her bow and produced an arrow from her quiver. She was set to let the arrow fly at her target when a small flying gargoyle landed on her outstretched arm and sunk its teeth into her. Elonda screamed, dropping her bow, but in her unencumbered hand she still held her arrow and she drove the tip into the eye of her attacker. The gargoyle screeched and fell back and Elonda quickly led Cyna away from the hallway and toward the gate.

Blood dripped down Elonda's arm and across her hand. The wound from the gargoyle pained her, but she ignored it. She pulled

Cyna to her, so she could look into her eyes. The girl had succumbed to fear. She was breathing hard, fighting back the tears.

"Breathe, Cyna, we can do this," she said. "Listen, we need to get you out of here. I can get you past the gargoyles. I don't know if I will be able to follow."

"No, don't leave me," cried Cyna, holding on tightly to Elonda.

"You have lived here a while now, do you know where you can go, do you know where you can hide?"

Cyna shook her head yes. A scream from one of the elves split the air.

"Great. I will do the absolute best I can to follow you. But first I have to distract these monsters, do you understand?"

Cyna shook her head again.

"When I say so, you run for that spot and stay there." Elonda gripped her sword with her good hand and marched forward.

Two gargoyles had just dispatched the second elf they had been fighting. So it was two against one. Elonda smiled and charged.

She leapt as she drew close to the first gargoyle twisting in the air and striking the gargoyle in the back as she leapt passed him. The second gargoyle responded by swinging its tail at her, but she was faster. She nimbly jumped over the tail and sliced it as it went past. She rolled to her left, putting herself between the gate and the gargoyles.

"Run, Cyna! Run! Run!" she screamed as she batted away the arm of one gargoyle.

Cyan ran as fast as she could toward the gate. The gate was ahead and to the right, Elonda was to her left and then the gargoyles. She watched Elonda side step one gargoyle and swing back at it, scoring a hit on its back. Elonda barely avoided the second gargoyle, but did. And then quickly repositioned herself, keeping herself between Cyna and the gargoyles. Cyna ran through the gate just as she heard a scream from Elonda. Cyna turned to see Elonda's bloody arm being crushed in the grasp of a gargoyle.

Cyna stepped forward, but Elonda shook her head. Cyna turned, and ran.

As soon as they had left the others Leah and Lalatco quickly made their way to the back of the castle. They had one goal. Get the key out of the castle and away from the fight. Once they reached the back watchtower, they quickly ran up the stairs. Half way up, they ran into a small gargoyle on the stairs. Lalatco was in the lead, and already had his scimitar drawn. With two quick swipes of his blade and a quick kick he sent the gargoyle into the wall, and they moved quickly past the creature.

Leah and Lalatco reached the top of the stairs and found the watchtower dark and empty. Just as they hoped. Lalatco drew a large knife from the bandelier over his shoulder and embedded it in a thick length of rope. Then standing on the stone edge of the watchtower, he swung the rope over his head like a lasso, before letting it go. The knife flew across the sky before driving home into the nearby mountain face. The throw was almost perfect, the rope creating a downward angle.

"You first, darling," said Lalatco.

Leah, holding the hilt of her sword in one hand and the flat of the blade in her other, jumped from the tower using her sword to fly down the rope line. She picked up speed as she neared the face of the mountain and dropped down to the ground before she would have smacked into the rock. She hit the ground hard, but dusted herself off.

Lalatco was already following her down the rope and he dropped from the rope, landing with a little more grace.

"Show off." She smiled.

Lalatco shrugged, and they were moving again. The waterfall roared behind them as they headed east. They stuck close to the base of the mountain. They could see gargoyles still soaring here and there above the castle. But with each step it brought them closer to the end of the valley.

Then they heard Gargan call out to the gargoyles and many of them took flight to chase him down. This allowed Lalatco and Leah to continue moving on unseen. No one seemed to take any notice of them in the dark and they continued their progress. As they neared the end of the valley, they slowed. The shadows laid thick about them and uneasiness fell over Lalatco. Instinctively, he took the key out from under his shirt and tossed it to Leah. Just as he did so a foot landed square in his chest.

"Lalatco!" shouted Leah.

A figure cloaked in shadow revealed himself.

Lalatco scrambled to his feet and eyed their attacker. "Who are you?" he yelled.

"Why, I am the Silver Shadow," the man said, placing one hand on his chest and giving a slight nod of the head. "Good to see you again, Lalatco."

"Sorry that I can't say the same. What do you want?"

"Simple really. I already beat Jyres, and now I will beat the great elven warrior, Lalatco."

Lalatco glanced over to Leah.

Seeing this, the Silver Shadow quickly said, "She is free to go. I am here for you."

Leah and Lalatco looked at each other. Leah shaking her head no. Lalatco said, "Go, I love you."

Leah, with tears streaming from her face, raced out of the valley.

28
FIGHTS AND FLIGHTS

Vurth shook off the last hit he took and grabbed Demorous' outstretched hand. Vurth clasped it and pulled himself up. Bram had long left them to battle with his other minions, which they continued to do. Had it not been for Demorous, Vurth probably would have been out for the count at this point. Demorous's awesome strength had been able to keep the gargoyles at bay. But Vurth knew that was all they were doing, surviving. They had no idea if Bram had caught Gargan and Jyres, who had called away some of the gargoyles. Nor did they know how the rest of the occupants of the castle were faring. Gargoyles took their turns keeping the two warriors occupied at the top of the gate.

The latest gargoyle charged them both and they sidestepped it. Vurth was tiring, and he put his hands on his knees. But he didn't have long to rest before they were fighting again. He still had his knife and he used it to slash at their attacker. Demorous connected on a punch to the gargoyle's midsection and it stumbled backward. From behind a gargoyle swooped in, knocking Vurth to the ground. Demorous was able to fend it off, but the first gargoyle he had punched charged Vurth and wrapped him up with his powerful arms. Vurth was trapped, he struggled to get free, kicking with his legs and pushing with his arms. But it was no use.

The gargoyle dug its claws into Vurth's shoulders and held him out. Vurth fought back a cry of agony as the claws did their damage. Before Vurth knew what was happening next, he was spinning through the air, thrown by the gargoyle. Vurth flew right into the castle wall. He heard a cracking sound as he fell to the ground. His vision started to blur, and then there was darkness.

Both Lalatco and the Silver Shadow drew their blades. They each took steps in opposite directions, as they slowly circled each other. The dance began with Lalatco striking first with a quick jab of his scimitar. The Silver Shadow deflected it and stepped back, staying patient. Lalatco struck again, this time with two quick swipes, but the Silver Shadow blocked them both and Lalatco backed off.

"What is it you hope to gain?" asked Lalatco, staying at the ready position.

"Just to restore my name, the Silver Shadow will be feared again." Trying to catch Lalatco off guard the Silver Shadow thrust out at the elf, but he quickly backed away, avoiding the attack. "After I take care of you, I will have bested both of the kingdom's heroes."

"But no one is here to see it," commented Lalatco. "How will the fear spread with no one to spread it?"

"Word of my battle and easy victory over Jyres will start to spread throughout your people. Your loss will spread easily as well."

They both fell silent and their blades met high in front of their faces. Lalatco pushed the Silver Shadow's blade away and spun, quickly bringing his scimitar toward the exposed left side of his enemy. But the Silver Shadow saw it coming and reversed his own blade in time to stop the blow. He then kicked out with his right foot catching Lalatco in the leg and sending him backwards. Lalatco went with the movement and rolled away as the Silver Shadow's blade struck the ground where he had just been.

Lalatco bounced up impossibly fast and spun toward his attacker landing a kick on the Silver Shadow's shoulder. Their blades clashed again in front of them, and then again and again as they each fell into the rhythm of the combat. They struck and parried, neither breaching the other's defenses.

Then, Lalatco, in a surprise move leaned back as the Silver Shadow's sword swung across. Lalatco's body bent back so far that he was almost parallel to the ground. Then he popped back up as the sword went by, just missing him. His own sword came around and scored a hit on the Silver Shadow side, leaving a significant bloody gash.

The Silver Shadow recovered quickly and was able to fend off the elf, who now looked for a way to finish the battle. Their swords found each other repeatedly, as the constant clanging of metal reverberated off of the mountainside. But the Silver Shadow was now breathing heavily and the wound was bleeding steadily. But still he was smiling.

Before Lalatco could even think about why he would be smiling, he all but disappeared in front of him. Lalatco sensed a movement, but the shape was not defined and he failed to block the sword. The Silver Shadow's blade scraped Lalatco's arm, causing him to drop his scimitar. Lalatco instinctively covered his wound with his other hand. But then the Silver Shadow, barely identifiable, punched him across the face and Lalatco fell to the ground. Before Lalatco could react the Silver Shadow fully materialized in front of him, his sword point touching Lalatco's chest.

"Well, well, well. What did I say?"

"You cheated," said Lalatco, spitting blood as he did so.

"No, no, not at all. Don't you use your natural elven abilities in battle. Such as your agility? So I used my delga ability, no difference."

The Silver Shadow flicked his sword to the right a few times and relished in Lalatco's pain as he scratched two Ss into his arm. "There now you are bleeding from both arms." He then took a bow and left the elf where he was.

Elonda was thrown and she landed hard. Her weapons were gone, knocked away or dropped, and her body hurt. She started to get back up, but only made it to her knees. Two gargoyles stood over her, and she swallowed hard. The gargoyles seemed like they were more than enjoying themselves and she saw no way to talk herself out of this one.

But then, somewhere just beyond the gate, she heard a growl. She couldn't see past the gargoyles so was unsure of what had made the noise she heard. The gargoyles seemed to pay it no mind, so perhaps she was hearing things. At that moment, two giant bears walked through the open gate.

One gargoyle slapped her across the face, sending her to the ground before they both turned to face the new threat. The bears advanced slowly, deep growls echoing from their bodies. Then they charged, each bear running right into its gargoyle and trying to bite or claw at their prey. The gargoyles fought back. Slapping the bear's muzzles away or clawing at the bear's back. The bears got their full weight on top of the gargoyles and the gargoyles screamed as the bears ended the fight.

After it was over both bears walked up to Elonda, still laying on the ground. One of the bears placed his snout in her hand. Sensing the bear's intent, she put her arm over the bear's head. The bear lifted his head, and with its help, she again got to her knees. She looked down at herself. Blood was smeared across her arm, hand and face. With what little strength she had left, she climbed on top of the bear.

Gargan continued to fly north, with a host of gargoyles in pursuit. Jyres held on tight, knowing that at this speed and with the sudden changes in direction, he could easily be in a free fall again. Although Jyres was glad that their plan had seemed to work, he didn't really have a second step in the plan. He hadn't thought that far ahead.

"I don't see a way out of this," he called to Gargan, who had to strain to hear him over the rushing wind.

"Nor do I. We won't make it far before we are surrounded."

Think, Jyres, think, he told himself. *There must be something we can do.*

He scanned the area around them, looking for something, anything that might present a solution. Gargan banked to the east cutting around a mountain peak, trying to slow down their pursuers. Slow them down, that's what they had to do. Gargan banked again and Jyres held on desperately. Gargan planted his feet into a side of the rocky peak and exploded back the other way as rocks flew up and around them from the maneuver.

Jyres reached out and snagged one of the rocks. He looked back behind him and saw Bram, changing his flight path to get behind Gargan again.

"Gargan, bring Bram in a little closer, I have an idea."

As Gargan turned in a little and slowed down, Bram came at them at full speed.

Jyres, still rock in hand, sat up tall. "You want it?" Jyres yelled as loud as he could. He held up his hand. "Fine, go get it!" Jyres bent his arm back and threw the rock. Bram and his gargoyles reacted immediately, diving toward the falling object. Whether Bram really believed it was the key or not, Jyres knew that the gargoyle wouldn't take the chance that it wasn't, and his hunch had paid off.

"Fly, Gargan, Fly!" yelled Jyres, as Gargan banked hard and let the wind speed him away back toward Serenity Castle.

Leah was all alone in the dark, key in hand and traveling to the southeast. She knew she had to find somewhere to hide. At first she had just gotten as far away from the valley as possible. Now she was in the grassy plains between the Valley and the Forest of Malkin.

She let herself sit down, taking a moment to rest and to collect her thoughts. She breathed heavily, cursing herself for getting out of shape. As her time with Lalatco had increased, her need for battle, swordplay, and exercise had steadily decreased. And she was paying for it now.

She moved just a little farther, before sitting down again next to the rushing river. She pulled the key out of her pocket, really examining it for the first time. She had not held this in her hand since she had first found it. Right before Bram ripped it from her. She traced her finger around the raised edge, the orange color almost seemed brighter as she did so. This key, it seemed, would continue to cause trouble. She stuffed it back in her pocket and sighed.

The weight of it wore on her. Just now did she really understand the pressure that Lalatco and Jyres were under, always having to protect this metal object. After this night was finished, and they all were reunited, they would have to come up with another plan, because protection was no longer the answer. They would all see each other, right? *Lalatco.* Her tears started again as she thought of him. She had left him by himself against the former knight. He would be okay, he had to be.

A noise suddenly burst from the quiet. The landscape around her had seemed so quiet and still, but now it was interrupted. She looked around, quickly trying to find the source. There, stalking toward her was the creature. Her hand instinctively shot to her pocket, as if that would protect the key. Actually, it probably did the opposite and the creature stared right at her, and charged.

Leah got to her feet as fast as humanly possible, but it wasn't fast enough. As she began to run the creature was all but on top of her. The creature reached out toward her as they ran and its finger just slightly grazed her arm. A quick jolt of pain flashed through her, and she fell to the ground. As fast as the pain had come it had vanished. Leah turned toward the creature who gazed down upon her. Her heart raced and she could feel herself sweating. With no other way to keep the key safe, she plucked it from her pocket and rolled quickly out of the way as the creature reached for her again. She brought her arm back and threw the key into the river.

The creature turned, trying to track its trajectory in the dark night. Leah didn't wait to see what the creature would do. She turned, ran, and screamed.

Jyres and Gargan had bought some time with their deception. But not enough. They were again surrounded by enemy gargoyles. They glided above the mountains, near the valley. Gargan had shown his magnificent ability to ride the winds, but they were vastly outnumbered. There was always another gargoyle to evade. Gargan banked again, before turning in the opposite direction.

This time Bram had anticipated correctly. Bram with one strong sweep and grab, plucked Jyres right off of Gargan. His awesome strength forced Jyres to let go of his friend. Gargan tried to react, but was immediately swallowed in enemy wings and arms. The enemy gargoyles got a hold of him, punched him and directed his flight right into the side of a mountain.

A victorious bellow leapt from Bram's throat. "It is ours! We have what we need. Gargoyles, to me." As if in one motion, gargoyles swooped after their leader. Both those in the sky and those still at the castle followed Bram to the west, over the mountains and to their home.

"No!" screamed Gargan, a sound of despair and sorrow, as he fell from the sky. His heart fell in his chest, aching over the loss of his friend. Tired, and emotionally defeated, Gargan controlled his descent enough to land on the walls of Serenity Castle.

A scream rang out into the night. Elonda—hurt, but not beaten—whipped her head around. The sound was a scream of fear, a human scream, a human woman's scream. *Leah!* Having traded her bear mount for her Wild Spirit, she thundered toward the noise. The gargoyles had recently left the castle, and the regrouping had barely begun. But, the scream could not wait for more regrouping.

Others heard the scream, as well. Rutu and the Wanderer, both on the back of the same black donosin, followed after her. Elonda easily outpaced the bear, but she was happy to know it was behind her. The bears had saved her once already.

The horse's hooves thundered over the grass. Through the dark, Elonda could start to see two shapes moving toward her. Before long, she realized Leah was in a dead run, with the creature right behind her. Elonda started to curve the direction of Wild Spirit's gallop. Then she swooped in from the side and Elonda and Leah grasped arms. Leah was able to propel herself onto the horse with Elonda's help. As she did so, a muffled painful scream came from Elonda, her arm still suffering from her battle with the gargoyles.

Elonda had almost come to a complete stop to get Leah and the horde was right there. The horde screamed with a gurgling, crackling sound as it lunged at them. Its outstretched arms hit and pushed Wild Spirit in its midsection and the horse immediately fell to the ground. The horse neighed a painful, desperate, sound. Elonda and Leah were tossed from the saddle as the horse fell.

Elonda didn't have time to be concerned over the health of Wild Spirit because the creature was only a few steps away from them. The creature, its features as indistinguishable as always in its gelatinous form, took a step toward them. Was that a smile she saw on the creature? Or was she just imagining things?

She started to move, but this time her arm pained her so much, she was frozen and despite the danger, she couldn't bring herself to move. Elonda stared at the creature, remembering what had happened to Jyres with one touch, what had just happened to Wild Spirit. But she would face it with determination. With gritted teeth and without blinking.

The creature reached out to grasp her, but a roar split the air as the Wanderer and Rutu rode in on the black donosin. The horde turned to size up the new threat before reaching back to Elonda anyway. Rutu jumped off of the bear and let out a sound like a squawking bird with a sore throat. A yixl's equivalent to a battle cry. Rutu landed right in front of Elonda and he turned his back to the horde. The horde reaching for Elonda came in contact with Rutu instead. The horde felt the spikes on Rotu's back, and drew itself back. The brown-orange color the horde normally had turned to a dark brown where it had touched the yixl's spikes.

Unsure of this development, the creature withdrew toward the river. Much like it had withdrawn from combat after being unable to penetrate Zar's spell three years before. It walked up to the riverbank, stopping and peered around as if it was searching for something.

"What is it doing?" asked Elonda breathlessly.

"Trying to find the key." Leah's heart raced and her words came out quickly. "I had it. I threw it in the river. I didn't know what else to do."

Elonda just nodded in response and watched as the creature waded into the river. It went slowly, pressing into the current and looking this way and that. The further it got into the river, the slower it seemed to progress. Then, in an instant, it was gone. The river carried it away with the current to the south.

Elonda, clenching her teeth, and holding her left arm to her chest, used her one good arm to crawl over to Wild Spirit. The horse's belly rose and fell with labored breathing. Elonda laid her good arm over the horse, letting her know she was there.

"He will be okay. He is already recovering his strength." After saying that, the Wanderer swung down off the bear's back, and kneeled down by Elonda. "Now, let's help you recover yours." The Wanderer revealed cloth from his bag at his side and put Elonda's injured arm in a sling. Leah and Rutu, both appearing to be unharmed for the most part, came and sat by the Wanderer and Elonda, who still had her good arm resting across Wild Spirit.

"Did you know that would happen?" asked Elonda, pointing at Rutu's spikes and then pointing at the river.

The yixl shook his head in response, apparently understanding the question.

"Well, we can be glad it did," said Leah, who laid down right next to Elonda. There they lay in silence for a long while.

29
RECOVERY

Cyna ran into the dark of the night. She had forgotten where Elonda had told her to go. She just ran. She forgot all about her little cave, her place, where she was supposed to go, and ran. Finally, she fell to the ground. She tried to catch her breath and panicked a little when she couldn't. After a few more moments, she had controlled her breathing. Now what, what should she do? Where was everyone? Jyres, how was Jyres?

Sitting up, Cyna turned to gaze across the river, not looking for anything in particular, and there in the dark, she could see two forms. She peered into the darkness trying to decipher what was happening on the far riverbank. She saw the dark silhouette of a person pull her arm back like she was going to throw something. Cyna didn't think, she didn't consciously react. She just did it as the person threw an object towards the middle of the river. She raised her hand and yelled "Stovea." In an instant, there in her outstretched hand was the key.

A scream rang out into the night from that same riverbank.

And Cyna ran. This time with a direction. Cyna ran toward the mountains she could still vaguely see in the dark. She ran towards her cave.

King Malick tried to bring order to the recovery. He sent runners here and called for help over there. But it was a disheartening process. With each new injury found, or each death discovered, all of which had taken place at the hands of the gargoyles, his heart grew heavy. But his determination grew tenfold. Their need for order, protection, and alliances in the kingdom had just been put on full display. As he was directing traffic and relief efforts, a slow-moving, bloody elf approached him.

"Lalatco! Are you okay? Quick, come this way."

"The wounds are superficial, no need," said the warrior elf waving him away. "Have you seen the others?"

"No, is the key safe?" the king asked with urgency.

"I don't know, last I saw it, it was. What about Leah, Jyres, Elonda, anyone, have you seen them?"

"Vurth lies unconscious, but breathing. I have not seen any of the others you mentioned. But don't lose hope. Help me regroup and we will soon find your friends."

As evening turned into morning, Malick and Lalatco spent the next few arcs aiding those who needed it and trying to account for those who were still missing. Brigand was kept busy, putting his powers of healing to use. The tragedy did seem to draw the Council of Peace together, because everyone was pitching in. Even Empress Octavia was helping. Her forehead dripped with perspiration as she moved quickly from one injured to the next, helping in any way she could.

Gargan had returned earlier and shared the terrible news that Bram had captured Jyres. And just as Lalatco was about to lose hope that he would see any of his friends, or his wife, anytime soon, Leah and Elonda walked through the front gate. Upon seeing each other, Leah and Lalatco rushed to each other, catching the other up in a full embrace.

Tears ran down Leah's face as she choked out the words, "I lost it. I had to. I...I...I threw it in the river."

"It's okay. You are safe now. And you mean more to me than anything else."

As the husband and wife hugged, Elonda smiled at Lalatco and put her hand on his shoulder. "Good to see you are okay," she said.

"Thanks. Why don't you go find Brigand, see if he can help you with that arm."

"I will. But what about Jyres, where is he?"

A pained expression crossed ever so quickly over Lalatco's face. Elonda wouldn't have noticed it had she not been watching him closely. And a fear started in her gut, building up to cause tightness in her throat.

"Sorry, Elonda, he has been captured by Bram." Lalatco looked down, not even able to meet Elonda's gaze, where he would have to see her sorrow.

Elonda wiped away a few tears before finding her resolve. "Well, we will just have to free him then. Anything else?"

"Vurth is unconscious, not even Brigand was able to help him. And no one has seen Cyna."

Elonda, let out a sigh, and stared at the ground. So much depressing news in a short amount of time. Jyres captured, Vurth unconscious and Cyna missing. She hoped Cyna had found her place to hide, and had just not come out of hiding yet. After another deep breath, she said, "Okay. I will go find Brigand." She then walked away, leaving her two friends in their comforting embrace.

Elonda learned from Brigand that she had indeed broken her arm. But after her visit with him, her arm felt amazing. She stood off to the side of the throne room, flexing and stretching her arm, still almost not believing it. She had taken a rest after the healing, but she only did so out of necessity. She almost felt guilty about it, with so much to be done. But she would not have been good for anyone if she hadn't gotten a little rest. She shifted her gaze over to the king and Lord Kapel who were running over the list of casualties and the missing. The number of missing people was down to five now, with one of those being Cyna. The casualty number had risen to 11. Although it saddened everyone, that number probably would have been a lot higher had Jyres not drawn so many gargoyles away from the castle.

Elonda was waiting to talk with the king about Jyres. She wanted to start making a plan to rescue him immediately. As she was waiting, Gargan entered the room. He paused for a moment, taking in the current status of the room, then walked over to where Elonda was standing.

"I must speak with the king," said Gargan. "Jyres must be freed."

"Well, I am glad you and I are in agreement."

"Yes," responded the big gargoyle while placing a comforting hand on Elonda's shoulder. "I failed to protect him. I feel responsible." "It is no one's fault. And you know better than anyone, that Jyres would not place any blame on your shoulders. Or anyone else's."

"You are correct. But I will make sure that the failure to protect him will be made up for immediately." Gargan said this with resolute determination in his voice, his teeth clenched, and claws balled in a fist.

Elonda returned Gargan's earlier gesture, putting a hand on his muscled shoulder. "We will get him back."

The Council of Peace was again gathered in the Throne Room. Thankfully, almost all of the members had escaped the battle with the gargoyles without major injuries. Vurth unfortunately, was still lying in bed, unconscious. Alive at least. The rest of the Council was here. A few minor injuries were obvious, such as the new scars on Shepherd Rowland's face. But they were all here after surviving an attack that, in retrospect, could have been a lot worse.

"Well, here we are again," began Malick. "I have gathered this Council together again as there are new pressing matters to discuss. As I am sure you have heard, Jyres has been captured. Many others, including representative Gargan, have expressed their concern and interest in freeing Jyres. But that is a decision that now rests with this Council."

The discussion began and most supported the idea, but the empress presented the strongest reason why the Council should take action. "The people of this newly formed nation now look to us for a response. We have just begun. The people of Heritage and all of Calridian see Jyres as a hero. There must be an immediate reaction by this Council to show everyone that this Council will do what needs to be done."

The decision was unanimous after that. Conversation then delved into how, and who would be sent, to free Jyres. Many were optimistic, seeing as they didn't know how Bram would protect him during the day. Gargan warned they shouldn't underestimate Bram, but the Council was undeterred. With the Captain of the Guard still incapacitated, Tagro volunteered to take up the role in place of his father and craft a plan to free Jyres.

Shortly after Tagro had said that, conversation turned to focus on the status of the key. King Malick had always planned on keeping any knowledge about the key strictly to a few people. But after the events that transpired, he was struggling to fend off the questions. Lord Kapel came to his aid.

"My fellow representatives. This Council has been formed with the objective to preserve peace. In fact, its name itself is a statement of that. I still believe that peace, as it relates to the gate, is most easily achieved by no one having any knowledge of the key or its location. In fact, many of us have never even seen the key or know what it looks like. That in itself provides an element of protection. The king has informed us that, as it stands, the key is not in the possession of the enemy. And that must be good enough for us."

Elonda was waiting right outside the throne room. As soon as the meeting was over, she found Gargan.

"Well?" she asked immediately upon seeing the green gargoyle.

"We will go rescue him," said Gargan. "Tagro has already begun the planning."

"Then I better wait for Tagro," said Elonda, with a bit of relief evident in her voice.

"We both shall."

As they waited for him, Elonda sighed. "I was also entrusted to keep Cyna safe. I am torn. Do I rush to help Jyres or go searching for Cyna?"

"She was safe last you saw. Lord Kapel and the king will continue to look for those who are missing."

"I suppose you are right. I just feel responsible."

Gargan put his large hand on her shoulder. "I know the feeling, I suffer from the same."

Leah tossed and turned in her sleep, evil dreams haunting her, denying her a restful sleep. Visions of the horde creature assaulted her. It reached out to grab her, the feeling that shot through her with barely a glancing touch. Then she saw herself throw the key. The small shield-shaped key that had caused so much grief already. It should have been thrown in the river long ago. It can't be recovered from there, can it? She saw herself throw it again, as if watching herself from above. Like a bird seeing the world beneath it. She saw it again and again. Her mind replayed through the whole sequence of events as she slept in a state of not fully asleep and not really awake.

She unknowingly rolled over again, this time facing her husband. And another playback of events started in her mind. This time the sounds of the dream seemed so vivid. The noise she had heard, the scream she had made. Wait? What about the splash of the key in the river?

Leah shot up, breathing hard. She tossed her blankets off, all of a sudden too warm to have them. Lalatco stirred next to her.

"What is it?" he said in a half-garbled tone.

"The splash."

"Uh huh," he said, still not really awake.

"Lalatco, wake up."

"What? Okay, I am up, I am up," said Lalatco as he sat up in bed.

"It never made a splash."

"What didn't splash?" replied Lalatco, his voice still showing he was not quite awake.

"The key, I didn't hear it splash," Leah emphasized again.

"I am sure you just don't remember it. It is lost in the river."

"No, I have had to relive this all night. It never hit the water. I am sure of it."

30
Tracks And Dragons

Tagro son of Vurth, Elonda, and two other elves were assembling just outside the castle's gate. It was just the third arc of the day. Tagro had decided they would stay small and hope to reach Bram's castle unnoticed. They could then slip into the castle while the gargoyles were sleeping and free Jyres without causing any alarm. It reminded Elonda of the last time they were at the castle and Lalatco had snuck in. This time, Meslar and his knights wouldn't be there to protect it.

Elonda was just about to go off to the stable and make sure Wild Spirit was ready to go when another group walked through the gate. Lalatco, Leah, and three elves, and all of them were armed and prepared for something.

"What's this about?" asked Elonda

Lalaltco grabbed her by the elbow and led her away from the group a little ways. "We have reason to believe that the key didn't actually fall into the river."

"But I thought…"

"Just trust us, there is a strong possibility that is not the case. We are going to investigate right now."

Elonda, still not sure she understood how this could be true, nodded her head. "Take Rutu with you. In case you run into that creature."

"That's a good idea," said Leah as she joined them. "We will do that. But, Elonda, you make sure to bring Jyres back to us."

"I will. Gargan will meet us when he awakes and Tagro has a solid plan."

"She will," said Lalatco with confidence. "I was hoping Cyna would turn up this morning. She will be anxious about Jyres as well."

"Me, too. I would be lying if I said I wasn't worried about her, too."

"She will turn up," Lalaltco and Leah both said at once.

"Any word on Vurth?" asked Elonda, changing the subject. She couldn't dwell on Jyres or Cyna for very long, it made her lose her focus.

"I just sat with him for nearly an arc," remarked Leah. "No change. But that also means he hasn't gotten worse. There is still hope."

"There is always hope." Elonda threw an arm around each of her friends and pulled them close. "I will return, with Jyres. And when I do, Vurth will have recovered and Cyna will be here. We'll all be together again."

Leah, Lalatco, Rutu, and the elves got to work. They spread out along the river, opposite the bank in which Leah had fought with the horde. The elves were skilled at this sort of thing, but they relied on Leah's memory for where she would have been and what direction she would have thrown the key. As she stood on the shore, looking back to the other side of the river, she doubted her ability to throw the small key such a distance in the middle of the night. But something nagged at her. Something told her to keep looking.

The arcs slid by them, and the moons moved across the sky with no result from their efforts. Leah started to doubt herself as they searched. Were they even in the right location, across from where she had been? Was she farther down the river?

As if in answer to her doubts, one of the elves shouted, "Lalatco, over here."

They all rushed to where the elf was. "See! Tracks, a small human or elf. They head off in this direction." The elf pointed back to the north

Lalatco bent down close to the grass, examining the depression in the green grass to see for himself. His fellow elf was right. Lalatco slowly followed each step in the grass. Some were harder to see than others, as time had certainly passed since these tracks were made.

"Keep following these tracks," said Lalatco. "Leah and I will scout up ahead in this direction and see if we can pick up the trail a little ways ahead."

Sure enough, they were able to pick up the trail as it headed back towards the Valley of the Dragons.

"Whose tracks would they be?" asked Leah.

"That I could only guess. But whoever it is may have the key. Come on."

A few arcs later the small group had been able to track their quarry all the way to the mountains that helped create the Valley of the Dragons. It brought them to a small entryway into the side of the mountain. Lalatco nimbly lowered himself down into a small cave, only to find it dark and foreboding. But his elven eyes adjusted well enough, and he moved on. The cave let out into a much bigger cave, which seemed to have tunnels everywhere. Lalatco looked around, but the rough ground and stone didn't leave a nice trail to follow as the grass had.

Lalatco returned to the others still waiting outside the small entrance. "Well, if we believe this person does have the key. We may never find them. Under the mountains is a labyrinth that I dare not venture on my own."

*****

The creature known as the horde washed up on the shore along the river. It laid there, confused, alone. The strength of the horde had always been in numbers. The horde together with a single purpose. Alone, the horde had struggled. It had struggled to understand the gargoyle Bram. This led to its being held captive. Once free, it had thought it would retrieve the key and unleash the others. And together they would be strong.

But again, it failed. This time, for the first time, experiencing a stinging sensation, something that had never happened to the horde in its entire existence. Somehow, another creature had hurt it. It had been trapped before, but never hurt. It could not do this alone.

Its purpose for so long had been to be free. Then its sole purpose was to find the key. Now, its purpose was to find help. Who would help? Not that Bram creature, it had thought putting it in a cage was helpful.

"Hey," someone said.

The creature sat up, looking around to find the source of the noise. For that was what it was, noise.

"You still alive?" asked the person who called himself the Silver Shadow. He had a fruit in his hand, cutting it with his knife before putting a piece of it in his mouth. "I was starting to wonder. As luck would have it, I happened to come by this spot and see you laying there. Seems odd to run into you here."

"Stung...I was....in the river," said the horde pointing back to the water.

"Okay. Didn't find the key, I take it?"

"No...key...in river."

"I was wondering about that, since a few friends were combing the shore looking for something. They are tracking something, back to the mountains." The Silver Shadow sat down clutching his injured side as he did so. The elf Lalatco had certainly left his mark as well.

"Key?"

"I am not sure, but thought you might want to know."

"Help...again...us?" asked the creature. Wondering if this could be the help it seeked.

The Silver Shadow smiled in return before cutting another piece of fruit and sliding it into his mouth off the knife. "Here is the thing, there is nothing in it for me anymore. I got my revenge."

"Power?"

"No, we talked about that already, I am not like those other beings. I don't need to control you, I don't need you to rule the kingdom for me."

"Other...reason...help?"

The Silver Shadow threw away the rest of his fruit and thought for a moment. Lalatco's words about no one being there to see his victory echoed in the back of his mind. Would the people and races know his name again, would they fear and honor it? Give it the respect it deserves. "Maybe, I am not done yet," he said.

*****

As Lalatco and Leah walked with King Malick in the Great Hall, giving him their report, the doors of the hall flew open. "Sire, you must come! Come look!"

The king quickly followed the elf who had made the announcement, as did Lalatco and Leah. They were led out to the terrace above the main gain, where others had already gathered. There, to everyone's amazement, were four silhouettes in the sky. Two of them, unmistakably being Esmeralda and Crimson. The other two, gargoyles maybe?

"Well, our two dragons have returned," remarked Malick.

"Not two dragons, sire," said Lalatco with a smile. "Four dragons. I see four dragons."

"Four?" the king exclaimed. "Are you sure they are dragons?"

But Lalatco didn't need to respond. For each moment that passed brought the flying silhouettes closer to the castle. And the king couldn't help but agree. Two much smaller, but no less magnificent, dragons followed Esmeralda and Crimson. All four dragons did a loop around the castle. This brought a round of cheers and other remarks of astonishment from the crowd that was gathered.

One of the younger dragons was a bright yellow, like a streak of sunlight it flew through the air. The other young dragon was more of a combination of colors, like an orange and blue that fought each other for dominance.

The four dragons circled again, well aware of the onlookers. A dragon liked to show off, and even as the adult dragons settled in toward the valley, the young ones zipped around the castle.

King Malick and others strode out of the castle as the two dragons landed in the valley.

"You have returned, and not alone!"

"We are no longer the last two living dragons. No longer a dying race," responded Esmeralda, who towered above the humans and elves that had come out to greet them.

"This is wonderful, but how is this possible?"

"A Dragon Pericarp was found. An essential item that we thought was lost to us."

"I know little of Dragon Pericarps I am afraid." The king shrugged.

"Some things are meant to be secret, and some things, thankfully, have been kept secret," replied the dragon.

"Welcome home! Serenity Castle is complete!" shouted Malick and the onlookers responded with similar words.

The two young dragons then came to land by their much larger counterparts. The yellow dragon was a little bigger than the other young dragon, but still no larger than Gargan.

"Well, do they have names?" asked the king.

"They do," said Crimson, who looked at the young ones in turn. "Sunbeam." And the yellow dragon let go a small roar in response. "And Kaleido." The dragon of multi colors put its head in the air and blew fire in response.

"Come and see the completed castle, and then we have much to discuss," stated King Malick in a much more somber tone.

After filling in Esmeralda on everything that had happened, Lalatco, Leah, Esmeralda and King Malick discussed the key at length. Ogla had given the king permission to search the mountains for whatever he was looking for, but warned that entering the mountains was a dangerous thing. Outside the mountains was the Kingdom of Calridian, but inside the mountains was the orcs' and goblins' domain, and the deeper you went, the more chaos you found.

"I see no other option," said Malick. "We must follow the trail. We believe that whoever left that trail has the key. So we must enter the mountains."

"I agree," said Esmeralda. "But, who and how many do we send?"

The king thought about that for a moment. "A large army will not be able to enter and move about the caverns. Only a few can be sent."

"The key is my responsibility, I will go," said Lalatco.

"We will go," Leah corrected her husband.

"Who else should accompany you? Only sending two of you seems like the wrong decision."

"Actually, I was thinking gargoyles. They are powerful and can thrive in the dark. And the sunlight will not reach them once deep inside the mountains and so won't be able to cause them to be stone statues." Lalatco smiled briefly, before adding, "I know Gargan is helping to free Jyres, but I am sure members of his clan will help us."

"That is an excellent idea, warrior elf," said Esmeralda.

"Very good, I will arrange it." After saying this, the king dismissed them.

Percy and Hawkins, two gargoyles that Lalatco had gotten to know, followed Lalatco and Leah toward the mountain entrance they had traced the key to the day before. Percy was a small gargoyle and, when standing, his head didn't quite reach Lalatco's elbow.

Percy was one of the King's Envoys and was able to speak well in the common language. Hawkins was a taller gargoyle, and had an appearance much like that of a bird. The four of them entered the initial cave and followed the path deeper into the mountain. It was not long before the distant cries, screeches, and calls from orcs or goblins could be heard.

Lalatco led the way for the group, leading with one small torch in his hand. His hair showed silver in the torch light, the elf's hair catching the color of the stone around him. They entered into a large cavern with many exits. The ceiling was much higher than three times their heights, and the paths, if you could call them that, were strewn with rocks and obstacles. The light from Lalatco's torch bounced off the cavern walls, casting shadows of the four intruders against the rock.

"So Ogla knows that we are here. Does that help us?" asked Leah as she climbed over a boulder.

"I don't think so. He made it clear that we are in their domain. I don't think any of the creatures that live here will hesitate to attack," replied Lalatco. He looked over at his wife and smiled, before almost chuckling.

"What? What is it?" asked his wife, while looking at herself, thinking something was out of place.

"I have not seen you in your hunter gear in a long time, I forgot how well it suits you." Leah was wearing the same clothing she had been wearing on the day they met. She wore a bright-green shirt that was tucked into her brown pants. And her unique leather coverings on each elbow and shoulder. From the patches strips of leather connected to each other and then again to a thicker leather pad that went around her waist. Strips of leather also curled around her arms and then around her fingers and connected to a patch on her palm. Lalatco never really understood the leather around the fingers and on her palm, but Leah swore by them, saying they helped with her control when firing an arrow and saved her fingers from irritation.

"I know, I am your lovely wife now, but I can still play in the mud when needed."

This drew a laugh from Lalatco. He then scanned the cavern one more time. "We better pick one of these other paths, I don't think we could stay unnoticed in this cavern long at all."

Lalatco quickly led the group to a side passage and stopped once they had gone a small distance. There the group paused, and looked at one another, almost as if communicating to one another without saying a word. But they didn't have to speak. They all saw the many different options there were to choose from. They knew how hard the task was in front of them. After the moment passed, Lalatco gave them a nod and led them further down the passageway.

Two arcs and many tunnels later, the group stopped to rest. They sat down and Leah rested her head on her husband's shoulder. Without a word, Hawkins reached over and snuffed out Lalatco's torch. Lalatco was about to protest, but Hawkins had his finger over his lips, asking for quiet. On the far end of the small cavern they had stopped in, goblin voices were heard.

Lalatco, Leah, and the gargoyles crouched down and hid themselves the best they could. Meanwhile the goblins who had entered the caravan from a different tunnel started walking in the direction of the hidden travelers. One of the goblins was talking, and his voice was a high-pitched scratching.

As they grew closer, Lalatco could tell that there were three goblins. Each had a rough looking sword of some kind hanging from their leather belts. Lalatco struggled to make out too much else in the dark. The goblins didn't seem to have much trouble in the dark, as they marched along, avoiding obstacles and choosing a new path out of the caravan.

The goblins' path took them awfully close to Lalatco and the others, but almost miraculously, the goblins walked right on by without so much as a glance in their direction. Lalatco let out a breath he didn't realize he was holding, but remained perfectly still for a long while more. Finally, he broke the silence.

"Well, that was close."

"Yes," responded Percy. "Perhaps we need to go without light from now on. Hawkins and I can guide you, as we can still see well enough."

"I won't be able to see anything!" exclaimed Leah in a voice full of worry.

"I know, but I think Percy is right. If we are going to get through this undetected, we are going to need to do so without the full use of our vision." Lalatco stood up, and offered his hand to Leah, who grabbed it and stood up.

"I know, but I still don't like it."

Another day into their adventure in the mountains and the group was starting to lose faith. They had been able to avoid the orcs and goblins, but their search for anyone else who had ventured into the mountains had not turned up anything interesting. In fact, they hadn't seen anything at all to tell them they were even on the right track.

The group of four had just started moving again after a long break for sleeping and eating and watching in shifts. The other issue that the group was starting to have was would they even be able to get back out of the caverns when they wanted to. After a lot of turns and similar looking tunnels, everything seemed to blend together. So the group had decided to attempt to make their way back to the large cavern they had first seen when they had started their search. That way they would be confident of where they were and still have the choice to explore more if they wanted to.

Although it took longer than they hoped, the next day they recognized the tunnel where they had seen the three goblins walk right past them on their first day. This came as a welcome sign, for they were confident they could retrace their steps from here.

After a short break, however, as they were about to move on, a handful of orcs and goblins stumbled upon the travelers.

"We can't let them tell the others," said Lalatco as he burst into action.

Knives went flying from his hands into the surprised orcs. Leah was almost as quick with her bow, sending two arrows into the closest goblin. Percy and Hawkins each tackled a goblin, leaving two orcs who started to run and screech. Lalatco let two more knives fly into the back of one of the fleeing orcs. Leah's aim was perfect, taking down the other orc with a well-placed shot in its neck.

Leah and Lalatco retrieved their arrows and knives while the gargoyles worked to drag the orcs and goblins away from the main path. Satisfied, they quickly moved away from the area and worked back toward the main cavern from their first day.

A few arcs later the group had reached their destination, and had positioned themselves in a side tunnel off of the main cavern. There they rested, keeping watch in shifts as they did so. Their question of where to go next was answered while Hawkins was keeping watch. Many shrieks, squawks, and yells ripped through the cavern. Something was happening, and it was something close by!

31
THE TWO LOST SANDS

Tagro, Gargan, Elonda, and two more elves had come across the mountain pass, then stayed close to the mountains, following them south. They continued south until the barren wasteland started to give way to dirt and plains. Elonda felt as though the trip was taking forever as they traveled in the shadow of the mountains. Elonda knew she had to stay patient, but Jyres was out there, waiting for rescue.

On the second morning after leaving the mountain pass, Tagro led the elves over the plains toward Bram's castle, leaving Gargan in his stone form in the shadow of the mountains. They hopped to reach the castle without being spotted by Bram or his clan of gargoyles. For that to be at all possible, they had to leave the safety of the mountains and travel across the plains during the day.

By nightfall Tagro and the elves were in the swampy terrain just south of Bram's castle. There they waited out the night, trusting in the trees of the swamp to protect them from the unwanted eyes of the gargoyles. Gargan had stressed the importance of keeping watch on the castle and Brams' activities. So now that the night moon was out again, Gargan and plenty of his own gargoyles would be keeping their eyes on the swamp and the castle.

When morning came, Tagro and the elves didn't wait. They immediately went toward the castle. The only way to enter the castle was across a land bridge. Elonda had memories of this bridge. The last time she was here, they were attacking the castle as Meslar and the knights tried to avoid them. She had climbed over the walls and distracted the knights long enough for another elf, Silvan, to open the gate. That distraction had almost cost her her life.

This time, there was no attack planned. Thars were not roaming around the castle and a wizard and his knights were not waiting inside. Only sleeping gargoyles awaited them.

After crossing the land bridge, the group started to prepare to climb the castle walls. They had the right equipment along to help make this easier work. Tagro still struggled with it a little, but the elves helped him and soon all four of them were over the castle wall.

Inside, it was as she and Tagro remembered. A small tower was on each corner of the castle. The castle's middle section rose up to even height with the walls, but another tower rose up then from the middle section, and was even higher. They quickly headed down to the courtyard, which would bring them to the interior of the castle.

Although they were moving rapidly, they remembered Gargan's warning that a gargoyle can awake if provoked. But almost all of the gargoyles were perched on top of the walls, and not near the interior of the castle. This left the small group confident they would not disturb the sleeping enemy.

Before long, the group had made it inside and they began to work their way down into the lower levels of the castle. They were searching for the cells where the prisoners would be kept, in this case, Jyres. After a few wrong turns, the hallway they were in opened up in front of them and small cells lined both sides of the hallway.

Elonda ran to the first cell, her skin full of goosebumps in anticipation. But when she grabbed the cell bars and looked in, her anticipation turned to disappointment. He was not there. She turned to find the cell on the opposite side of the hallway, but that was empty as well. She quickly moved to investigate the rest of the cells. Each one was empty. Empty.

She collapsed to the floor in despair. Where was he? Why wasn't he here? Her heart felt as empty as the cells around her. She screamed once, and the elves came to try to soothe her, but she pushed them away.

She didn't understand. Gargan had said that Jyres was captured by Bram. He wouldn't lie; Gargan wasn't capable of such an act of betrayal. So where was he? Tears fell from her eyes and landed on the dry ground at her feet. After a moment, she wiped the tears away. Finally, she turned her head and saw a hand already reaching out for her. She grabbed it and Tagro helped pull her up.

"They knew we would come for him. They knew they couldn't defend him from us during the day," said the dwarf. "They must be keeping him somewhere else."

Elonda nodded her head, the dwarf's logic pushing through the chaos of her emotions. "But where? Where else could they keep him?"

"I don't know. Perhaps Gargan would have some ideas. Let's get out of this castle before we have other gargoyles to deal with. I would much rather discuss the day with Gargan, then with an awakened Bram."

The group quickly retraced their steps, hurrying to leave the castle. Elonda followed the others in a haze. She had felt so confident that he would be here. That Jyres would be all right and they would free him. Now that that was not the case, she had to reorganize her thoughts. But she couldn't. She longed to be with him again, and that longing kept her from focusing on the task at hand. Her body went through the motions needed with practiced agility, but her mind was elsewhere.

*****

Cyna had run to the mountains, and to the place she called her own. At least, that is what she had thought she did. She had slid into her cave, only to find out that it wasn't the right cave. Somehow in the dark, she had made a mistake. Now she found herself in a new dark cave. Unsure of what to do, she didn't do anything. She stayed where she was, staring at the key in her hands.

Should she climb back out of this cave and try to find hers? Should she stay right where she was? Should she go further in this cave? What if the creature who wanted the key was somewhere outside, somewhere in the valley searching for it?

Her decision on what to do was forced upon her, she heard noises, scary ones, and she ran. She ran blindly in the dark. She shoved the key in her pocket. Then she tripped over a rock in the path and stumbled, scraping her arms in the process.

Before she knew it, beady little eyes stared down at her. She tried to back away, but she backed right into a pair of legs. She looked up and saw that she was surrounded by green, ugly, smelly and nasty creatures. Goblins. She started to scream as their grubby hands grabbed her and hoisted her up. Her screams only made the goblins snicker, and they carried her away, deeper into the tunnels.

They met up with some other creatures in the tunnels. These creatures were a little bigger, a little smellier. Orcs. The orcs bound her hands and feet together and threw her in a corner of the small cave they were in.

That was three days ago.

Now, she still sat in the same corner, all but forgotten and unsure of what they had planned for her. She had been given just enough water and scraps to keep her alive. She was hungry, thirsty, tired, and alone. She cried every night. But no one cared. She cried every day. But no one cared. Where was Jyres? Anybody? Wouldn't somebody help her?

As those thoughts started to torment her, she began to lose track of time. She began to lose track of her surroundings. At one point she was moved, but she didn't remember when. She only knew that she was moved, because this place was a little bigger than the last place, more orcs and goblins.

One of the bigger orcs stood up and started talking and making noises, and the whole group started to get loud. A fire was started in the middle of this cave they were in. The noise became louder, as if they were anticipating something. But then the type of noise changed. What had sounded like celebrating turned into screams. Excitement turned into chaos.

Cyna forced herself to focus on what was going on. She found the fire and used it to focus her eyes, and bring her back to herself. She blinked, forcing her eyes to stay open. Then she saw it. The creature, the horde. The horde creature moved into the area thick with goblins and orcs. It reached out with its arms, grasping the two nearest green creatures. The poor creatures immediately screamed and convulsed before falling to the ground. Dead.

Cyna, still tied up, felt helpless. But she felt a need to get away from the creature. She inched herself across the hard floor, moving as much as she was able with her hands and feet bound. She backed up until her back was tight against the cavern wall.

The creature continued its destruction. Grabbing and holding orc after orc and watching them fall. Orcs and goblins would rush wildly at the creature, attacking it with clubs or swords. But they seem to do little or nothing to the horde. The swords would go right through it, and the creature just needed to hold the green enemies for a moment to see them fall to the floor. A room full of orcs and goblins was quickly becoming a room full of dead orcs and goblins.

And then another figure was in the room. Its movements were a blur of shadows. The shadows formed and reformed as its slender sword found orc and goblin flesh. The shadow warrior added more bodies to the cave's floor. When the last of the orcs and goblins had fallen or escaped the carnage the warrior completely materialized. He was dressed all in gray and carried a sword in his right hand. The warrior marched forward until he was standing over Cyna. Using his sword, he sliced the ropes on Cyna's hands, freeing her hands, but not her feet. "I am the Silver Shadow. Hand it over, and you will not be harmed."

Cyna pushed back the hair that had fallen in front of her face, but did not respond. The Silver Shadow raised his sword until it was under her chin.

"I have no desire to hurt someone as young as you. Hand it to me, now!" The Silver Shadow's voice was no longer calm, but forceful.

And Cyna's resolve broke. She dug her hand into her pocket and produced the key. The Silver Shadow reached out and grabbed it, leaving his sword where it was to ensure Cyna didn't try anything.

"Thank you," he said. Before putting the key into his own pocket. Without another look at Cyna, he yelled to the creature. "Time to go. I have what we need." The creature and the Silver Shadow then disappeared into one of the side corridors.

Cyna, breathing hard, burst into tears. The tears turned into gasps as she tried to catch her breath. Get it together Cyna, she told herself. You are still alive. You need to find your way out and get help. Someone needs to know about the key. Finally, her breathing slowed, and she found the courage to reach down with her now free hands and untie her feet. Just as she did so, figures burst into the room at the other end.

Panicking and fearing she would be captured again, she got up and tried to run. But she had no strength. Her legs failed her. She only went a couple of steps before she fell again. "No!" she cried. "It can't happen again." She pushed herself back up and forced herself to stand again. But then it didn't matter. Someone was around her and she was too late, the creatures would capture her again.

"Cyna!" someone cried. "What are you doing here?"

"What, who is it?" Cyna collapsed again, but was caught before she hit the ground.

"Quickly, we need to get her out of here."

EPILOGUE

After Lumpkin's arrival and the discovery of the organization system that had been used at one point at the old library, work had progressed quickly for Zar, Flick, and Lumpkin. This Zar was grateful for, as it seemed as if any later would have been too late. The wizard was feeling it in his bones.

He came to the last corner of the library that he was interested in this evening and rested a moment on his cane. He let out a sigh. "Almost done," he said to himself, "and then you can rest." He reached his hand up to the shelf on his right and as he did so he bumped the books resting there and they tilted and fell. Some of them fell to the ground, and others just fell to the bottom of the shelf. "Darn it all," he said.

"But what do we have here?" For there behind the fallen books was a cutout of sorts in the back of the shelf. The old man reached and pressed the indentation and a trap door in the shelf above dropped down. And on the little wooden trap door was a scroll. Zar reached up and grabbed it, already having a thought as to what he had just stumbled upon.

Zar slowly returned to his desk where he inspected the scroll. On the outside was a familiar looking image. The same image and design that was displayed on the key. Zar slowly undid the scroll and smiled. "Lumpkin," he called. "Where is that dwarf now? Lumpkin!"

Finally, the dwarf, bobbing up and down as he walked, came and stood before the wizard.

"Lumpkin, I will need you to do something for me. This scroll here will need to be brought to the king right away. Do you understand?"

"Yes, king, king," said the dwarf as he accepted the scroll.

"Excellent, you must leave at first light."

The dwarf nodded excitedly before returning to wherever he had been before he was called. Zar smiled as the dwarf walked away. *Very good*, he thought. *Very good.* Zar leaned back in his chair, sighed, and smiled. He had enjoyed his time at the library. But his work here was done. Then he closed his eyes and took a deep breath. He opened his eyes again and saw Flick standing by his chair. *That is fitting*, the old man thought. Then the powerful wizard closed his eyes again and breathed his last.

Lumpkin had just finished packing his belongings for the trip to see the king. The last thing he did was to carefully place the scroll in his pack and pick up the wizard's staff given to him by Zar. Before he left, he wanted to go see if Zar needed anything else. He walked up to the desk and thought that the old man was sleeping. Had he fallen asleep at his desk last night?

But as he leaned closer to him, he realized he wasn't sleeping. The poor old man had died in his sleep. A tear slid down Lumpkin's cheek as he looked at the once great wizard. He had come to enjoy his time with the man very much. And now he is gone. As Lumpkin stood there, the body of the great wizard, Zar, disappeared.

Lumpkin stood there unsure of what to do. In the end, he decided there wasn't much left to do. He put his hand on the old man's desk, tapped it with his knuckles, and hoisted up his pack for the journey. After looking for Flick for a little while, but finding no trace of him, Lumpkin left the library on his journey to Serenity Castle and the king.

*****

Cyna woke up. She stretched her arms above her before relaxing again and then realizing that she was in a bed. How did that happen? She blinked away the sleep as her eyes adjusted to the light. Then she saw Leah sitting at the end of her bed.

"Leah, what happened?"

"Hi, Cyna, I was going to ask you the same thing. We found you under the mountains, you passed out right after we found you. It looked like you had been through quite the ordeal." Leah slid down the bed to be closer to Cyna.

"It's gone. I had to let them take it." Cyna's lips began to quiver, but Leah put her hand on her arm in an attempt to calm her. "Who was it, Cyna?

"The creature and the Silver Shadow, I didn't want to give it to him. But he had his sword at my neck."

"It is okay, you should have never been put in that situation, and that is my fault."

"Where is Jyres, is he here, can I see him?" asked Cyna hopefully.

"I am sorry Cyna, he is not here. We don't know where he is."

And Cyna's tears returned.

*****

Darkness. Complete darkness. Complete darkness enveloped Jyres. But Jyres knew where he was. He was thrown into a cell. A cell that he had been in once before. Only last time his stay in the cell was very short term, as the elf, Silvan, had freed him and the others who had been captured almost immediately. This time there was no elf hiding in the shadows. Nobody else was even here. The old ruins of the castle Stone Heights were empty.

Once a night a gargoyle from Bram's clan would visit and provide Jyres with water and a little bit of food. Other than that, Jyres was alone. His thoughts more often than not were on his friends. He hoped they were safe. Jyres had not seen his friends since they split up in an effort to keep the key safe. He hoped the key was safe. He hoped his distraction was enough for Lalatco to get the key away from the battle and somewhere hidden.

Bram hasn't talked to him at all yet. He had searched Jyres aggressively for the key and then left Jyres to guess at what had happened. Jyres told himself that he had to stay positive. Had to think that the plan worked, that his friends, and Elonda, were safe. Because if he let himself think otherwise, well then he would not last long in this cell. All alone. Dark. Lonely. Lost. Forgotten.

*****

Most of the members of the Council of Peace had returned to their regions for now, but the king, Esmeralda, and Lord Kapel were gathered in the Throne Room. The room had gone silent, as they considered the events that had transpired in the last few days. It had been a rough turn of events for Calridian. Finally, the king spoke again.

"Our Captain of the Guard is still unconscious. Jyres has been captured and is being kept somewhere where we cannot find him. Cyna found the key, only to give it to the enemy. The Silver Shadow and the creature are now in possession of the key that could open the Gate of Fire. This would most certainly bring destruction upon the kingdom. Did I miss anything?"

"Well, when you put it like that, it does put a negative light on our situation," replied Lord Kapel.

"Is there any other way to describe our situation? It is bleak."

"It is bleak. But it is not over yet. Rutu has the ability to hurt the creature. We need to figure out how and why. We don't know for

227

sure what the Silver Shadow's intentions are; if we are lucky, he will not immediately head towards the gate. And let us not forget, we now have four dragons." Lord Kapel had put great emphasis on the word four.

The group fell quiet again. Until a dwarf came running into the throne room. "Sire, sorry to disturb you. But someone is here for you. And he will only talk to you. He is a rather peculiar dwarf, if I do say so myself."

"Lumpkin," said the dragon. "He was with Zar. He had the Dragon Pericarp."

"Show him in," replied Malick.

A moment later Lumpkin was led into the room. Lumpkin came forward slowly. He unconsciously drifted to the right, away from the dragon as he approached the group.

"Lumpkin, I presume?" asked the king.

"Yes, yes, Lumpkin. I am Lumpkin, son of Lustor," stammered the dwarf, removing his pointy hat as he did so.

"Welcome. I am King Malick. To what do we owe the pleasure?"

"Um. Well, Zar. He, Zar. Zar sent me." Lumpkin focused on his pointy hat instead of the king.

"Very good. How is Zar? We may need to call on his aid again."

The dwarf continued to stare at his feet. He shifted back and forth before finally looking up. "He died. He is…he died," said Lumpkin shyly.

The mighty dragon let out a low angry growl and a puff of smoke out of its nostrils that floated to the ceiling. Lord Kapel lowered his head in quiet reflection and Malick' face was one of pure shock.

"Zar has died. How?" Malick paused. And all was quiet before he said, "How is this possible?"

"Age. Yes. Age, Age," said Lumpkin, so softly that the others struggled to hear him.

"Age, but he is a delga!"

"Yes, a delga. But a delga who has lived long. Delga are not immortal like the elves. His time has come," said Esmeralda, sending another puff of smoke toward the ceiling.

"Does any hope remain?" said the king as he flopped onto his throne.

"He did send me, send me," said Lumpkin as he tried to get something from his pack. "This, sent me, with this. He did, sent me." Lumpkin handed the scroll to the king.

King Malick took the scroll, examining it. Then he unrolled it. And at the very top of the scroll it read, in bold and bright script, "The making and the unmaking of the Gate."

ACKNOWLEDGMENTS

It takes a lot of people to bring a book to life, and I wouldn't be a self-published author without the time and talents of many others. First, a special thank you to my wife and my father who were the initial editors. Your thoughts and suggestions made great improvements to the story. I would also like to thank Belle Manuel for her excellent editing and for making sure all the i's were dotted and t's were crossed.

Where would a book be without a great cover? I owe my daughters extra hugs for their ideas for the cover and for being the initial artists. Love you girls! I am so pleased with the final cover of the book and the credit for that goes to Morgan Johnson. Thank you, Morgan, for all the time and energy you put into creating a great-looking book cover.

My eternal gratitude goes out to all my supporters and readers. Joshua Vick, your encouragement, advice, and humorous conversation are appreciated more than you know. And thank you for lending your voice talents to my website! Sam, my biggest fan, I hope you love this book; I am already working on book 3! And thank you to all my supporters on Kickstarter, you made this possible.

A special THANK YOU to these fantastic Kickstarter Supporters:

Austin Hoffey
Greg Schmidt
Mom & Dad
Jensen Hinton
Collin Vanderhoof
Spencer Wright
Ellen Pilcher
Sharon Johnson
Justin Burgess
Nick Simmons, My Third Brother
Gregory A Pollack
Brian Cretzmeyer
Justin Vanderhoof
Debra ann Wilson
Rita Kabaso
Brandon Thielen
Jason D
Meghan & Kevin Brennan

ABOUT THE AUTHOR

The Keepers of the Key is B. J. Vanderhoof's second novel. His love for fantasy and science fiction inspired him to begin writing. When he is not writing, Vanderhoof is working at a YMCA as a Program Executive. He enjoys playing board games, watching movies, reading, and spending time with family. Vanderhoof lives with his wife and three children in Appleton, Wisconsin. Visit his website at https://bjvanderhoof.com